Arthur, *Rex Brittonum*

A Light in the Dark Ages, Book Five

By Tim Walker

Text copyright © 2020 Timothy N. Walker
All rights reserved

Arthur *Rex Brittonum*

"The twelfth battle was on Mount Badon in which there fell in one day 960 men from one charge by Arthur; and no one struck them down except Arthur himself, and in all the wars he emerged as victor."

Nennius, *Historia Brittonum* (History of the Britons) c. 820

Acknowledgements:

Beta reader, proofreader & critique partner - Linda Oliver
Copyeditor - Sinead Fitzgibbon (@sfitzgib)
Cover design - Cathy Walker (cathyscovers.wixsite.com)

Published by:

http://timwalkerwrites.co.uk

Arthur *Rex Brittonum*

Table of Contents

Map	3
Place Names	4
Character List	4
Prologue	6
PART ONE	8
Chapter One	8
Chapter Two	14
Chapter Three	22
Chapter Four	27
Chapter Five	36
Chapter Six	41
Chapter Seven	49
Chapter Eight	56
Chapter Nine	70
Chapter Ten	84
Chapter Eleven	94
Chapter Twelve	106
Chapter Thirteen	118
Chapter Fourteen	132
PART TWO	143
Chapter One	144
Chapter Two	148
Chapter Three	157
Chapter Four	171
Chapter Five	177
Chapter Six	185
Chapter Seven	191
Chapter Eight	198
Chapter Nine	212
Chapter Ten	221
Epilogue	230
Author's Note	243

Arthur *Rex Brittonum*

Map

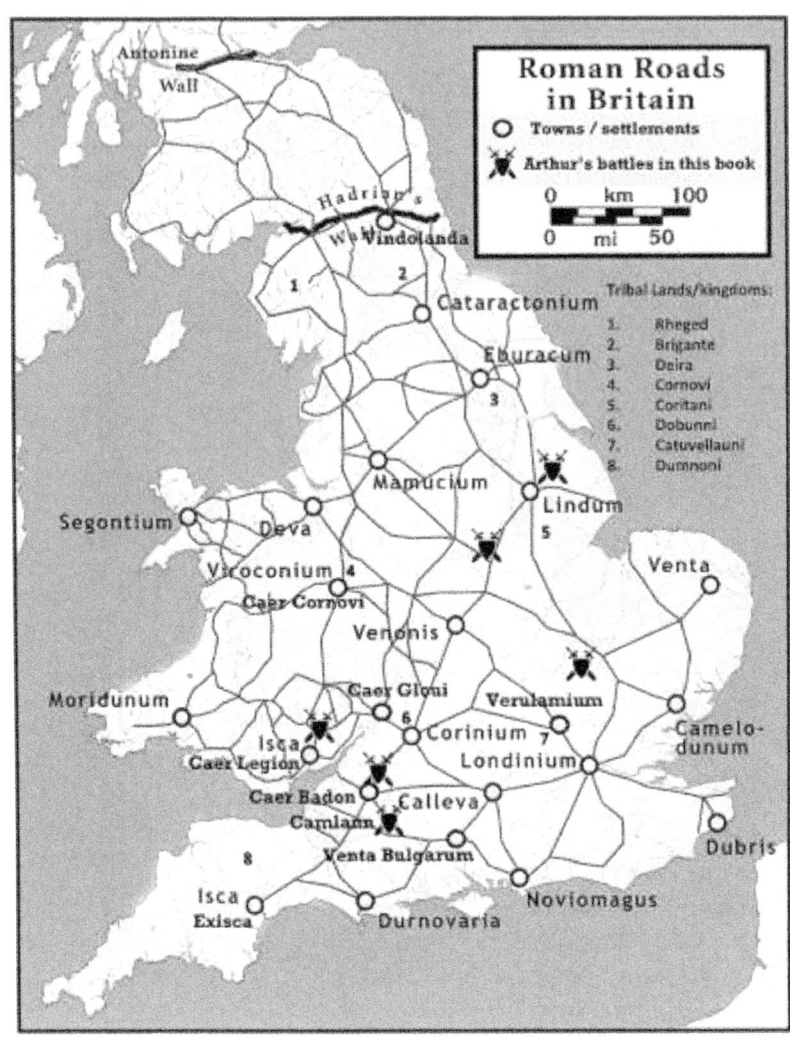

Arthur *Rex Brittonum*

Place Names

Modern	**Roman**	**Briton***
Britain	Britannia	Albion (ancient name)
Ireland	Hibernia	
Wales	Cambria	Cymru
Scotland	Caledonia	
Chester	Deva	Caer Ordovici
Anglesey	Mona	
Winchester	Venta Bulgarum	Dunbulgar
Exeter	Isca Dumnoniorum	Exisca
Silchester	Calleva Atrebatum	Calleva
London	Londinium	Lundein
Gloucester	Glevum	Caer Gloui
Lincoln	Lindum	
York	Eboracum	Ebrauc
Bath	Aquae Sulis	Caer Badon
Caerleon	Isca Silurium	Caer Legion
Wroxeter	Viroconium	Caer Cornovia
Carlisle	Luguvallium	
Hadrian's Wall	Vallum Hadriani	The Wall/Great Wall
Hadrian's Wall fort	Vindolanda	

* Some Briton place names are 'best guess' due to lack of evidence

Character List

Arthur - King of Britannia/*Rex Brittonum*
Gunamara - Arthur's wife and queen, daughter of Meirchion
Llacheu, Amhar, Gwen their children
Merlyn - Healer and former adviser to Arthur
Anne - Arthur's sister, Queen of Powys (married to Owain)
Morgaise - Arthur's half-sister, Queen of Dumnonia
Guinevere - Arthur's second wife and queen
Morgana - Uther's firstborn daughter, Arthur's half-sister
Mordred - Son of Morgana, King of the Britons (in south)
Ambrose - Arthur's Chancellor, son of Maddox
Asaph - Arthur's chaplain, later an abbot

Arthur *Rex Brittonum*

Gildas - A monk in Asaph's priory
Peredur – Prince of Rheged, Arthur's brother-in-law
Bedwyr - Knight, commander of Arthur's army
Lucan - Knight sub-commander
Pinel - Knight sub-commander
Agravane - Knight sub-commander
Mador - Knight sub-commander
Gaheris - Captain of Dobunni, made a knight
Herrig - Arthur's bodyguard, a Jute
Dermot - Arthur's cook
Barinthus – A merchant from Armorica (Brittany)
Gerwyn - Bard and spy for Arthur
Viroco - Captain of the Coritani
Caratacus - Cadwallon's champion

Tribal Kings and Chiefs
Meirchion Gul - King of the Rheged
Maddox - Chief of the Coritani, based at Lindum
Owain Ddantgwyn - King of Powys (Cornovi tribal chief)
Cado - King of Dumnonia (succeeds Geraint)
Adminius - Chief of the Catuvellauni
Malachi - Chief of the Dobunni, grandson of Ambrosius
Cadog - Chief of the Silures
Caradog - King of Gwent
Cyngar - King of Demetia
Vortipor - King of Dyfed
Cadwallon - King of Gwynedd 'the Head Dragon'

Angliscs and Saxons
Cerdic - King of the South Seax
Octha - King of Ceint (son of Hengist)
Icel - King of the Angliscs
Beowulf - Icel's champion

Arthur *Rex Brittonum*

Prologue

To the Most Honourable Maddox, Chief of the Coritani, Residing at Lindum Colonia

My dearest father,

I send you blessings in this year of Our Lord, five hundred and fifteen, and add to this my most heartfelt wishes for your good health and contentment in these difficult times. The warming sun of spring is most welcome, and this very morn I walked through a meadow aglow with primroses, reminding me of my childhood at Lindum. Happily, I resolved to take up my quill and write this missive.

My lord and master, King Arthur of the Britons, sends to you his blessings and hopes for a continuing friendship with the Coritani, and I must tell you that his queen, Gunamara, and their son, Llacheu, are in good health. He keeps me busy as his Chancellor in this wild and windy northland. We have made some improvements for our comfort in the royal enclosure of King Meirchion Gul of the proud Rheged people, here in the former Roman town of Luguvalium at the western edge of the Great Roman Wall. Gunamara knows her father's interest in such matters and invited him to inspect the finished work. Hot springs service our bathhouse, and our villa is heated from beneath the floors, restored by clever tradesmen who have studied the Roman system of circulating warm air in the space below the buildings, causing droves of unhappy rats to take their leave!

I am grateful for your advice, Father, and now employ your methods of tax collection from market traders and farmers, who are reminded that they rely on protection from our soldiers. Thus, we are able to share the burden of revenue collection with our Rheged hosts, and to pay and equip Arthur's oath-sworn riders and spearmen, who number one hundred mounted and one hundred on foot.

Arthur is restless and keen to move southwest and announce himself to the hard-pressed people there, for he is already well-known and much loved in these northern lands, and in the lands of the Brigantes and Deiran people to the east, who owe him their allegiance and have provided many warriors. In addition, Lord Percival now commands the training school at Vindolanda, where warrior skills and leadership are taught to an eager group of youths – many of whom are the sons of nobles who wish for advancement and to make their name.

Arthur's noble sister, Anne, now queen to Owain, King of Powys, has given him a reason. She has requested his help to repel border raiders to their lands, and Arthur has now received the blessing of his father-in-law, King Meirchion, to undertake an expedition. I shall accompany him, and promise to send a messenger to you once we arrive at the Powys court at Viriconium – I know not what the locals call it.

Dear Father, if you look at your map of Roman Britannia that takes pride of place in your study, and place a straight-edged rule across it, you will see that Lindum in the east aligns with Viriconium in the west at no greater distance than one hundred miles as the pigeon flies. Sadly, our messengers are earthbound and must navigate the mountain range that is the backbone of our island.

We have received reports from scouts that the unwelcome sails of raiders' ships have been seen off the east coast, reminding us all of the dread dangers of these warming days. I pray for your safety from Anglisc raiders who have for many years blighted our coast and coveted our meadows and farmlands. Please, I beg you, adhere to Arthur's advice to keep watchful men on your walls and towers. I know you will.

Dear Father, I beg you send a rider to King Owain of Powys at Viriconium with your reply to this missive and tell us of your situation – I am anxious for news. King Arthur has pledged to keep safe our island from hostile raiders and their attempts to forge permanent settlements – although the southeast lands are already occupied by Saxons, Franks and others. I pray that the Coritani are spared this fate, for we are a proud people with Roman ways who would make poor and unhappy slaves to the pagan Saxons!

Your loving son, Ambrose

Arthur *Rex Brittonum*

PART ONE

Northwest Britannia, close to Deva, in the year 515AD

Chapter One

"PULL HARDER YOU wretches!" bellowed the captain, turning his warty head away from the pursuing ships to urge his crew to greater effort, gnarled hands gripping the tiller so firmly his knuckles shone white in the gloom. Low grey clouds scudded overhead, driven on by strong westerly gusts that blew into the lone sail intermittently, like puffs of air from bellows feeding a fire. Soft rain slanted across the faces of the desperate crew and passengers on the deck of the thirty-foot merchant rig, its eight oarsmen dashing their oars into the choppy green of the Hibernian Sea as angry whitecaps pointed the way to the green and grey shorelines rising before them.

"Row for your lives, the western savages are gaining on us!" Random words were snatched away by the fitful rage of Manannan, the dread god of sailors, who inhabited the narrow sea between Britannia's western coast and the land of Hibernia. It was across these waters that wild tribesmen habitually raided the comparatively wealthy and orderly Britannia, now left unguarded following Rome's withdrawal.

A cluster of six passengers huddled beside the burly captain at the stern, holding onto ropes or the side rail as their ship rolled in the waves that carried them to shore. Those who had voided their guts on deck or over the side turned pale faces to see the three black sails gaining on them through the gathering storm.

Barinthus clasped the charm around his neck and muttered a prayer to Fortuna. "I shall sacrifice the finest kid I can find in your temple at Deva, should you see fit to deliver us there in safety."

The well-fed Armorican had chartered the ship in the port of Dinan on the northwest coast of what had once been Roman Gaul and was transporting his cargo of fine wines, jars of olive oil, rolls of silk and linen, and some live quails in crates to sell to the nobles of western Britannia. He pulled the fox fur collar of his cloak tighter against the rain and looked down at his sodden calf leather boots, then to the crates of squawking birds that slid from side to side across the deck of the lurching vessel, noting their clucks of displeasure at every roll and shower of sea spray.

"I fear they will soon be upon us!" he yelled at the captain, who fixed him with a filthy look that spoke of regret at accepting the charter. "I have outrun many Frankish pirates around the rocky bays of Armorica where I know the reefs, but these waters are unknown to me. Let us hope we make beach before the rocks rip out our keel."

They were now in surf that sent rows of churning white-capped waves, like advancing lines of ghostly shield men, towards a shore that revealed itself as a shingle beach before towering pock-marked cliffs. The shrill cries of gulls seemed to foretell their impending doom as the roar of waves breaking on the beach filled their ears. The captain expertly kept the boat pointed straight ahead, and they were carried forward with great lurches as if being thrown out of his kingdom by the hand of Manannan himself. Stones scraped the hull as the boat made an inelegant beach some ten yards from the shore.

"Form a line to the shore and pass the cargo!" the captain yelled, picking up a crate of terrified fowl as he barged his way to the prow. The other passengers followed suit with their possessions and anything else they could lift. Barinthus buckled his sword belt around his generous girth and lifted his bag strap to his shoulder. Then he fell in line with the queue of soaked passengers and sailors, shuffling along the narrow deck between oarsmen's berths to be helped over the side into the churning surf by two of the crew.

"Head for the path between those bluffs," the captain shouted at Barinthus as he lowered him into the thigh-high waters. "We have ten minutes to clear the beach before those devils are upon us."

The portly merchant waded to shore and fussed over his precious cargo as the bundles and cases were piled haphazardly on shiny pebbles and strands of seaweed. He implored his fellow passengers to help carry his wares, and some agreed, slinging their bags on their backs and carrying one crate between two up the crunching shingle towards grassy dunes and the path beyond. He looked back and saw the three similar-sized ships of their pursuers negotiating the waves as they approached the shore. He made the difficult decision of which items to leave behind, opting for the lesser value crates of fowls, and scrambled over the loose stones with the captain and crew towards the hoped-for safety of the cliff tops.

"We must hide in the woods and pray to the gods that they do not find us nor take my ship," the portly captain grumbled as he followed his scrambling crew over the pebbles, seaweed and driftwood with arms full of the merchant's precious goods. The stony beach soon gave way to sandy hillocks crowned with marram grass and a worn path that had served fishermen well for countless generations. The straggling line of twenty made their way up it, heaving their burdens towards a pillow of pale sky squeezed between the steep cliffs that loomed on either side.

From the top of a dune, Barinthus looked back to see the raiders' ships beach and dozens of fur-clad warriors leap out, roaring at the crates of terrified quail they found. Fights broke out as some picked up the crates, tussling with their mates before wading back to their boats, whilst their huge leader waved a battle axe and urged his men up the beach in pursuit of their fleeing quarry. Barinthus had stopped to catch his breath and watch the scene below, and now moved as fast as his plump thighs would carry him up the rocky path that wound its way to hoped-for salvation. Water squelched from his boots and he ducked his head as angry sea birds dived towards him in defence of their nests on the cliffs to his left and right, their aggressive shrieks mimicking those of the covetous raiders behind.

The threatening oaths of the raiders grew louder as he neared the clifftop. Stopping briefly, Barinthus sucked in a lungful of air before making his final dash to the top. The others had disappeared from view ahead, but no sooner had he staggered onto level ground than two leather-clad warriors rose suddenly from the thick sage grass and grabbed his arms and bags. They dragged him without a word towards a copse some fifty feet away. His cries of protest were ignored and his mind was beset with the fear that they had avoided one set of pirates only to walk into the clutches of a band of thieves. Glancing back, he noted a line of men lying on their bellies in the greenery that fringed the clifftop, waiting for other unfortunates who came up the path.

Arms numb from being held so tight, he stumbled through thick gorse and a line of stunted trees into a clearing, to be thrown to his knees before a rank of soldiers. Barinthus noted a pair of high-quality calf leather boots before him, not unlike his own, and his gaze warily inched up well-stitched leather leggings to a thick, silver-studded sword belt, from which hung an ornate scabbard that held a hilt of shining silver. The torso of this man, perhaps their leader, was protected with a padded leather gilet, and his biceps were shrouded by sleeves of a finely woven woollen shirt. What fate had befallen the previous owner of these fine clothes? This well-dressed leader now stood looking down on him, with legs apart, thumbs hooked into his belt, his forearms adorned with intricately carved bronze bands.

"Stand up, sir, and address your rescuer," the man commanded in a firm but not unfriendly tone, at odds with the drama that was unfolding around him. Barinthus struggled to his feet, aware of the shouts and cries of men and the clash of swords to his rear as the ambush of the raiders was executed by these unknown warriors.

"To whom do I have the pleasure of thanking for our… rescue…?" Barinthus stuttered, bowing awkwardly to the imposing figure before him. Looking up he locked onto shining green eyes that exuded confidence, a handsome and noble fellow whose shoulder-length nut-brown hair was banded by a simple leather thong, his clean-shaven dimpled chin at odds with the men around him. A raised white scar ran across his right cheek, suggesting a brush with danger. He was not the chief of the local tribe, the Cornovi, who was an established customer of the merchant. Nor were these Cornovi warriors.

"I am Arthur, King of the Britons. You are forgiven your ignorance, as those in these parts do not yet know me." He turned to grin at his comrades, eliciting some gruff laughs. Arthur was enjoying the discomfort of the grovelling merchant before him.

"My apologies, my lord king. I am Barinthus, a merchant from Armorica, come to sell my wares to chiefs and, erm… kings, such as yourself, in the westerly places of this windy island." His head bobbed up and down, face turned away in deference and fixed with an appeasing grin as salty droplets fell from his pointed grey beard, and his plump hand instinctively clutched the purse at his belt.

"Well then, Barinthus of Armorica, we shall escort you and your fellows, once we have disposed of these Hibernian raiders. Our paths lie in the same direction as I come to seek the lord of this land."

Arthur pointed to the south and then brushed past the grovelling merchant and the frightened clutch of passengers behind him, to emerge from the treeline shouting commands to his men. They were swarming with deadly purpose across the meadow, some still engaged in duels with raiders; others binding the hands of those they had not killed, or picking trinkets from the dead. Some had chased the few who had escaped the slaughter down the path to the beach. Arthur strode to the cliff edge to see his men fighting on the beach and in the surf, noting that just one pirate ship had managed an awkward retreat into the waves - a couple of desperate raiders were lunging for it, diving awkwardly into the churning water. He turned to his men and laughed at the almost comic scene below.

"Bring the prisoners and secure the ships!" he shouted down to the beach. Then to his men he said, "Tie the prisoners in a line and make ready to leave this place."

Returning to the sheltered copse, Arthur resumed his exchange with Barinthus. "So, you know my brother-in-law, King Owain of the Cornovi people?"

"Yes, my lord king, I have been supplying him for some three years with many goods from Gaul and the Roman world beyond." Barinthus bowed with a flourish of his damp cloak, regaining his composure.

"Then you may accompany me to his court at Viriconium. But first, we shall pay a visit to their northernmost town of Deva and introduce ourselves to King Owain's man. Do you know who is the master of that town?"

Barinthus's face darkened and he bit his lip. "Indeed, I do, my lord. I usually skirt the place. He is a lusty warrior called Caratacus, named for the rebel leader who escaped the Romans to ferment rebellion in these parts. But his master is not King Owain of Powys, but King Cadwallon of Gwynedd, known as the Head Dragon, whose lands lie from here to the west. He is a frugal customer…"

"Ah, Caratacus, a rebel name indeed," Arthur mused, looking over the heads of the expectant throng before him. "So, this corner is where the kingdoms of Gwynedd and Powys meet. I know little of Cadwallon, except that he is descended of mighty Cunedda, who was sent here by Vortigern, the tyrant some called emperor, after Rome departed. He came to oppose Hibernian raiders such as those we fought today and planted his seed in this land."

Arthur brought his attention to bear on the stout ship's captain. "Captain, you may return to your ship and sail up the estuary to the port at Deva, together with the two captured ships. We shall make a gift of them to this Caratacus." He stepped forward and pointed away to his left, through a gap in the trees, to where the battlements of a fortified town with fluttering flags could just be made out across the channel in the hazy distance. "My men will assist you. Take those that you need to return your cargo to the shore and man the captured ships. We shall meet there before the day is done. Come, let us prepare to leave. Bring the prisoners!"

Arthur *Rex Brittonum*

Chapter Two

THE TOWN WALLS rose from the ground like a row of dirty grey teeth as the column crested the last hillock before spilling out onto a plain kept clear of trees. There were gaps in the crumbling wall, Arthur noted, but also something else – dark objects hanging on ropes draped from Deva's battlements. A flock of crows took to the air at their approach, cawing a warning.

A returning scout shouted, "My lord, the walls are lined with the dead!"

The grim sight of mangled bodies encased in iron cages brought gasps of shock from the priest and other sensitive souls in the column. Arthur called a halt before a dry ditch littered with the detritus and foul smells of human waste, beneath the curious and watchful gaze of spearmen clustered on the battlements.

Deva's gates remained open, and Arthur ordered his army to remain outside whilst he entered through the high stone gatehouse with a dozen followers and Barinthus. His hundred horsemen and a similar number of foot soldiers, with four ox-carts of supplies and camp followers, clustered in groups on the plain and waited.

Inside, curious townsfolk and lolling guards watched as they progressed along a main thoroughfare to the forum at the town's centre. Its size and layout reminded Arthur of the other great Roman legion towns he had visited – Corinium to the south and Ebrauc to the northeast.

"Long have I wished to visit this town," Arthur remarked to his personal guard, Herrig. The six-foot flaxen-haired Jute grunted and resumed his slow sweep of the faces lined up above them on the upper balconies of town houses, ever watchful for the glint of a blade. "The Romans controlled this island with five legions, Herrig, each of five thousand men, strategically placed in four legion towns and at The Wall. This is the home of the legion who marched over the north and west, subduing rebellions and making pacts with wary tribal chiefs. If only I could command such an army," he added wistfully, bowing and smiling to those who cheered.

"They have gone, my king, and left their mark on your land. Now it is yours to rule," Herrig replied in a slow, grating drawl. "These people are curious at your coming. I doubt they have many visitors."

"Given the welcome on the walls, I doubt it too."

They entered a square lined with people standing beside market stalls, and Arthur dismounted before the steps to a two-storey stone building dominating one side of the forum, doubtless the main administration hall. Behind him, his two banner-bearers stood, holding high his emblem of a bear and dragon grappling. Roman letters spelled, 'ARTHUR REX BRITTONUM', in thread of gold, for those few who could read it.

A line of six men dressed no better than the people in the streets, save for cloaks and sword belts, waited for him at the top of the steps before a pair of great oak doors. Arthur left his two bannermen with the horses and the rest climbed the worn stone steps to be greeted by a bowing steward, who requested they should surrender their swords and daggers to his guards. The great oak doors were opened by surly spearmen and they entered into a dark hall, partially lit by oil lamps on the walls and some strips of daylight through high windows of broken glass.

Birds fluttered in the rafters and cringing hounds scurried aside as Arthur strode on fouled reeds and hay strewn across the stone flags towards a raised platform on which sat a man locked in conversation with subordinates. Arthur stood patiently until the man turned to face him.

"Who are you that have entered the land of the mighty Head Dragon, Cadwallon of Gwynedd?"

"I am Arthur, son of Uther, chief of the Brigantes and Deirans, Lord of the Great Wall and King of the Britons. My commanders are Peredur, Prince of Rheged; Bedwyr, a noble knight; and Herrig, my champion."

"Ha! I did not know the Britons had a high king, save for that mewling brat in the south, Mordred!" He turned to his attendants to elicit their laughter. Then returned his huge, smiling, black-bearded face to Arthur and added, "I am Caratacus, the Keeper of this fortress of Deva. You are welcome Arthur, son of Uther. We have heard of you and look forward to hearing your tales of battles in the north lands in our hall this evening. How many are you?"

"I thank you, Lord Caratacus, for your welcome. We number two hundred warriors, and a ship's crew and passengers we have rescued from Hibernian pirates. We captured two of the enemy ships and present them and those we captured to you to do with as you will." Arthur had already persuaded the unhappy Barinthus to give up a crate of quails and some vials of wine to present to their host. He now waved Barinthus and his attendants to step forward. "This merchant from Armorica has brought some fowl and fine wine for your table."

"Ha! This is good and shows you are well-mannered folk who know the value of honouring your host. You are all most welcome. My men will see to your accommodation in our barracks and provide stables for your horses, although most will have to camp outside the walls. We shall meet again as the sun goes down. Welcome to the once Legion City of Deva!"

ARTHUR PLACED BARINTHUS and the other passengers from the ship into the care of his chancellor, Ambrose, knowing his learned friend would glean what information he could about their various businesses and connections. He also called forward the bard, Gerwyn, who had once travelled in Armorica, and charged him with entertaining the ship's passengers to soothe them after their brush with calamity.

That evening, Arthur and his commanders dined with Caratacus at his high table, exchanging tales of battles, winning tactics and the nature of their enemies. It soon transpired that Caratacus was the champion of his king,

Cadwallon, charged with governing this town, manning watchtowers along their north coast and sending out patrols on a daily basis to check for raiders. The threat came entirely from the sea, as their neighbouring tribesmen caused little conflict. The Head Dragon, Cadwallon, was based at a fortress on a high rocky bluff overlooking the sea, some fifty miles to their west, and would habitually tour the fortresses that bordered his lands three or four times a year.

"You still call this place by its Roman name, Deva. Why is that?" Arthur enquired of his host.

"Ha! It trips off the tongue more easily than 'Caer Ordovici' which the locals use."

Caratacus wiped his greasy hands on his jerkin and leaned towards Arthur. "We fought a bitter battle last year with Hibernian settlers on the Isle of Mona, once the lair of the leaders of the druids. They had killed or enslaved our people and were occupying the villages in that place. Our fiery Head Dragon led his men by boat across the narrow straights, and I led a second group of warriors to attack their port on the western shore. Battle raged for one month until we overran the island and captured their king – a fat, boggle-eyed fellow who smelled of fish. He was ransomed to one of the kings of Hibernia, and others were kept as slaves to work our mines. We freed hundreds of our people and there was great rejoicing."

He grinned at the cheers and banging of goblets by his men, and poured wine for himself and his guest. "I am intrigued, Lord Arthur, that you claim the title, 'King of the Britons'. Did you have a coronation from kings and chiefs in the north lands?" He signalled for a waiting girl to clear their empty platters and threw some bones to his hairy wolfhounds.

Arthur was now aware that outside of the safety of the Rheged and Brigante lands, this would be a contentious claim. "Yes, my father-in-law, Meirchion Gul of the Rheged, did gather the northern chiefs and placed a crown on my head, charging me to follow in the footsteps of my father, King Uther, and defend this land from the many raiders that beset it. It was his will."

Arthur *Rex Brittonum*

"Ha! But a king needs a kingdom and the consent of the people to rule. Where is your consent? I doubt if the other kings of this island would willingly submit to you, my lord." His black eyes gleamed in the torchlight, his smile and slight bow spoke of mischief. But Arthur had warmed to this huge, well-humoured warrior and would not rise to the bait.

"Your words are well spoken, Caratacus, and I do not take them as mocking jibes, as some might." This drew laughter from the assembled higher-ranked warriors on both sides of the table. Both men smirked to show their pleasure at playing to the assembled throng of burly warriors. "I am aware that Uther's firstborn, Morgana, has dismissed my claim and has crowned her son, Mordred, who sits on Uther's throne at Dunbelgar in the south lands. They are a threat to our peace, and we believe they have formed an alliance with the South Saxons who are menacing the Dumnonians, whom we hold dear as allies. But we are bound for Powys on your southern border, where King Owain and my sister Anne, his queen, feel the threat of the Saxons growing to the south and east."

Arthur paused to let his words sink in and supped his wine. He saw he held their attention and continued. "The advance of the Saxons in the south and their brothers, the Angliscs to the east, is a concern to all the kings and chiefs of this island, and I intend to lead the resistance to their spread. Whether I am welcomed as king or commander, I am here to help."

Arthur sat back and surveyed the faces of black-bearded warriors across the table, who merely stared at him without expression. This was the first test of his well-prepared speech to the holders of these western lands.

Caratacus merely grunted and tore a strip of meat off a bone with his teeth. They ate and exchanged stories until Arthur chose his moment to ask his host about the bodies hanging from the walls.

"Ha! Some are captured raiders and some are criminals. If you are to be a king, Arthur, then your people must fear you as much as love you. Otherwise, maintaining order becomes impossible and your rivals will prey on your weakness. Public maiming and execution leave a powerful memory in the minds of the onlookers." He noted Arthur's stern, unsmiling look.

"Will the Hibernian pirates we have given you meet the same fate?"

"Some will be burnt at Beltane in offering to the gods. The strong will be sent to the king's salt and iron mines to work out their days. We are not barbarians, Arthur, but the peace must be maintained with an iron will."

Caratacus diverted his attention to Bedwyr, seated next to Arthur. "And you, Bedwyr, have the dark looks of our people – you could pass for one of my men. I am curious to know that Arthur introduced you as 'knight'. To my knowledge, there have been no new knights made since the time of Ambrosius, before I was born. How are you a knight?" His dark eyes gleamed and a smile played above his greasy beard.

Bedwyr exchanged glances with Arthur and cleared his throat to speak. "I have trained under Gawain and Percival at Vindolanda on the Great Wall, the last of the knights of Ambrosius. My king, Arthur, did lay his sword on my shoulder and proclaim me a knight, in that tradition. As for my looks, my mother is from this land."

"And your father?"

"He was the grandson of an *optio* in the famed Second Augusta Legion, who marched across these western lands, and may well have served time in this place. I was raised on a *colonia* and trained to fight in the Roman manner, my lord."

Caratacus coughed, spat and emptied his goblet. The men were becoming drunk and rowdy – oaths, barely disguised insults and challenges were exchanged. The dark-looking Cambrians were fascinated by the fair-haired Herrig, and many offers to arm wrestles were laid. The Jute was losing his composure and had leaned forward, about to speak, when Arthur stood and thanked Caratacus for his hospitality and indicated he was ready to retire ahead of their continued progress south in the morning. There was nothing more to be gained here.

Caratacus looked affronted, but then broke into a smile. He pushed back his heavy oak chair and banged his goblet to silence the noise. "Our meal is at an end and I must bid you a good night. There will be no more insults or challenges for our guests. Arthur, my steward will escort you to your lodgings. We have enjoyed your stories of war and guile, and I believe you have a powerful destiny, if you stay alive." He belched and swayed slightly with the effect of the rich wine. Arthur clasped his host's forearm, and then signalled his men that they must all take their leave. "And I shall convey the substance of your words to my lord and king, Cadwallon," Caratacus shouted to their backs.

ARTHUR GATHERED HIS men in the grey morning and they left through the great stone gatehouse, following the Roman road that led south towards their destination, Viriconium. He turned back in his saddle and saw the great bear-cloaked figure of Caratacus standing on the parapet above the gatehouse, staring solemnly down on them. The foot soldiers and wagons that waited outside fell into line behind the horsemen.

The normally silent Bedwyr rode beside Arthur, also looking behind. "My lord, this Caratacus has the look of a fierce warrior who commands the respect of his men. He would make a powerful ally."

"Indeed, he would," Arthur replied. "But we cannot know the minds of these people until we have met with the King of Powys at Viriconium. He shall tell us of these kings and warlords that inhabit this wild, westerly land. It is the bulging belly of our mother island of Britannia, but we are yet to know the nature of its offspring."

Peredur, the youthful brother of Arthur's wife, rode forward to join the conversation. His slight frame bounced up and down in his saddle and his high voice squeaked in the cool morning air, "My lords, it is my father's will that you make peace with these sons of the mighty Cunedda, the kin of us Northmen who did colonise these lands…"

"Yes, yes, I know, my eager young brother," Arthur said, cutting his words. "I carry letters from your father to that effect, intended to smooth our welcome from the kings of Gwynedd and Powys."

"Then you did not give the letter for the King of Gwynedd to his man, Caratacus?" the youth persisted. He was still irritated at not being invited to dine with Caratacus, Arthur having chosen only his burly commanders.

Arthur smiled down at his young deputy. "I shall ask our host, King Owain, to call a council of kings of these lands, and shall choose my moment to give the letters. Patience is an important part of diplomacy, young Peredur. We must meet them, talk with them, break bread with them, and get the measure of them. What I will ask of them they will not willingly give. In truth, I wish my old friend and adviser, Merlyn, were by my side to give me his counsel."

Bedwyr grunted and replied, "You are well rid of that sorcerer and meddler in the affairs of kings. He abandoned us to our fate in the Forest of Celidon and owes his allegiance to the druids and dark gods of the forests."

Arthur threw back his head and laughed, causing his black stallion, Mars, a leaving gift from the Rheged king, to snort and toss its head. "You were always suspicious of Merlyn, my friend, because he is one of a kind. I have known him since I was a child, hiding behind a curtain and peeping at the mysterious visitor to our farm. He has always watched over me and always told me since I remember that my destiny is to lead the peoples of this island against our many enemies. He inhabits the fringes of two very different worlds – the one moulded by Rome, and the ancient world of the old gods who once held sway over our people. He holds much knowledge in his grey-bearded head. But I know not if he is alive or dead."

They lapsed into silent reflection as the purposeful, straight road the Romans had named Watling Street guided them beside streams, through wooded vales and across plains where wary herders drove their cattle and sheep away from the marching soldiers and rumbling wagons.

Arthur *Rex Brittonum*

Chapter Three

"MY DEAREST BROTHER!" Anne gushed, flinging her arms around Arthur's neck and kissing him warmly on both cheeks. "I am so pleased to see you journeyed safely from the Northlands." She held him by his dusty arms and looked into his deep green eyes; mirror images, she knew, of her own. Arthur beamed his pleasure at seeing his sister again, at a loss for words. "But I am standing between you and my noble husband. This is Owain Ddantgwyn, King of this kingdom of Powys."

Arthur gathered his wits and handed the reins of his horse to his young squire, Dermot, and faced the royal couple. "My little sister, Anne, it is with a glad heart that I see you again. And my noble brother-in-law, King Owain. I am much pleased to make your acquaintance." Arthur bowed to his host and the two men clasped forearms, grinning at each other. Arthur noted Owain's prominent front tooth, standing out like a pale grey tombstone.

"Arthur, my brother, well met! It is my pleasure to welcome you to Powys, land of the Cornovi, and to Caer Cornovia, once called Viriconium, our great town and fortress. Please, come into my great hall where food and drink await, and let your saddle-weary friends and commanders join us." He swept a welcoming arm towards the entrance.

Arthur's gaze widened to admire the great double doorway before them, the height of two men, prompting Owain to explain its grandeur. "This once was the Great Basilica, where tradesmen and healers touted their services." He then clapped his hands to send his attendants scurrying to their duty.

The cavernous interior, richly hung with tapestries, was lit by oil lamps in recesses in the walls and on bronze stands beside the massive stone columns that supported the high roof beams. Anne placed her hand on Arthur's arm to draw his attention and asked him, "But where is your queen, Gunamara?"

"I have left her and our infant son, Llacheu, in the care of her father. She was weakened after the birth and I feared for their welfare on such a long and arduous journey. I shall send for them once I am settled here," he said. Then he was compelled again to look curiously about him at the great space, where attendants in colourful livery now stepped towards the trestle tables, bearing jugs and steaming platters, and the local nobility lined his path, bowing as he passed.

ASAPH, ARTHUR'S CHAPLAIN, strode purposefully through the marketplace, bowing his tonsured head to left and right at the respectful traders. Rotten plums squelched under the tread of his leather boots, and he held up his woollen monk's habit to protect its hem. He was from the first crop of novices who had been ordained by Bishop Samson at Luguvalium, beside the Great Wall. Because of Asaph's inquisitive mind and adventurous spirit, his mentor had assigned him to accompany Arthur on his expeditions as his chaplain and spiritual advisor. His mood was light and full of the joys of God's presence on finding this town well-ordered and without the signs of pagan worship he had encountered on his journey across the sparsely populated northlands.

Beyond the square that provided sheltered alcoves for the market stalls, he found a cobbled street of single storey thatched houses that had animal pens beside them. He turned left and marched up a slight incline to the church located in a sizeable corner plot at the end of the street. He nodded his approval on finding that a sturdy wooden hut, long and plain with overhanging thatched eaves, now occupied the stone foundations of what once must have been an imposing and ornate temple. The church sat to the back of the slab, Asaph noticed, behind a low wall with seat grooves that bordered the temple forecourt. He looked behind and saw that he was at the highest point in the enclosed town, with streets sloping away to the stables and barrack blocks by the far wall.

Turning back, he approached a crafted wooden cross taller than a man, which was set on the polished stone of a central plinth. Was it haughty Jupiter who had been toppled to make way? Asaph guessed that barely a hundred years ago, townsfolk would have bought fowl from sellers arrayed across this open space. They would have carried them by their legs, squawking and struggling, into the temple, to have them slaughtered by pagan priests in ritual supplication to their chosen god. Idolatrous nonsense, he thought, and a sinful waste.

The familiar and welcome smell of incense assailed his nostrils as he pushed open the door and entered into the subdued, dimly lit interior. The nave was open, save for timber roof supports, as the congregation would stand to sing and chant during the saying of the holy mass. Along the walls, benches ran for the elderly and lame to sit beneath paintings of scenes from the gospels. The room was empty, and Asaph walked across worn stone flags to the altar, a simple wooden table. He bowed low to the crucifix on the altar, before passing through a narrow doorway at the rear into the sacristy, where the priest kept his vestments, candlesticks, chalice and copper plate. Beyond that, another door led to the priest's quarters. He knocked and waited until he heard a faint voice bid him enter.

"Ah, fellow priest, you are most welcome!" An elderly white-haired cleric, much shorter than the tall and robust Asaph, rose from a simple wooden cot to greet him.

"I am sorry to have disturbed your repose, Holy Father," Asaph whispered, somehow feeling a hushed tone to be appropriate.

"Come in, my brother. I have few enough visitors, come in. I am Father Ederyn. He gripped Asaph's arm and led him to a table with two chairs. "Sit. I'll call my housekeeper for some refreshment." He rang a small bell that was on the table and sat opposite his visitor.

"I am Asaph, from the Northern Diocese, come yesterday with Arthur and his men."

"Ah yes, the whole town turned out, myself included, to welcome the queen's noble brother. I was much relieved and pleased to see the chi-rho and fish banners draped from your wagon as you passed by, dear brother Asaph!" He chuckled and looked up as a woman came through the outer door, carrying a tray laden with a pewter jug, two cups, a wooden spoon, a platter of cut bread and a jar of honey. "Ah, Theresa, you always know when I have a guest," he chortled.

Asaph smiled at the retreating woman and replied, "I can assure you, Father, that my king is a devout Christian who prays with me every day."

"King, you say? We had not heard that."

"He was crowned King of the Britons by Meirchion Gul of the Rheged, some three months before our departure. The ceremony was attended by nobles from across the northlands, both below and above the Great Wall. I have never seen such hairy and rough-looking fellows. But I have heard from their talk that there is a rival claimant to be King of the Britons in the far south."

"Ah yes, the twisted politics of our vexing age. Does that make Arthur a rebel? Since Uther has gone, everyone wants to be king. We are fortunate here to be free of troublesome raiders." Ederyn poured some mead into the cups and offered bread and honey to his guest. "We keep our own hives outside the walls and ferment our own mead from the honey. Eat and drink, my friend – you are a big fellow I can see."

After washing down a hunk of bread with the sweet mead, Asaph asked, "Is there much pagan worship in this area?"

"There is. Many of my congregation visit a shrine to the water goddess, Coventina, about half a mile upstream, where a dam has created a pond. They bathe there and throw offerings into the waters to have their prayers answered. A strange druid fellow lives in the woods beyond, keeping out of sight of Owain's soldiers, who are under instructions from our most noble king to chase him off if they see him." Ederyn chuckled at the thought. "I admonish them from time to time, but don't overdo it as I know that old beliefs linger in some hearts, as was the way in Roman times. Do not look so horrified, my young brother in Christ. Have faith that His word will prevail."

The younger priest finished his bread and honey and washed it down with a gulp of mead. Eying the older man he said, "It will soon be the festival of Beltane, to welcome the spring. What is your... view of the people celebrating such pagan festivities?"

Father Ederyn sighed and sat back in his chair. "Our bishop expects us to stage a rival spring festival, with a procession through the town, at the same time as the Beltane festivities."

"And will you?"

"I am of a mind to hold a procession after our Sunday service and pay no heed to the maypole dancing and lewd, ale-soaked cavorting that will take place on the meadow by the river."

The idealism of youth burst from Asaph. "Are we not shepherds? To let them fall into such liberality..."

"Our king allows the people their festivals," the cleric assured him, patting his arm, and continued to give the younger man the benefit of his experience. "Because they celebrate the passing of the seasons, they rouse each man to his yearly tasks. When such a song and dance is made, young Dawid or Jack cannot swear he knew not that it was time to sharpen his plough. And which proud mistress can leave undisturbed the grubs that are fattening themselves? They chomp away in her oaken chest, but the festival signals the time for spring shaking and sweeping, and so domestic order is rescued."

"Then I shall join you for your service and procession, dear father," Asaph replied with a smile.

The two priests talked of church and lay politics until the orange sun dipped below the walls. "I will take my leave of you now, Father," Asaph said, standing.

"Please invite Arthur to my mass tomorrow, an hour after sunrise," Ederyn replied, rubbing his hands and smiling with pleasure at this unexpected and informative visit.

Chapter Four

"I HAVE SENT riders out to the other four kings of this westerly part of Britannia, asking them to attend a council here at the rise of the next moon," Owain said to his brother-in-law as they strolled from the great hall in search of privacy. "There are urgent matters. Foremost is the common defence of our lands. I mentioned your coming, but held back from naming you 'King of the Britons'." He coughed and dropped his eyes to a pointed shoe that carved a curved line in the dust.

"So, who am I to them, my lord?" Arthur asked plainly.

Owain met his eyes and replied, "I described you as the brother of my queen, and a powerful lord of the north lands who commands the loyalty of the mighty Rheged, Brigante and Deiran peoples. I named you as Arthur, son of Uther, inheritor of the Roman title, *Comes Brittonum*, Lord of the Great Wall."

Arthur scratched his clean-shaven chin and pondered on this. He had told his brother-in-law of his crowning by King Meirchion of the Rheged as *Rex Brittonum* - Uther's successor - but this had only been met with a look of mild alarm by Owain. Nothing had been said at the time, the subject had been changed, and he now saw that his words had melted away into the smoky air, a mere suggestion, almost a challenge, that had drifted to the rafters and out through the vents.

"I have been called '*Dux Bellorum*' and '*Comes Brittonum*', both imperial titles with little meaning now, decades after the Romans have departed," Arthur reflected aloud. "You are not the first to pour doubt on my claim to be King of the Britons."

"Some would say that title also belongs in the past." Owain put his arm around Arthur's shoulder and guided him to a wooden ladder that led to the parapet of the town walls. It leaned at an angle against an earth bank that bolstered the external wall, and led them to a platform of wooden planks that ran around the perimeter, offering views of the surrounding countryside over the top of the grey stone wall. A pair of spearmen lolling against the gatehouse stood to attention in the presence of their king. Owain nodded and they relaxed, but gave a cursory, habitual look across the gentle landscape for any signs of movement.

Arthur followed his host's gaze and admired the sweep of green pasture, dotted with white-fleeced sheep and the occasional shepherd's hut, which fell away to a river snaking across a wide valley floor.

"This is indeed a fair place, my lord," Arthur murmured.

"Aye, and one well chosen by the Romans, Brother. This fort commands the only ford for miles in both directions, across the cold and rough River Severna. Coventina has taken many lives." Owain shook his head.

"This is not the first time I have heard of Coventina," Arthur muttered, the image of the white-bearded Merlyn briefly coming to mind. "I was once guided by Uther's adviser, Merlyn, who would visit a shrine near Vindolanda sacred to this mysterious water nymph."

"The Lady of the Rivers and Lakes, and greatly feared by the people, as much as the Christian God is revered," Owain replied, nodding. He then pointed north. "The road on which you arrived was called Watling Street by those who made it, and our stonemasons have done their best to maintain it. It runs southeast to our second fortress at Letocetum, and I fear one day it will guide the enemy to our gates."

Owain spread his hands on the thick wall and turned with a smile to face Arthur, strands of his dark brown hair fluttering across his face. "Come Arthur, I wish to tell you about my fellow kings and so prepare you for the council." He led the way along the platform, away from any prying ears at the gatehouse.

Owain's flowing gown of green and gold wool buffeted in the breeze, and he pushed his hands into his generous sleeves. They turned a corner by a watchtower, placing the river at their backs and a distant range of snow-capped mountains ahead, before he spoke again. "You know, this land to the west of the Severna, with its wild mountains where they say dragons, fairy folk and giants dwell, was a challenge to the Romans. It is quite unlike the more manageable, temperate lands they had met south and east of us, and they did not strive hard to exert their influence here. Of course, they built this place and the forts on the southern and north-western coast, by the island of Mona, where the druids once ruled."

He paused and turned to see Arthur watching him intently. "I see," Arthur said, nodding. "And what would the Romans make of this place now, my lord? How do you fare, Brother? Where are your grim giants and sly fairies?"

"Kingdoms of hardy farmers are now established, and each eyes their neighbour with suspicion. But they are more uneasy on other counts. Whilst many elsewhere have suffered raiders from Gaul and the barbarous lands east of the isle, our kingdoms on this western shore have suffered raids from the Hibernians. Your party has already encountered them, you say."

Arthur nodded. "Do they think you are easy prey?"

"We are not many. Few call these westerly rocks and forests home. Our kings of Gwynedd to the north, Demetia to the west, Gwent to the south and Dyfed to the south-west, together with ourselves to the east and centre, rarely meet, and when we do, old conflicts inevitably surface and squabbles break out."

"Are they so unruly then? Is there no native sense among these kings?"

"I will tell you of them in a while, but first, let me prepare you for their hostility to your coming."

Owain stopped halfway between raised corner watchtowers and faced Arthur. "They will tell you they have their hands full defending their lands from seaborne raiders and their treacherous neighbours. They will tell you the threat from Hibernian raiders can be contained, and they care not for what happens in the other parts of this island. They will tell you that since the passing of King Uther, some ten years ago, they have not bent their knees to any high king, nor will they do so again."

"And that goes for you as well, my lord?" Arthur asked.

Owain's previous playfulness had now gone, and his face wore a serious expression, but he sidestepped the question. "Our situation in Powys differs from our neighbours, in that our lands stretch far away to the east of the Severna, where the soil is rich for farming, and pastureland covers the rolling hills."

"Ah," said Arthur, realising now the undoubted envy surrounding his sister and Owain.

"The chiefs of the Ordovici and Cornovi pay homage to me and expect me to patrol our borders with the lost lands of Lloegyr, to the east, where the dreaded Angliscs and Saxons roam the land and subjugate the people. I am wary of the threat from them and fear their greedy eyes will soon turn to us. That is why I need you here, by my side, Arthur. You have fought those devils and know their nature."

"Yes, you are right to fear them," Arthur replied, climbing down the ladder to the base of the east gatehouse. When Owain was beside him he continued. "On each spring tide more of their fellows, with wives, children and livestock, arrive on the east coast. They have a footing and intend to stay and settle the land. Their men are strong and fearless warriors who fight with sword, spear and axe, a match for our stoutest of men. Yes, I have fought them, at the Rivers Glein and Dubglass near Lindum and at Guinnion and Ebrauc further north, each time driving them back to their boats; but they always return in greater numbers."

Owain sighed before continuing, "My position is weakened by a bitter dispute with my southern neighbour, King Caradog of Gwent. Because of this, I must keep thirty or so men patrolling the mountain passes and river vales. News of bitter border raids and disruption of trade causes me sleepless nights and a poor appetite. Caradog has been invited to our council but may only send an emissary to find out what is said. In truth, Arthur, I must keep a watchful eye on all my neighbours."

Arthur nodded sagely as the two men progressed along a busy main street, past market stalls selling vegetables, loaves, dried fruit and meat, earthen pots and reed mats. Houses of wood panels and thatched roofs lined the street, built on solid foundations where brick and stone Roman buildings had once stood. He noticed Barinthus haggling with a couple of stall holders. The plump merchant briefly broke off to bow to Arthur and Owain as the two noblemen passed by.

"I am impressed by the extent of your labours. I see you replace and maintain what was left by the Romans." Arthur had stopped to handle a gaily painted wine jug, featuring Bacchus playing a lyre, before handing it back to its owner and turning to Owain. "May I ask, my lord, how many warriors are at your command?"

"I have a garrison of fifty gate and wall guards here, in addition to a hundred mounted guards who patrol the outlying areas. I have charged local settlements to be vigilant and maintain a pyre that can be lit to signal if they are attacked by border raiders. I can raise a militia from the townsfolk and farmers of up to five hundred men in a few days."

"The Rhegeds too like to be prepared," said Arthur. "I hope my arrival does not disturb this orderly town."

Owain pointed down a side street of uneven cobbles to a wooden building close to the outer wall and smiled. "The old Roman horse stables have been maintained over in the northern quadrant, next to eight rows of barrack blocks for our guards and their families. We can stable your horses there and we can provide beds for no more than fifty – perhaps your personal guards and attendants? Your other men will have to camp outside on the higher ground away from the river, which is prone to flood at this time of year."

They had arrived at the town centre, where Owain pointed to the four quarters from a central square as he spoke. Close by, a donkey trod a miserable circle around a well, its water spilling in jerky flows into the stone troughs where chattering women filled their basins. Arthur looked about as Owain indicated the locations of civic functions that included smithies for working iron, a warehouse for carpentry and the storing of wooden beams and planks, a bath house that was now used for the storage of grain, and a Christian church recently erected on the site of what had once been a temple to Jupiter.

"Ah, the baths are now filled with grain," Arthur laughed. "I have enjoyed taking the waters in other places in our island, but many are no longer used for rinsing the grit from our townsfolk."

"Our people make use of well water and a stream outside the west gate that feeds the river for bathing in the summer; but in the winter, the air here is very rank!" Owain held his nose and they returned in high spirits to the great hall.

As they mounted the steps to the great oak doors, Owain turned to his brother-in-law and casually remarked, "You mentioned Merlyn earlier. Perhaps you do not know that he resides at a white fortress in the mountains to the west – on the wild and inhospitable edges of my kingdom. He has been here once or twice for supplies."

Arthur stopped walking, open-mouthed.

Owain laughed and marched towards his queen and her attendants, who engulfed him with questions about meals and accommodation. Arthur took his leave, saying he wished to settle into his quarters, as he had much to dwell on after his conversation with his brother-in-law.

"MY LORD! A messenger has come from Lindum with grave news!" Ambrose, clad in sandals and toga, stood in the entrance hall to the senior office holder's villa that had been allocated to Arthur.

Arthur jumped to his feet instantly, throwing aside the towel with which he was wiping his hands. He had been enjoying a bowl of sticky preserved figs with the young prince, Peredur, who was sharing his accommodation. "What grave news is this?"

"I have received a most vexing reply from my father to the missive I sent him before our departure from the Northlands. He says that the Angliscs sailed on an early spring tide in great numbers, led by their one-eyed king, Icel, and have captured their town of Lindum, enslaving those not able to make their escape!"

"By our God and Saints! That most Roman of towns, overrun! And did the noble Maddox make good his escape?"

"Indeed, he did, along with his fellow council members and their families. They have fled to the western edge of their tribal lands, and are hiding in the villa of a farm estate. They are pleading with you, my lord, to send an armed troop to collect them and escort them to this place. The messenger without knows the place where they are staying." Ambrose lifted his shoulders, attempting to retain some dignity, but his eyes held a desperate appeal to his boyhood friend and lord.

"Come with me. I shall consult with King Owain to decide on the best response." Arthur turned to Peredur and waved him to join them, and then let an attendant affix his red woollen cloak to his leather gilet. His squire, Dermot, and guard, Herrig, came running from the kitchen and fell into line behind the three men. They marched to the gate of the royal enclosure and waited outside whilst a guard conveyed Arthur's request to see his host.

They were admitted into a courtyard where a fountain spilled water into a circular pond. Anne met them and invited them to stone benches between ornate columns.

Owain appeared, bucking his sword belt. "What is the matter? Are we attacked?"

"No, my lord," Arthur said, standing to greet him with a bow. "My friend and chancellor, Ambrose, has received a message from our eastern cousins, the Coritani, telling us his town of Lindum, in size not unlike this, is overrun by Angliscs. Ambrose's father, Maddox, was leader of their council and has fled to the woods with others. My old ally is begging for me to go to his aid."

"This is dread news indeed." Owain sank to a seat, took a goblet from a tray and sipped. "What will you do, Arthur?"

"I ask for your consent to rescue them and bring them to your lands. I would need scouts and also land between here and your border for them to settle. Out of kinship, will you consider this, my lord Owain?"

Owain paused to think, instructing his attendants to bring refreshments. "We cannot know how many there might be until you find them… but we do know from others of their tribe that the Coritani are civilised folk with Roman ways, like ourselves. Perhaps you should bring their leaders to us so we might talk to them. Indeed, their leader can describe their plight to our council, and thus impress upon my neighbours the dangers that lie on my borders."

He brightened at this thought, casting a smile at his dour guests. "But direct their people, dear Arthur, to our other Roman fort of Letocetum. That place is lightly populated and has abandoned farmland surrounding it. There was a plague there a few years ago and many of those that did not perish moved on. But that is not all. It is said that a giant inhabits the rocks there and the people are frightened by it. Without doubt, there is something unnatural that has scared them away from that luscious valley. We keep a small garrison at the fort to defend our southern border."

"You are wise, my lord," Arthur replied. "Then I will take my mounted men and leave my foot soldiers here, camped outside your walls. We shall leave with your scouts after our morning victuals. I take my leave to make preparations."

"The captain of my guards, Viroco, and a troop of our men will guide you across the central mountains and valleys of this island to the borders of the lost lands," Owain said, clasping his brother-in-law's forearm. Arthur hugged his sister before leading his men to the garden gate. "Do not tarry in the east, Arthur," Owain shouted after them. "Remember, our council of kings will take place at the rise of the next moon. May God protect you!"

Outside, Arthur turned to Bedwyr and remarked, "And I am curious to find out more about this unnatural giant.

Legends abound of such creatures. We shall survey that land and investigate this mystery."

    The town was soon a hive of activity, as soldiers due to ride out met with family and friends and sought supplies for the road. The solitary tavern was teeming with local and visiting soldiers, the air full of laughter and oaths, with drinking challenges and scraps spilling into surrounding streets. Arthur, his preparations made, toured the town with his commanders to assuage his restless spirit. He laughed and joked with the men, his yearning for adventure barely contained; the image of the leering king of the Angliscs revived in his memory, his sinews taut at the prospect of battle.

Arthur *Rex Brittonum*

Chapter Five

ARTHUR JOINED HIS sister, brother-in-law and commanders for a church service and blessing from Father Ederyn, before riding out of the east gate on the road that dipped down to the ford. They crossed where the gently flowing river bubbled around stone slabs that had been laid across the riverbed for ease of passing. Townsfolk cheered the two hundred horsemen and the solitary supply wagon that followed them, shouting words of encouragement to the wagon as it struggled up the far bank and headed towards the rising sun that peeped from behind distant mountains.

"You know the place where we should camp?" Arthur asked Viroco, proud captain of the Cornovi Guard.

"Yes, my lord. We can reach the base of the far mountains by evening if we keep to this pace. There is a meadow with shepherds' huts beside a stream. Beyond that, there is a pass through the mountains that will bring us to the land of the Coritani."

"Do your Cornovi people have much contact with the Coritani?" Arthur asked.

"They look to the south and east for their trade, and we look to the west. There is some trade, mainly in livestock, across the mountain pass, but in truth, we rarely see them. I cannot recall there ever having been conflict between our peoples. Thus, we do not have a garrison in the east, merely passing patrols."

"This will be a long trek," said Arthur, after some time, "and not an easy one."

"You prize the safety of the elder, Maddox, to make such a journey when your army is barely rested."

"Yes, our fortunes have long been entwined. And so, for him I brave Letocetum's giant."

"Ha, you have heard of that? Now and then, scouts claim to have glimpsed a giant, hairy man disappearing amongst the rocks. This, understand you, is a wild, uninhabited place through which few people pass. And sometimes people are reported missing. We send out a patrol to investigate, but no one is ever found."

"And do you believe in it?" Arthur persisted.

Viroco looked at Arthur with a steady, black-eyed stare. "It is hard to believe fantastic tales, my lord. I am more inclined to believe that bandits live amongst the rocks and the odd traveller is waylaid. If our plan is to lead the Coritani folk who are fleeing from persecution to those lands, as my king charged me, then we must search that wild place and flush out any bandits… or giants."

Arthur grunted and they lapsed into silence again. The land was farmed to left and right of the road, and often children ran beside the horses, holding up bunches of lucky purple blooms, or chunks of bread for the amiable riders. After two hours, Arthur called a halt at a crossroads where crude shacks had been made for the sale or exchange of farm produce to passing travellers. The horsemen dismounted to stretch, and bartered with the farm women and children, or simply led their horses onto the grasslands, where they sat amongst the daisies to chatter and drink from their gourds.

In the supply wagon, Derward, Arthur's loyal cook, jumped down from the front board. With his travelling companion, Father Asaph, he then set about inspecting the foodstuff on offer. He carried a purse full of bronze and silver coins stamped with past emperors' heads that Arthur had given him, together with a bag of woven tapestries, for wall or table decoration, rolled into lengths that stood hip-high. Ambrose jumped from the covered wagon and followed behind. He had not been to war with Arthur since his days as a squire, but this time he knew he must go to find his father and bring him to safety. Remaining in the wagon was a healer who had learned his skills from Merlyn at the dispensary in Vindolanda.

"Popular with houseproud wives, those are," Derward said, as he pushed the bag of tapestries into Asaph's long arms.

"And what are you looking to barter that you couldn't get in Caer Cornovia?" Asaph asked.

Derward grinned through broken teeth. "I have barrels of salted pork and strips of cured venison aplenty, but some fresh cuts on the spits tonight would be welcome. The men are always cheery on roasted fresh meat!" He led the priest in an awkward shuffle towards the chattering farmers' wives, leaning on a staff as he dragged his lame leg and muttered curses.

"I will pray to Saint Madron, that you may find relief," Asaph said, his clean-shaven chin resting on the heavy bag in his arms.

Derward turned and grimaced wryly, clutching a carved charm that hung around his neck. "Save your prayers, Father. I have offered a sacrifice to the water goddess to watch over me and make the enemy blind to me. They will not see me cowering beneath the wagon, and pass by. We are heading to war, something you have yet to experience." He sighed as he approached the row of shacks and fell into haggling with the locals.

BY THE END of the fourth day they had cleared the mountains without serious hindrance or incident. Arthur led his column onto a grassy hilltop where there was already a chill in the evening air. A shepherd had driven his sheep to one side and stood gawping at the banners depicting a bear and dragon, and the rows of leather-clad helmeted horsemen, their round shields painted with differing emblems, clutching spears flying coloured pennants at the ends. Below them the land sloped away to a wide plain on which farmsteads were dotted and copses of trees stood on lone hills. To the north, a dense forest wall ranged, but to the south and east, the land had largely been cleared for farming. Arthur noted a column of thick smoke curling upwards, perhaps some ten miles distant. The sun was dropping behind the mountains to their back and long shadows fell across the land.

"Shall we set our camp here for the night, my lord?" Viroco asked.

"Aye, tell the men to make camp. Send your scouts to the nearby farms to allay their fears at our coming and get news of the movement of the enemy. We shall investigate yonder column of smoke at dawn."

That evening, Arthur ate with his commanders around a crackling campfire, its flames dancing yellow and orange. Bedwyr leaned towards him and noticed the scar across his right cheek glowed white in the firelight. Arthur saw where he was looking and put his hand up to it.

"It always seems to rise before battle," he chuckled, running his finger along the ridge. "It serves to remind me of my mortality, dear Bedwyr."

"I was there that day, my lord, but came late with Gawain and his men, to find you bloodied and bruised, your shield and helmet smashed. We were fearful for you."

"You had good cause to be. We were surprised in our camp and unprepared to defend ourselves from the Deiran assault. Noble Varden, who had taught me to fight with sword and shield since I was a lad, had fallen by my side from his wounds, his snowy white hair flecked with his own blood, and Herrig staggered with wounded arm hanging limp to my other side."

Arthur glanced at Herrig, sprawled at the other side of the fire, listening. "Grime was his name, a captain of the Deiran guard. He had singled me out in the battle. I still see his leering visage, Bedwyr, eyes wide in anticipation of slaying me, his warm, sour breath in my face as he leaned in, pushing me back with his shield. I could not move, my legs buckling beneath me; I could only turn aside as his knife carved into my face. In that moment, as his hot blade cut open my cheek, I felt my time had come."

"The fear of death in the rage of battle is no disgrace, my lord," Bedwyr said, clasping his master's arm.

"No, it is the extremes of emotions, my friend. Exhilaration, then dread fear. Cruel blood lust, then uncertainty and doubt. All in a rush of madness. It twists and binds us, making us stronger, those of us who survive. Others are maimed and live on as half-men, dreaming of what once was. But I lived, and he died; his bones now lie in a burial pit close by the walls of Ebrauc. Your coming swayed the tide of battle in our favour and saved us, dear Bedwyr. I remember how fiercely you and Gawain fell upon our enemy. I could do little more than nurse my wounds and watch, as my loyal guardian, Herrig, swung his sword with his one good arm, bellowing defiance as he kept the enemy at bay. I came close to meeting our maker that day."

"But you did not, lord," Herrig growled in his deep voice, poking the fire with a stick. "It was not your time."

"Our Lord God watches over you, for your cause is just, my lord," Asaph added.

Arthur scanned the loyal faces around him, reflected in the glow of the fire. He spotted his young squire in the gloom and called to him. "Bring a gourd of wine from my tent, young Dermot, I have a thirst for it."

The fire crackled and an owl hooted as the men tore strips of meat from animal bones with their teeth. Dermot bowed as he presented a gourd to his master. Arthur was still in reflective mood and leaned forward before speaking. "And after that battle, we did subdue the Deirans and they came under my rule. Their dying chief, mortally wounded by the Angliscs, did commend the care of his son, young Dermot here, to my care. I became their chief and pledged to raise this boy to be a warrior and wise leader, who may one day return to his land and rule over his people." He ruffled the boy's hair, and noted his eyes shining with pride and determination.

Arthur dismissed the boy and addressed his entourage, "I could not ask for better company. I know you are all with me and our task is simple – to rid our land of these unwelcome raiders who mean to settle and push our farmers aside. Tomorrow we shall rescue dear Ambrose's father and kin, and get the measure of our enemy. Now let us join the men in song before we sleep the sleep of just men."

Chapter Six

THEY BROKE CAMP in eerie silence and rode off the plateau into a blanket of mist that covered the farmlands. Sullen farm workers stood by as the soldiers filed past in pairs, each man wondering what the day would bring. Viroco's scouts had reported that there were many refugees from the great town of Lindum at the magistrate's villa, in the direction of the rising column of smoke.

By mid-morning, they had reached the back wall of the magistrate's estate, and Arthur's scouts had reported that the front wall was heavily barricaded against a rabble of Anglisc warriors clustered around a huge bonfire they had made some one hundred paces from the villa's gates. The thick brambles that lined the inside of the stone wall and tumbled over the top between sharp spikes would dissuade many from attempting to scale it.

"Bedwyr and Viroco, you will go left, leading half of the men around the estate walls, and I shall proceed with my men and Peredur with his Rheged guard to the right. We shall meet at the front and form up in a line facing the enemy. Eight men will remain here with the wagon." He looked at his eleven-year-old squire, Dermot, mounted on a frisky pony, his eyes wide with excitement. "Dermot, you will stay close to Ambrose and keep him safe for me. Your time to witness battle shall come."

Arthur intended to waste no time on speaking to the defenders of the estate. No sooner had the two lines of horsemen met before the front ditch, to cheers from the wall behind, than he ordered lances braced and a slow trot towards the Anglisc warriors. The morning fog had lifted, as if God himself had lifted a curtain to reveal the enemy. Arthur's confidence and eagerness to engage the enemy gave heart to his men, many of whom were novices. Their enemy, numbering more than a hundred, ranged in two loose shield walls on either side of their bonfire that had now burnt low to a mass of glowing embers. Another thirty or so wandered about the countryside, returning with arms full of plunder from nearby farms.

The Angliscs shouted war cries and curses in their guttural tongue and beat their swords and axes on cowhide shields. Only four of their leaders were on horseback, Arthur noted. He nodded to his horn-blowers who sounded the charge, then kicked his heels into Mars' flanks and screamed at the top of his voice. Feeling Excalibur in its sheath slapping his hip, he gripped his long lance firmly in one leather-gloved hand and clasped the round shield that protected his thigh and side in the other.

The earth shook with the vibration of two hundred horses galloping as one, generating a drumming that filled the ears of both the horsemen and their enemy. The war cries turned to screams as the line of horses crashed through the Angliscs, knocking many to the ground. Others were impaled on lances, as the purpose behind months of practice came to fruition for the eager horsemen. Arthur ran his lance into the throat of a burly warrior whose long moustache hanging in twin blond plaits, whipped around his face as he fell. After twenty paces, Arthur pulled up his horse and spun around, drawing Excalibur from its scabbard. The blade that had once been wielded in battle by Ambrosius now shone in the sunlight, and Arthur paused to wait for his riders to line up beside him. He glanced behind and smirked at the sight of Bedwyr and three others chasing the Anglisc leaders on their ponderous farm horses.

Holding Excalibur high, and with another roar, he kicked his snorting black stallion forward and they fell upon the dazed Angliscs, who staggered about and tried to raise their fallen comrades to their feet. Arthur knew to broadside his intended victim and slash to his left, where his shield gave him some protection from counter thrusts. His razor-sharp steel blade carved through any impediment beneath it, whether helmet, shield or chain mail vest. This gave his sword a seemingly magical power to onlookers, who knew not that it had been fashioned to steel from highest quality iron in the hottest furnace by a master swordsmith. He rarely needed a second slash or stab to fatally wound an opponent.

His men made short work of their enemy, and few prisoners were taken. The numerical advantage and use of horses had been a decisive factor, and Arthur could see that barely a dozen of his men had been killed. However, at least two dozen were nursing wounds.

"Fetch the wagon – we have wounded men that need attending!" Arthur shouted. "Do not slay any more of the enemy - we will need them to dig a burial pit. Herrig, question the prisoners to find out what you can of their plans. Come with me, Peredur. We shall meet with those inside. Our work is done."

AMBROSE'S JOY WAS mixed with grave concern at meeting his father inside the estate compound. Maddox limped towards him, leaning on a stick, his white hair matted and unkempt, his robe dirty and cloak torn.

"Father! I praise the Lord God at seeing you alive... but am sorely vexed at the state of you. Come, sit beside me and tell me all." He guided the old man to a stone bench and they fell into deep conversation.

"My son, there were too many of them for our valiant soldiers. First, they overran our port at Gleinmouth and rowed their ships upriver to the bridge at Dubglass, and then they marched the remaining miles to surround our town walls."

"Then how did you escape?"

"Some of our men rode hard from the port to give us warning. We had barely time to pack our most valued possessions into carts and flee westwards. Only two dozen guards accompanied us - I know not the fate of those brave soldiers we left behind to defend our town." He paused to stifle a sob, wiping his eyes with the sleeve of his grubby robe. "Our noble magistrate, Allius, led us to his estate with its stout walls. But you have come just in time, as those devils followed us, arriving in the night. They were plotting their assault on us, like wolves eying an unguarded flock... Oh, Ambrose! I am proud of you, my son, and grateful to your lord and protector, Arthur."

Maddox bowed his head and let emotion overcome him. Ambrose patted his shoulder and looked up to Arthur and Peredur, who stood close by surveying the defences.

The portly Allius bustled up and clumsily embraced Arthur. "Ah, my lord Arthur, our saviour! Your coming is most timely. As you can see, our walls and gates are manned by a mere twenty Coritani guards, together with thirty or so of my estate workers. We would not have withstood their assault." He waved his white sleeve to the walls and its crude wooden walkway, on which stood boys and men armed with pitchforks and knives lashed to wooden staffs.

"They would only have spared those they could use as slaves," Arthur replied.

Peredur was bouncing from foot to foot, still high on his first taste of battle. "They were no match for our cavalry charge. We rode them down like the mangy curs they are…"

"They were unprepared this time, my young brother," Arthur interrupted. "The next time, we will face a much more determined shield wall. But it was the perfect day for you to dip your lance and blood your sword." He lightly punched the youth's shoulder, laughing at his exuberance.

Bedwyr and Herrig rode in through the gates and dismounted next to Arthur. "My lord," Bedwyr said. "We have burnt the siege ladders they were constructing and have set their men to dig a burial pit."

"And what news did you glean from the captives, Herrig?" Arthur asked.

"They are proud men and would say little, but one told me, on threat of being thrown on the fire, about their one-eyed king, Icel. The brazen fiend intends to take up residence at Lindum and rule the surrounding lands. Their people are in Gleinmouth with their livestock and seed for planting, waiting for the lands to be portioned out."

"And how many warriors are there?"

"He told me more than four hundred, of whom we have killed about eighty today. There are two hundred women and children, and so far, they have captured over a hundred Coritani for slaves, my lord."

Arthur ground his teeth and glowered in rage. He turned to Allius, who had been joined by Ambrose and Maddox, and said, "Our mission is to bring as many of you who are willing and able to cross the mountain pass to safety in the land of the Cornovi, where King Owain extends a warm welcome…"

"But my lord!" Allius blurted. "We had hoped you would lead us in driving these devils from our lands!"

"I do not have enough men for that," Arthur replied dismissively. "This venture is to rescue those who wish to be rescued. We are amassing an army in the west to take on these Anglisc and Saxon invaders, but for now, we are unable to challenge King Icel in open warfare. I am sorry, my friend, but you must choose - remain here and try to hold your estate against others who will come, or travel with us to safety beyond the mountains and live to return another day. We leave tomorrow."

Allius groaned and hugged Maddox for comfort. The realisation that they must face the difficult choice of resisting alone or leaving with Arthur weighed heavily on their minds.

One more distasteful task remained. Arthur called Bedwyr and Herrig to him and spoke in a low voice, "We cannot risk taking Anglisc captives across the mountain, for if they were to escape, they would tell their fellows of the wealth of that land."

Bedwyr nodded, understanding his master's intent. "Once the burial pits are dug and their comrades interned, we shall despatch them also."

"I will see that they are buried with their weapons in hand and feet pointed towards the rising sun, so their departing spirits may find their way to their great hall," Herrig added.

"You are kind to our enemy," Bedwyr grunted.

"Would you have their unhappy ghosts walking this land?" Herrig replied.

"You know their beliefs and ways," Arthur said. "And it is right that warriors who fall in battle are honoured." He slapped his two trusted commanders on their backs. "Let us get to our tasks, for we shall leave in the morning."

THE MEN SANG songs into the night, drinking the mead provided by the monks who had fled with carts of farm produce, exchanging their stories of the battle and showing trophies they had taken from their dead foes. Some silver crucifixes and other trophies spoke of ransacked churches, and Father Asaph, drawing himself up to his full height, wrestled them away from grudging soldiers, reclaiming them for God.

In contrast, the Coritani were distraught at the prospect of having to flee from their lands, knowing that crude, pagan Angliscs would take over their farms. Ambrose worked on Arthur's behalf, persuading them that their best interest was served by travelling west and going to a rich valley where abandoned farms awaited them. In the courtyard of the villa, Arthur probed Maddox and his council members about the coming of the Angliscs, gathering as much detail as he could, and shared news of his expedition from the Great Wall to the Cornovian capital, Viriconium, now Caer Cornovia, and his favourable impression of King Owain.

"This King Owain has never travelled to our lands, nor have any of our council travelled there," Maddox commented. "We only have traders' reports that it is a peaceful and prospering place."

"And yet their town is barely five days ride from here," Arthur added. He stood and warmed his rear in front of the fire. His calm nature in a crisis and air of certainty had a soothing effect on those around him, though they knew their journey would take far longer, even walking in dry weather, and could be treacherous because of the winding inclines. He exuded the confidence of a man born to lead, and always felt at ease in the company of other leaders. "I am truly sorry for your woes, good fellows, but your testimony to the council of western kings that will convene at the next rising of the moon will persuade them to go to war against these devils."

Maddox sighed, as if his life essence was slowly dissipating. "If we remain here, our doom seems inevitable. Our best hope, Arthur, is to join forces with you and draw them into battle, as your father, Uther, did to great effect. His defeat of them halted their spreading by many years. Now it must happen again."

Allius glanced at the glum faces around him and stood, clasping his hands in front of him. "We are decided, then. We shall abandon this estate and the surrounding farms, and follow you across the mountain pass. It is springtime, and we must hope and pray for renewal, under the protection of our neighbours, and Our Lord Jesus Christ."

Asaph's "Amen" was solemnly echoed by a half dozen cowled monks hovering on the fringes of the meeting.

"Tomorrow we leave, after breakfast and morning mass," Arthur said, bowing to his host and taking his leave for a wooden cot in a hastily prepared guest room.

THE WARM SPELL extended to the next morning, and bright cowslips, attended by butterflies and chirping finches, seemed incongruous when set against the bitter and bloody battle that had taken place the day before. The churned-up earth and silent burial mound in the distance bore witness to the fight, as the column of riders led out a sullen trail of walkers interspersed with ox and horse-drawn wagons. Virtually the entire neighbourhood had decided to leave, shocked by the violent battle they had witnessed or heard of. Others had joined their ranks in the morning to swell the numbers of refugees to over three hundred.

Arthur was pleased to see Bedwyr, Viroco and the Coritani captain laughing at a shared joke. They had bonded well in the heat of battle, and he was certain he would have need of their loyalty in the future. He glanced behind and smiled at the sight of Peredur riding beside a fair young woman of a similar age, trying his best to impress her with boastful claims. A memory flashed in Arthur's mind, of his kicking a wounded Anglisc towards the terrified youth in the heat of battle, yelling at him to finish him off – not unlike a cat pushing a wounded mouse to its kittens. The first kill is always messy and sorely vexes the conscience. He fell back to ride beside the wagon that carried Ambrose, Maddox, and the elderly councilmen.

They exchanged pleasantries and then Arthur addressed the question he knew to be on their minds. "We will clear these mountain passes before nightfall and camp on the other side. Then we shall be guided by Viroco and his Cornovian guard on a southern trail to a sparsely populated land guarded by an old Roman fort."

"Then we are in their hands," Maddox intoned with little enthusiasm.

"You mistrust your neighbours," Arthur replied, "But so far all that I have seen and heard from the Cornovi has been true and honest. Have faith, dear friends." Arthur decided not to tarry and give them the opportunity to voice fears or doubts. He dug his heels into Mars and galloped to the head of the column. He would not add to their woes by mentioning giants or bandits – such things would be dealt with in due course.

Arthur, looking back over the long column to the green lands beyond, had an idea. He called the captain of the Coritani guards to him and detailed him to hang back with his men and cause a rock fall to block the narrowest pass once they had all passed through. "It may dissuade our enemy from attempting to follow our road, at least for a short while."

Chapter Seven

AFTER TWO DAYS of slow progress through a rocky and wooded wilderness, scouts reported that the fort at Letocetum was two hour's ride away. Arthur asked whether there were any settlements on the way, and they replied that the land was eerily quiet, with dogs roaming around abandoned farmhouses the only living things they had seen.

Arthur called his commanders to him and gave his orders. "The main column shall follow these scouts to the fort and camp there. I shall take my men and Viroco and his Cornovi guard to scout the wilderness to the west of our road, and Bedwyr and Peredur shall take the Rheged guards to the eastern wilderness to scout the woods and rocks. The Coritani guards shall remain with the main column and escort it through the valley ahead. At the sight of any trouble, blow your horns and send riders to warn the main column."

A stream ran the length of a wide, flat valley, devoid of life except for a pair of hares boxing in the long grass and a hawk circling above. Arthur called a halt and then approached his officers. "I'll ride ahead through the trees before yonder rocky outcrop and see what I can see from the top. Viroco, take your men into the woods here and follow any trails you find. Be ready for outlaws."

"Yes, my lord," his earnest captain replied. "We shall look out for you on the outcrop. Beware, for these are wild lands where few men have ventured."

With that, the two groups of riders parted, each numbering about fifty. Arthur picked up an animal trail through an ancient wood of oak and ash carpeted with bluebells and littered with fallen trees. His path rose away from the valley floor and soon trees gave way to bush scrub and large rounded boulders.

"This is good country for an ambush, for sure. Keep your eyes open," he shouted behind.

"Movement, my lord!" one of the men shouted, and Arthur caught the flash of a spear thrown in his direction, sailing harmlessly by. Reining in Mars, he swiftly detached his shield from his saddle as he turned to face the threat. Ten or more figures had emerged from the thick bushes, with spear arms ready to throw.

"Advance on them!" Arthur bellowed, and then crashed into the brush, his shield braced before him to deflect missiles. A hail of crude spears, rocks and clubs assaulted the riders as they pressed ahead. Yells and curses rang out when a weapon found its mark, but most batted away the objects with their shields. As they closed in on their attackers, Arthur's soldiers saw a ragged bunch of bearded, dark-eyed wild men wrapped about with animal pelts. They growled and howled like starving wolves, shaking clubs in the air, but they were backing away from the advancing horsemen.

The horses walked steadily, testing the uneven ground with delicate steps, their riders with lances at the ready and shields held high. Arthur fixed his sights on a hulking, hissing youth wielding a club and at ten yards distance yelled, "Attack!"

Screams sliced the air as Arthur's men stabbed with vicious lances at their primitive foe, sending them crying in pain and fear, and clutching their bleeding wounds, into the sanctuary of the forest. Arthur killed one man with lance and sword, and looked along the line to see a pattern of retreat.

"Hold steady!" he yelled, as some impulsive riders started to chase their fleeing quarry. "We shall not enter the dark forest. Back to the path!" He turned Mars and made his way back to where they had a clearer field of vision. Seeing that all his riders were unhurt, he shouted, "We make our way to the high ground and then dismount to survey the area!"

The wild men had melted away into the cover of the trees, and so they continued uphill until they reached a rocky outcrop. Arthur dismounted and detailed six men to remain with the horses. He then led the remaining men onwards, jumping from rounded rock to rock until they reached the highest point. On the way, he had marvelled at crude depictions of animals carved into the weathered rocks by ancient folk.

"This is a fine view," he puffed, as his men gathered around, "and one that the ancient peoples shared."

They could see for miles in all directions, even as far as a rising twist of smoke from a fort at the far end of the valley beneath them. In the other direction, thick forest stretched for miles, interspersed with white crags. Behind them, the blue mountain range lined the horizon. Above, white clouds scudded across a blue sky, and swifts ducked and dived on the blustery breeze. Arthur was reminded of the wild lands north of the Great Wall.

"This is the wild heart of our island, my lord," one of his men remarked.

"Indeed it is, and I suspect those uncouth fellows live in caves below us, living off the bounty of the forest."

"And any unsuspecting travellers passing by, no doubt," another added.

"Shall we flush them out, my lord?"

Before Arthur could answer, the faint sound of a horn, carried on the wind, reached their ears. "Our friends are calling for us. We must leave the wild men for another time. Back to the horses!"

In short time they left the treeline and entered the grassy valley. Viroco licked his lips, pursed them against the silver rim of his polished goat's horn and blew three long blasts skyward to summon a reply from Bedwyr. Arthur waited, his ear cocked, almost without breathing, for a reply. It came from the trees on the opposite side of the valley, from where Bedwyr and Peredur had led their men. This at least ruled out an attack on the column, which by now must surely have reached the safety of the fort.

"The Rheged guard are under attack. We ride to their aid!" Arthur shouted, guiding Mars to a shallow stream and crossing it. He led his men to the forest, where they worried at its edges impatiently, at first finding only briar-snagged paths suited to badgers. When a narrow lane at last was found, they ventured into the mysterious hush under the leafy canopy, filing forward over soft leaf-mould with as much urgency as the dim light allowed. Arthur sent his scout ahead, instructing him to sound his horn at regular intervals and then listen for the reply. They crossed glades and re-entered the trees, sending families of wild pigs and dappled deer scurrying into the undergrowth, as the horns of their comrades grew louder.

Arthur's scout was waiting for him at the forest's edge, and beyond him he saw a wide clearing on which a battle was raging. It was no ordinary battle, and he now understood the gasp and look of amazement from his scout. Barely a hundred yards away was a scene of chaos, with wounded and dead horses and men littering the meadow. Two giants swung huge clubs the size of tree trunks at the riders who were attempting to stab them with their lances. The giants roared and bellowed in pain and anger whenever their hides were pricked, swinging their deadly weapons in slow arcs, with riders ducking and pulling hard on their reins to steer away from them.

"What is this madness?" one of Arthur's men asked, as they fell into rank on either side of him.

"They are giant men, that much we can see," Arthur replied. "Advance in line."

As they approached, Bedwyr called his men back. Now the two giants, one holding a bloody wound in his side, turned to face the new threat. Each stood taller and more massive than a bear. The wounded one frowned and shook his great shaggy head, sending his tangled locks swinging and revealing eyes as dull as sea coal, that blinked as if he was stunned. He wiped blood on the pelts tied round his torso, which was so hairy the fur looked like part of him. The other creature raised itself to its full, terrible height and bared its teeth to emit a stomach-churning growl.

Arthur, at the centre of his men, signalled his intention to target the nearest giant, the wounded one. "Charge!" he yelled, urging Mars to a canter, driving him forward across the knee-high grass towards their target. A raised club slammed down towards Arthur, but he jammed his heels into Mars's flanks and ducked away from the blow. As his horse veered away from the solid object in front of it, Arthur thrust his lance hard into the chest of the monster, then let go of the shaft to ride on. The giant groaned in pain and bent low as the next rider pricked its other side with his lance.

Arthur turned to see that the other giant had smashed the head of the horse that had first attacked it, sending whinnying animal and screaming rider to the ground. But the second rider had held his course and pierced its side, leaving his lance quivering in the creature as he rode past. The pattern had been set. Wave after wave of riders rode past the giants, attacking from both sides, thrusting their lances into them and dodging away from retaliatory blows. A few terrified youths failed to come close enough to strike. At last the giants dropped to their knees, groaning in pain and losing their strength to defend themselves.

Arthur dismounted and drew Excalibur, approaching the dying creatures with caution. Bedwyr was soon by his side, and they eyed the groaning monsters, that knelt in agony, their blood seeping from between giant fingers.

"Their blood is red, like men," Bedwyr said, edging forward with his sword out in front.

"An aberration of nature, no doubt, but as mortal as we are," Arthur replied. Soon the wounded giants were surrounded by warriors with swords pointing at them. Arthur made eye contact with the nearest giant, and saw rage and pain in his black eyes. Thickset brows hung over deep eye sockets, and its nose was flat and broad. Its skin was brown and wrinkled and fuzzy brown hair covered the arms and body. Arthur approached and it growled a warning, and then tried to get to its feet. One foot was raised, but it was still on one knee when Arthur attacked. He rushed forward and aimed the sharp point of Excalibur at the giant's throat.

The speed of his attack was sufficient, and he drove the point into its leathery skin. The creature gurgled and rolled its head. Arthur felt its hand knock him sideways and he stumbled, but quickly regained his feet as the giant rolled onto its side. Excalibur was still lodged in its throat, and he decided to wait until the creature was still before retrieving it.

Arthur looked across to hear the dying roar of the other giant as his men swarmed over it, stabbing it with their swords from all sides. Soon, both giants were lying dead in the trampled and blood-soaked grass. The men gave a cheer and clambered onto the bodies of the giants, cutting off locks of hair, or a finger, to keep as trophies.

"Cut off their heads and let us leave their bodies here for the wolves," Arthur shouted above the noisy celebrations. "We will display their heads on spikes at the fort so that all can see and believe that giants did live here - and two were slain by Arthur and his men!"

THE GARRISON OF some twenty soldiers, together with their families, welcomed their captain, Viroco, their friends amongst his guards, and Arthur's men. They were bemused at the wagon train of three hundred refugees from their neighbouring lands to the east. Arthur, Ambrose and Viroco calculated that they had eight days before they must return to Caer Cornovia, little time to help the Coritani refugees settle into farms that lay abandoned in the lands surrounding the fort.

The garrison soldiers had good knowledge of the area, and so led the expeditions with clusters of farmers to find suitable lands, and to organise work details to repair walls and roofs of dilapidated structures. Meanwhile, Arthur, Bedwyr and Viroco led patrols to root out bandits and search for evidence of other giants. There were no more sightings of the strange creatures, or their lair, but they did clear the rocky lands of primitive folk who dwelt in caves, driving those they did not kill into the forest beyond. What pity they may have felt for them was secondary to the desire to create a safe haven for the new settlers. The valley was reclaimed for cultivation and settlement, and the garrison detailed to make regular patrols.

As the rising of the new moon approached, Arthur said his farewells and led his men, together with Viroco, Ambrose, Maddox and the Coritani council leaders, onto Watling Street and the two-day ride to Caer Cornovia, in a north-westerly direction. He drew raucous laughter from his men when he threw a sack containing one of the grizzled giants' heads into the back of the supply wagon, sending Asaph scrambling to a corner, clutching his crucifix and muttering prayers.

"This is an evil thing, lord Arthur, an unnatural monster that should be burned," the priest moaned.

Arthur guffawed and replied, "It was a living thing, but from where it came, we do not know. I shall show it to the council of kings to add wonder to my tale of the daring rescue of their Coritani allies."

"Pride is a sin, my lord," Asaph chided.

"Then find it in your heart to forgive me, Father, for my intention is to show my qualities. This will advance my case to be accepted as their high king and lead their combined army. I must win their faith if I am to save our land."

"I shall pray for you, my lord," the priest replied in a whisper, creeping as far as he could from the offending sack.

Arthur *Rex Brittonum*

Chapter Eight

CROWDS OF PEOPLE, townsfolk mixed with visiting soldiers, surrounded the simple wooden-fenced amphitheatre that stood outside the north wall of Caer Cornovia. Viroco was intrigued and proposed that they follow a connecting footpath to see what was attracting everyone's attention. In the opposite direction, away to their left, the entire meadowland between the town and the river was hidden under gaudy tents and crude wooden shacks, smoke rings curling from campfires and banners fluttering in the breeze, indicating the arrival of the kings of western Britannia.

Arthur detailed the wagons to proceed to the town with most of the men, and followed Viroco with a handful of followers. Mars picked his way along a dirt track that skirted the west wall, carrying his rider beside the picket fence of a cemetery where simple wooden grave markers surrounded a compound for the imperial stone sarcophaguses at its centre. Gravediggers working in the far corner stopped to stretch their backs and gaze at the passing horsemen.

Viroco had stopped to speak to some idling fellows and then turned to beckon Arthur to join him. "These fellows say that warriors from the differing kingdoms are fighting a mock battle in the arena."

"Then let us dismount and look at their efforts," Arthur replied.

Two men attended to the horses as the remainder pushed through the crowds and climbed up the tiered stands to make a space for watching the spectacle below. There appeared to be four teams, each of about twenty warriors, clad in leather and animal furs, and armed with wooden shields and swords. Two teams were lounging by the sides, shouting abuse or encouragement, whilst two sets of warriors fought each other in the centre of the sandy arena, eliciting grunts and groans. Three judges, clad in bright orange tunics and carrying white flags, would tap a downed man on the shoulder and point to the side. The eliminated men were jeered and had vegetables and other objects thrown at them as they made the walk of shame to the far double gates enclave.

Arthur noticed a box for nobility on the far side, where Owain and other kings keenly followed the action, whilst Anne was waving with gusto at him. He smiled and waved back. "This is a fine sport for the men to prepare for battle," Arthur said with a wide grin.

"Yes, my lord, and the winning team will be feted with roast meats and ale by the kings, so there is much to fight for!" Viroco shouted back, above the noisy crowd.

"And no doubt bed the loveliest maids," Bedwyr added, to roars of laughter.

"Such is a soldier's lot – bitter defeat or glory," Arthur noted.

In a short while, only two burly, bruised brutes remained on their feet, circling each other in a tired motion. Their blows were slow and easily blocked, and it seemed a stalemate was inevitable, until one twirled around, dropped to his haunches and swept the other's foot away with an outstretched leg, causing his opponent to tumble to the ground. This was enough to win the match, and a much shorter judge held the victor's arm up. The crowd clapped, hollered and hooted their pleasure, as the winner and his team lined up before the western kings.

King Owain stood and raised his hands to silence the mob. "Our mock battle has been won by the Mighty Red Dragons of Gwynedd!" Cheers and boos rang around the packed arena. "Step forward their champion, Caratacus, and receive a purse of silver."

Arthur now recognised the mighty warrior who had hosted him at Deva as he conducted a slow lap of honour, wooden sword in one hand and money purse in the other. He looked up and recognised Arthur, making a mock bow in his direction. Arthur laughed and applauded him, shouting, "All hail the mighty Caratacus!"

"Let us hope we never have to face him across the field of battle," Bedwyr breathed in his ear.

Arthur *Rex Brittonum*

"I shall do my best to appease his master," Arthur replied. "Besides, I have my own mighty champion, Herrig, should the fates betray us."

Herrig smirked, his huge biceps bulging beneath his shirt, his great arms folded before him.

ARTHUR'S VILLA WAS a buzz of activity, with unfamiliar attendants hurrying hither and thither. He unclipped his cloak and handed his helmet and belt to a house slave as he entered the shaded portico.

"Ah, Arthur, there you are!" Anne exclaimed, beaming a broad and welcoming smile as she came through the doorway and embraced him. "But you carry the dust from the road," she chided, stepping away and brushing her gown.

"I am sorry, dear sister, the road has laid claim to me…"

"Never mind that, look who is here and anxious to see you." Anne grabbed his arm and pulled him into his hall, where the first person his eyes fell on was his wife, Gunamara. She let out a little cry of pleasure as she rushed into his arms. Arthur hugged her tightly and bent his cheek to her lush, honey-brown hair, breathing in her rosy scent. A silver cross dangled between her breasts and she wore the silver tiara studded with gemstones that Arthur had given her on their wedding day. He gasped in wonder at her presence and the memory of that blessed day.

"But I had not heard that you were coming," Arthur gasped, tilting her tear-stained face up to drink in her familiar beauty, and then kissing her soft lips with his cracked ones. She trembled and blinked away her tears.

"My love, I am happier in this moment than at any time since our wedding day," Arthur crooned, his face fixed in a joyous smile.

"Arthur," she barely breathed, "I had to come to you, with little Llacheu." She turned and waved forward a nurse, who held their sleeping son in her arms wrapped in a trailing blanket. Arthur's eyes widened in joy and he reached for the baby bundle, holding him up and studying his smooth skin and delicate lashes.

"He has his mother's hair now!" Arthur declared, causing a ripple of smiling agreement. "But I shall not kiss him till I have washed off the dust of the road," he added, handing the murmuring baby to his nurse and following with his gaze her swaying retreat to where a basket crib waited.

"He is dreaming of meeting you, I think," Gunamara said, firmly hugging her husband around his waist, as if to keep him from leaving her again.

Arthur returned her embrace and saw over her shoulder a cluster of young men, all unknown to him. They were looking hesitantly on the scene of reunion from a discreet distance.

Gunamara noticed where he was looking and said, "My husband, I was escorted to this place by these four warriors. They are the best of those schooled by Percival at Vindolanda."

"Ah, fresh blood for our cause!" Arthur laughed and bade them approach.

The young men came forward in turn and made their homage to him on bended knee as Gunamara presented them. First Agravane, a broad and confident fellow; next Mador, his brother, who had darker looks, a weak chin and brown wavy hair; then Pinel, a narrow-faced youth with dancing eyes; and lastly Lucan, a well-barbered fellow dressed in the manner of the son of a courtly noble.

Arthur's heart pumped with joy at this surprise visit, and the return to his borrowed villa seemed to be a true homecoming now that his wife and child were in it. Flanked by the two queens, he stood before four earnest young faces and summoned up a fitting response.

"Your service is welcome to us, young lords. It is no small thing to receive recruits primed to command under my experienced deputies. But these are matters for the future. Today, you have my greatest thanks for escorting my brave queen and our precious child safely from the northlands. And I am keen to know of your tutor, my good friend Sir Percival?"

Agravane cleared his throat and replied, "My king, we are honoured to enter your service. Our tutor, Percival, is now an old and frail man with silver hair, who hobbles about the place with a stick." When Arthur frowned, he lifted his tone, "...although his mind remains sharp as he watches our training, calling out any errors he perceives..."

His comrades sniggered at the unravelling description, and Lucan took up the briefing: "He rarely takes to horse or leaves the fort, my lord, but Sir Percival sends us to you with these words. Taking a deep breath first, he recited aloud:

"'My noble King Arthur, I commend these four young commanders to your service. I have done my best to prepare them for the challenges of leadership, taught them the ways of our weapons and horsemanship to the best of my ability. I did send them north, into the Gododdin lands, by way of test, to spend time with Gawain, who has cast his rigorous eye over them, him being the best of us.' Those were his words, my lord." Lucan bowed low with a sweeping gesture of the hand, then stepped back in line, causing Anne and Gunamara to make brief eye contact and exchange mischievous smiles.

Arthur's expression was one of amazement, his brows lifted high. "That is an excellent briefing. Indeed, I can picture my noble friend and mentor, Percival, speaking his words so eloquently reported. But I am most pleased to hear that you have met with the greatest knight and field commander of our age, Sir Gawain! I learned more about the ways of warfare and how to lead men from him than any other, and I look forward to hearing more of your time with him, for you shall dine in our hall tonight."

The four thanked their king, bowed and took their leave, following Queen Anne. She promised a lad would see them to their quarters. Arthur turned to Gunamara again and held her close now they were alone.

"But you smell of many days in the saddle, my lord," she lightly remarked, turning to order a bath be drawn for him. "You must wash and then rest, and enjoy bouncing our prince on your knee. For matters at the council of kings will drag you away tomorrow."

"There is dragging away to be done now," he said, slipping his arm around his wife's waist and guiding her towards his bed chamber.

THE GREAT HALL was decorated with the banners of the seven kingdoms represented at the council, plus the grappling dragon and bear banner of Arthur. A large semi-circular table of thick oak stood before the raised dais on which their host, King Owain of Powys, sat on his throne. Arthur, then Maddox representing the Coritani, then Peredur representing his father's kingdom of Rheged, stood before their chairs as the other four kings marched the length of the building, acknowledging with subtle bows the hollers of solidarity from their supporters bunched in the wings beyond the ornate columns.

A herald announced their arrival: "King Cadwallon, the Head Dragon of Gwynedd; Cyngar the Wise, King of Demetia; Vortipor the Viper, King of Dyfed; Caradog the Stag, King of Gwent."

The kings of western Britannia, each clad in a cloak and wearing bands of gold or silver around their heads, took their seats at the table. Attendants poured ale into golden goblets and silver platters of roasted birds' legs and other delicacies were placed on the table. The new arrivals nodded to the three unfamiliar men to their left as they took their seats.

Owain stood and held his arms out. "Welcome, mighty kings and their representatives to our council meeting. We five kings of the western lands know each other well, and our discussion on matters related to our common security will be given a broader vista through the shared experiences of our noble guests. May I introduce my brother-in-law, Arthur, King of Britannia and chief of the Brigantes and Deiran peoples…"

He paused as a rough cough, taken to be a disputation of his naming Arthur 'king', rumbled from the throat of King Cadwallon. "Are you well, my lord?"

Cadwallon fixed Owain with a black-eyed stare and replied, "I know of only one King of Britannia, and that is

Uther's grandson, Mordred." He picked up his goblet and drank, sitting back in his chair whilst looking straight ahead.

"I shall continue," Owain said quickly. "Arthur may speak for himself after the introductions are concluded. Next to Arthur is Prince Peredur, son of King Meirchion Gul of the Rheged, our powerful northern neighbour, and next to him is Maddox, Chief of our eastern neighbours, the Coritani, and representative of their Council of Elders. I shall begin proceedings by inviting each of you to speak in turn on the matters most urgent to your security, starting with Arthur to my right. When all have had a say, I shall speak for my kingdom of Powys, and then we may raise questions and concerns."

He paused to read the stern faces before him, and seeing no objection, called on Arthur to take the floor.

The hall fell silent – even the chattering supporters, the yapping dogs and the birds in the rafters seemed to stop their noise in expectation, as Arthur walked from his seat to the front space between the curved table and the king's dais. He wore a band of intertwined gold and silver thread that kept his shoulder-length nut brown locks to the sides of his face, exposing his battle-scarred cheek. His keen green eyes carefully scanned the kings before him and roved over their heads to the hundreds of warriors, noble women and assorted townsfolk who now filled the entire space of the great hall.

"Noble kings, chiefs, princes and fellow Britons, I stand before you as the son of King Uther, and brother of Queen Anne." He turned and smiled to his sister who clasped her hands and returned the smile with warmth. "She will bear testimony to my parentage, if you cannot see the likeness of our parents in our faces." This caused some murmurs and polite laughs. "It is true that my half-sister, Morgana, seized Uther's crown and tried to place it on the head of her tiny son, Mordred. At that time, I was languishing in his dungeon." This time raucous laughter.

He could see his audience was warming to his story and continued. "It was the bravery of both my sisters, Anne and also Morgaise, now the Queen of Dumnonia, that saved me from an untimely end." Arthur drew his finger across his throat, now fully in storytelling mode. "That bravery allied to the quick thinking of the healer Merlyn. Mayhap you know of him?" His audience was curious and edged forward to hear more.

"On our travels north, in the company of Uther's famous knights, Gawain and Percival, I was made *dux bellorum*, leader of battles, by my growing band of followers. You may raise your eyebrows, but it is true. Barely twenty years old and I was their leader. We fought many battles against invading Angliscs in the eastern lands, briefly liberating the Coritani, Deiran and Brigante peoples from their torments at the hand of these determined raiders. But they returned on fresh spring tides and now settle those lost lands we call Lloegyr."

At these words, a melancholy sigh for Lloegyr escaped from Maddox.

"I then pressed on northwards to the mighty Roman Wall," Arthur continued. "And it was in that snowy outpost that we found another of Uther's knights, Bors, commanding a band of well-schooled warriors and defending the wall from northern raiders. We joined forces and made a peace with their neighbours, the Rheged. In recent times, Gawain defeated the northern tribe, the Gododdins, slaying King Lot, and taking his crown for himself."

Arthur paused to take a sip of ale whilst his tale settled on the minds of his murmuring audience. He heard more than one voice questioning the point of his account.

"By this tale, I hope to impress on you all the many dangers that beset our much-troubled island home. You have your worries about Hibernian raiders from the west, but also know that the south coast is menaced by Saxons, the east by Angliscs, and the north by wild Picts from beyond the Caledonian forest. They all seek the same thing – our churches to loot, our homes to burn, our fields to take and our people to enslave."

Arthur *Rex Brittonum*

Arthur paused again to note the concern etched in the furrowed brows before him. He turned to signal Herrig to enter from the wings, carrying a bulging sack. Arthur nodded to his champion, who opened the sack and lifted the fat, round head of a giant by his long black hair. The audience gasped, and some cried out in fear at the sight of the huge, maggot-eaten head, the eye sockets hollow, as priests crossed themselves and clutched their crucifixes.

Arthur pointed to it and shouted, "And there are other dread things hiding in the wild places of our land, like this vicious giant I slayed with lance and sword as we reclaimed the settlement near Letocetum!"

He waited for the cheering to die down before moving to his conclusion. "I am my father's son, and I would do as he did – I will lead an army of the best fighting men of the kings of the Britons to clear our coast of our unwelcome settlers. We will overcome them. We will send them to their graves, or we will chase them back to their ships!"

The hall erupted in wild shouts, hoots, stamping of feet and banging of staffs. Arthur bowed to the kings and took his seat, sending Herrig away with his grim sack.

He looked at Anne, whose plea for support he had answered by dangling this colourful bauble of an offer before the neighbours of Powys, an attempt to distract them from infighting and turn their ire on a common foe. She was applauding him, but her eyes were fearful and her bottom lip was caught anxiously between her teeth. After all, this was only the beginning.

Once the noise had died down, Owain stood and thanked Arthur, then invited Peredur to speak.

The pale youth took his place at the front and ignored the sniggers of burly warriors to project his small voice as forcefully as he could. "My lords, I am the son of a mighty king who commands over a thousand spears and as many horsemen. He has subdued the tribes north of the wall, and has homage paid to him by chiefs in the northwest portion of this island. All bend their knee to him as far south as the great river by the legion town of Deva. It was he, Meirchion Gul of the Rheged, who placed a crown on Arthur's head and proclaimed him the true King of Britannia."

He paused whilst chattering rippled across the hall and the kings before him whispered to each other, gripping his wrists tightly in the sleeves of his gown. "I will ride at Arthur's side in the battles ahead," he shouted to quell the din, "and pledge three hundred riders to his cause. We have already dipped our lances in the blood of the hated invaders and are eager for more." The young prince bowed and escaped gratefully to his seat.

The next was Maddox, rising slowly and leaning on a staff, who received a fair hearing out of respect for his bent back and grey hair. "Noble kings, I speak for the Coritani, your neighbours to the east, beyond yonder mountains. Our once-Roman town of Lindum has been seized not two moons ago by the dread king of the Angliscs, Icel, and his bloodthirsty warriors. We barely escaped with our lives and meagre possessions. We barricaded ourselves into a walled estate in our western-most lands and prayed to God to keep us hidden. But the enemy hunted us down, even there." He shook his head to emphasise his disbelief and paused to catch his breath, as indignation ran around the open-mouthed audience.

"They laid siege to our walls and lit a huge fire, taunting us in their vile tongue, and jumping through the flames with axes in hand, long into our sleepless night. We knew what fate to expect. Then on the second morning, horn blasts to our rear signalled the arrival of Arthur and his men. Those stout warriors lined their horses before us and rode at the enemy with terrible yells. They scattered them! They speared them on their lances! And they hacked the thieving devils with swords!" His voice cracked as it reached a crescendo and he pointed his staff to the rafters, where birds took to their wings as the hall erupted in shouts and applause.

As the noise receded, he continued. "I tell you this: Arthur, Peredur and Bedwyr, together with your noble commander, Viroco, did show their fierce quality and skills, slaying our enemy, sparing only those who dug the burial pits. They saved us that day from murder, rape and slavery. But then we had little choice than to surrender our lands to their plunder and flee across the mountains to the safety afforded us by your noble king, Owain." He turned and bowed to King Owain, then said, "Our people have been settled in your abandoned farmland around Letocetum, and our warriors pledge their lances to Arthur's cause in the battles ahead that we hope will clear a path for us to return to our lands." He bowed to the kings and took his seat to warm applause.

    Owain thanked him and invited the first of his neighbours to speak, King Cyngar the Wise. The smallest and most lavishly dressed of the western kings stood at the front and raised his tiny hands in a call for silence. "My fellow kings and dear friends, I have listened in wonder to the stories of our noble visitors and trembled at the horrors to our north, south and east. These pagan beasts will show us no mercy, something we know from our own bloody battles with the fierce Hibernians, who raid our shores and have torn families asunder by snatching the young for their slaves." Much nods of agreement and murmurs greeted his words.

    "I care not if Arthur calls himself 'King of the Britons', and do not doubt he is Uther's son. But our battles lie in securing our borders from sea raiders, and on occasion, with our troublesome neighbours." His eyes narrowed as he met those of Vortipor, who was to speak next. "I wish Arthur well in his war with the Saxons and Angliscs, but am unable to pledge any men to his cause." With that, he daintily picked his way around the table and sat, reaching for a dried fig.

    Vortipor was a fat and unruly man, with the longest and most unkempt beard of all - black and wiry, to match his long, greasy hair. He dug his fat thumbs into his thick leather belt and eyed the crowd. His voice was deep and unfriendly. "I care not for Arthur and his war with the Saxons. I will remain in the far west and look to defend my rocky coast and northern border with my silvery-tongued neighbour." He glared at Cyngar and swaggered to his seat, scraping his chair before spilling ale down his beard as he downed his goblet.

    Owain could not hide his discomfort, nor hold the malevolent glare of his southern neighbour and foe, King

Caradog of Gwent. He almost stumbled over naming him and quickly returned to his seat as the tall, brooding presence showed him his back to face the throng, silencing the hall.

"I am Caradog, called the White Stag of Gwent, summoned to this meeting of 'kings'," here he paused to sneer at Arthur, "and share the view from the south of our island bulge. From my eastern outpost, I can see to the lands of Dumnonia across a wide estuary. Thankfully, a very wide estuary." He paused again to smirk at his own joke. "Yes, the white-capped waters of the angry goddess Severna form a barrier that most of the year is too treacherous to cross. I feel this is for a good reason, as the gods do not wish us to become embroiled in the messy affairs of the south and east. My lands are fruitful, with fair harvests these past years, and my borders are well guarded from land or sea raiders. Since the time of Uther, we have not bowed or bent a knee to any high king…"

Owain stood to interrupt him, "Except a delegation you received from King Mordred, and your friendship with the grandsons of Ambrosius are well-known…"

"I mind my own business and you would be advised to do the same!" Caradog snapped back, facing his worrisome neighbour.

Owain, now on his feet and steadily approaching, persisted. "You are not above dabbling in the politics of this land, Caradog, and no doubt have many schemes boiling in your cauldrons!"

"Do not lecture me, you miserable milksop!" Caradog edged towards his slighter neighbour, hand on sword hilt. Arthur had hoped that one of their fellow western kings would intervene, but they all sat forward in their seats, intrigued at the prospect of a possible fight. Arthur put his hands on the padded arms of his heavy chair, ready to stand, when the king's champion, Viroco, appeared and stood between the two men.

"My most noble lords, I entreat you to conduct your discussions in a civil manner," Viroco said in a deep, firm voice, eying the King of Gwent. In turn, Caradog's champion pushed forward from the crowd, his hand also firmly on his hilt.

It was only then that Cadwallon, the Head Dragon, stood and shouted for silence. "If you would back away from my noble cousin, King Caradog, and let me take my turn." This icy threat was delivered in a rumbling voice that demanded respect, and Caradog felt it prudent, when faced with the powerful northern alliance of Gwynedd and Powys, to back away and return to his seat.

"Yes, King Owain is my cousin," Cadwallon began, "and we share the bloodline of Cunedda, who did clear the north and western coast of our hated enemy, the Hibernians. We are charged with the same duty and must look to the sea day and night, for sight of their black sails. I too have enjoyed the tales of Arthur's bravery and share the concern in this hall for our eastern neighbours. They are woefully abused by these devilish Angliscs, who spring from their ships and lay claim to the lands that Ambrosius and Uther manfully fought for."

He paused to eye the quietened crowd. "But my first duty is to the safety of my people, and to this end, I respectfully decline to send men on Arthur's expedition to the south and east. They are distant lands to us, and we must look to our own borders." He bowed to his cousin and took his seat.

Some submissions of a cautious nature were taken from minor nobles before King Owain, still visibly shaken by the confrontation with his difficult neighbour, took to his feet to close proceedings. His fragile confidence was further dented by the knowledge that his fellow kings mocked him for his courtly ways and spoke of him as 'Owain White Tooth'. His lips worked feverishly in a futile attempt to conceal his shame, but he knew once he opened his mouth, it was there for all to see. "My fellow kings, chiefs and nobles, we have spoken in an open and forthright manner. And I can say with certainty that we all know the minds and will of our neighbours."

Two hours of heated debate had sucked much of the exuberance from those in attendance, and most just nodded with hunched shoulders, no doubt attuned to the rumblings in their bellies. "Despite our differences, we all live in fear of invasion and prepare for the defence of our lands and our people. We are one race of Britons, who outlived the long years of Roman occupation, seeing them leave us to our own governance. Now that governance we have enjoyed is under threat from those who come from less prosperous lands. Those who covet what we have and would take it for themselves."

He paused to let his words sink in. "We must be thankful, therefore, that Arthur Pendragon has come to us with an offer to lead our men in warfare against the worst of these invaders. Powys shall join with the Rheged and the Coritani in providing men and supplies to his campaign. We hope in time that our fellow kings of the west will see fit to join us in this most noble and holy endeavour – yes holy. For the pagans who come burn our churches and bring their own vile beliefs that are alien to this land."

Although the priests tutted and crossed themselves, most were too tired to respond. Owain moved swiftly to conclude matters. "But no more of this. I invite all our noble visitors to join us this evening in this hall for feasting and to be entertained by the travelling bard, Gerwyn, and his band of minstrels. Thereafter, we shall see what the 'morrow brings."

Chapter Nine

THE FEAST WAS a solemn affair, and Gerwyn worked his hardest to raise laughs amongst his dour audience of kings and their nobles. Largely ignored, he earned little coin. Arthur's alliance whispered amongst themselves as courses were served and taken away, as did the other huddled groups of disunited and suspicious kingdoms. Most wanted the evening over to return to their camps and prepare to leave.

"Let us meet on the 'morrow at my villa, Arthur, but not too early," Owain said, as he stood to take his leave. Anne hugged and kissed her brother, her tired eyes telling of a busy day spent preparing the hall for the council and the subsequent feast.

"My deepest thanks to you both for espousing my cause. For your passion, Owain." Arthur's speech was slurred. He had drowned his disappointment in wine and now welcomed the prospect of his bed.

"It is our cause too, dear brother," Anne said, taking her husband's arm. With King Owain's departure, the remaining guests took their leave, wandering in silent stupor between the high columns, as attendants followed at a discreet distance dousing the oil lamps. They ambled out through the open doors into the balmy spring night and on through the gatehouse to their camps dotted around the surrounding fields.

"You are king to many on this island who look to you with hope in their hearts," Ambrose said, guiding his forlorn master through a side door and along a path to their villa. An owl hooted nearby and Ambrose instinctively clutched the charm that hung from his neck to ward off evil spirits, glancing behind to see if the disapproving Asaph had noticed his pagan habit. But Asaph was not there, having retired earlier, along with Ambrose's elderly father and the other weary Coritani counsellors.

Ambrose helped Arthur to his bed chamber, sitting him on the bed beside a sleeping Gunamara, then kneeling to remove his sandals. "I know you are of an impulsive spirit, and cannot wait to ride to war, my lord, but I beg you to be cautious and wait for more intelligence of the enemy, and to see if more allies flock to your banner," he whispered in the gloom. Gunamara shifted but did not wake. The baby in his cot gurgled in his dreams.

Arthur stared at him through glassy eyes, struggling to keep them open. "Dear Ambrose, you are ever the peacemaker," he slurred, leaning on one arm to steady himself, "and I note your air of caution. But my mind is set, and we shall make the best of it. Good night, dear friend. Tomorrow we plan our campaign." He sighed as he fell backwards, asleep before his head hit the bedding. Ambrose positioned him more comfortably, placed a cushion under his head, covered him with a blanket and quietly withdrew.

ARTHUR AWOKE at the crowing of a cockerel with an idea. He pondered on it as he dressed and drank water from a jug brought to him by a yawning attendant, and then went out in search of the bard, Gerwyn. He found him in the great hall, searching the floor on his hands and knees where they had performed their play.

"Searching for coins, Gerwyn?" Arthur said from behind, startling him.

"My lord, you are awake early. I was, erm, looking for missing props from my act…"

"Of course you were," Arthur laughed. "But I must have your ear for a moment. And I will tell you how you can make up your slender earnings."

Gerwyn stood and dusted down his woollen tunic, giving Arthur his full attention. "I am at your service, my lord."

Arthur led the shorter, rounder, man into the shadows. "I want you to ask King Caradog if you may accompany his wagon train back to Gwent, to entertain his court, before moving on to your next royal appointment."

"But to what end, my lord?" Gerwyn whispered, conspiratorially.

"To find out what you can about the comings and goings of other nobles, in particular the grandson of Ambrosius who is based close by at Caer Gloui. And I want to know of any contact the king has had with Mordred and Morgana."

At the mention of Morgana, the blood drained from Gerwyn's face and he visibly trembled. "I still recall your flight from Morgana's soldiers and the fear that she instils in those who cross her path. My attempts to entertain her and her cruel son were as well received as last night's performance," he muttered.

"You have performed this service admirably in the past for Merlyn, on my behalf, Gerwyn. And now I wish you to apply your courtly skills again." Arthur calmed his impatience, glancing about at the movements of slaves sweeping the floor and others passing by. "I shall give you silver now and again on receipt of useful intelligence. One of my boldest scouts shall join your troupe, and he shall ride to this place with any news you can gather of Caradog's allegiances with those who might oppose me. That includes possible collusion with the Saxons."

Gerwyn's troubled face soon changed to a brighter outlook as Arthur pressed half a dozen coins into his palm. "I will look for King Caradog now, my lord, and see if he will permit us to follow his wagon train." Gerwyn bowed and scurried away, leaving Arthur to look about from behind a column to see if anyone had noticed his presence. The side door to the hall was close by and he wrapped his cloak about him and slipped away.

Arthur made a detour to the barracks to seek out his man, before returning to the villa. Gunamara greeted him with a plate of cut fruits and they joined Peredur and Bedwyr for some bread, honey and juice. "Before we disturb King Owain and Queen Anne, let us walk to the parapet and look out on the western kings breaking their camps," he remarked to his comrades. Bedwyr crammed a piece of bread into his mouth and stood, followed by the dainty Peredur, who wiped his hands on a towel and threw it at an attendant.

"Shall I call for Herrig?" Bedwyr asked, buckling his sword belt around his solid girth.

"No, leave him be. We shall not need him," Arthur replied, knowing his bodyguard had bedded a comely serving girl. The three men marched onto a busy lane, making their way past goat herders and cart pushers to the main gatehouse that faced Watling Street, and climbed the wooden ladder to the platform. From the walls they could see much activity in the surrounding fields, with canvas tents being rolled and lifted into wagons, wooden lean-tos pushed to the ground and chopped for fire wood, servants carrying pots and boxes of utensils, oxen being yoked and tethered, and riders brushing down their horses.

"They are leaving without ceremony to return to their lands," Bedwyr airily remarked, trying to draw out Arthur's thoughts.

"Aye, and without pledging men to our cause," Arthur replied. His attention was directed to the south, where a rising dust trail hinted at approaching riders. He pointed and said, "Quickly, to the south tower to improve our vista."

They were not the only ones making their way to the south tower. Viroco, captain of the guards, met them there. "My lord," he said, bowing slightly. "Riders approach, but we know not whom. I have sent three scouts to find out who they are."

Three horsemen could be seen galloping towards the gathering dust cloud, whilst the riders and wagons under the banners of the white stag of Gwent delayed their departure in that direction. Arthur smiled as he noticed Gerwyn's wagon join the Gwent party, with his own man's horse tethered to the tailgate.

After thirty minutes, one of the scouts returned, jumping from his horse and climbing the ladder to report to Viroco. "My lord, there is a long procession led by the Queen of Dumnonia, for we could see the white swan of her banner

Arthur *Rex Brittonum*

and that of the black boar of Cornubia. My comrades have waited to greet them and escort them here."

Viroco and Arthur's eyes met. "Were you expecting them?" Arthur asked.

"No, my lord. There has been scant news from that troubled land these past months. I must report to my king."

Arthur, Bedwyr and Peredur followed Viroco through the town to the king's enclosure, where two spearmen stood to attention at the gate, allowing them all to pass. Owain and Anne were sitting in their courtyard, where the remains of their breakfast were being cleared away by attendants.

"What news, Viroco?" Owain asked, rising from his chair.

"My lord, a procession of unknown size is approaching from the south. My scout reports that the banners to the front are the white swan of the Queen of Dumnonia, and the black boar of Cornubia."

"My sister, Morgaise!" Anne gasped, also rising from her seat. "Let me ride out to meet her, my lord." She gripped Owain's arm, and fixed him with her wide green eyes, knowing he could not refuse her.

Owain smiled and patted her hand. "Then take Arthur, so that your family may be reunited. Viroco, accompany my lady."

ARTHUR'S MIND WAS a swirl of possibilities and unanswered questions, as he trotted beside his sister's long-maned dapple mare. Anne wore linen and leather leggings under a tunic and rode astride confidently as any man, her hair held in check by a costly scarf glittering with gold thread. Her expression was pensive. "When did you last meet her?" Arthur asked as they approached Viroco's scouts, who were leading the slow-moving train.

"I have not seen her for two years, and that was at Caer Badon where we took the waters," Anne replied. "She had just birthed her third child." She squinted at the banners in the approaching procession, which was led by a dozen warriors bearing lances with black triangular flags fluttering at the ends. "She must be in the wagon with her children," Anne added.

Viroco had ridden forward and was talking to his men. When they caught up with him, he said, "The Queen of Dumnonia is in the royal wagon, in the middle, my lady."

Anne jabbed her heels into her mare's flanks and galloped past the dusty soldiers, followed by Arthur and his men. Morgaise could see her sister approaching and called on the wagon to stop. She climbed down and waited for Anne to dismount before they embraced tightly, crying out with pleasure mixed with relief at their reunion.

Arthur had only seen Morgaise fleetingly during his escape from Mordred's dungeon some twelve years ago, and marvelled at this tall, elegant lady, whose raven-black hair, banded by a golden tiara, was tied in braids that fell to her waist. He also dismounted and approached, waiting to be noticed.

There were tears of joy running down Anne's cheeks as she turned and pulled Arthur's sleeve. "And here is our dear brother, Arthur, now a fine warrior as you can see," she said.

Morgaise and Arthur were of the same height, and appraised each other for an instant before Morgaise flung her arms around his neck and kissed his dusty cheek. "My little half-brother, you have the looks of Anne and both your parents, whereas I have inherited my father's proud, black looks. But there is our mother in both of us. Well met, baby brother!" She squeezed his arms and pushed him back to arm's length to study him some more.

"I am joyous at this reunion, dear sister. Let us not talk of halves. You are both my dear sisters, and the only family I have remaining." Arthur pulled them both to him and they hugged in silence as dust swirled around their ankles.

Morgaise wasted no time in addressing the question that was on the faces of Anne and Arthur. "I have fled my husband's kingdom in disarray, for he is dead, cruelly slain in battle with the Saxons and Mordred's army." Her face fell and tears welled in her eyes.

"Are you saying that Mordred and the Saxons joined their forces to attack Dumnonia?" Arthur asked, incredulous.

"That is exactly what I am saying. We had little warning to raise the levies from surrounding farms and settlements. Speed and stealth were their intention. Cerdic, the king of the South Saxons, attacked our town by ship and along our coast, and Mordred's army attacked from the north, along the course of the River Ex. Our men fought bravely, but my noble husband, Geraint, fell in battle, as did the aging knight, Tristan, who despite his advanced years, gained us time to make our escape to the moors by riding out at the head of our guards. He died leading one last charge." She turned her head and sobbed on Anne's shoulder.

"This is heavy news, and I am deeply aggrieved for your loss, dear sister," Arthur mumbled. "But we must move swiftly to the town and share this news with King Owain and his guests, the kings of the west, for they are ready to break camp. Anne, will you travel with Morgaise in her wagon? Bedwyr shall take the reins of your horse. Come, we must make haste."

THE KINGS OF the west gathered with Owain in the great hall, anxious for news of the unexpected visitors. Arthur led in his two sisters, and an elderly woman with long grey hair and grief-stricken eyes was helped by Peredur and Bedwyr.

Anne introduced her sister, Morgaise, and then beckoned the old woman to come forward. "And this is the Lady Isolde, widow of our beloved knight, Tristan, who died bravely leading the guard in defence of their town. I will let my dear sister tell her tale of woe."

The kings stood in mute dismay at the unfolding of the tale, and then asked questions, as Arthur had, to confirm that the armies of Mordred and Cerdic had attacked in unison. The great Roman sea port and fortress of Exisca had fallen, and the southwest lands were now at the mercy of Mordred and the Saxons.

Arthur took Bedwyr to one side and said, "Go and find the captain of the Dumnonian guard and get as much information as you can about the battle, the route they followed, how many fighting men he has with him and how many remain scattered across that unhappy land."

"Yes, my lord," Bedwyr said dully, still reflecting on the report that the old king's favourite and legendary knight, Tristan, was no more.

"This is the gravest of news," Owain moaned, "and comes on the back of the tale of disaster told by our Coritani neighbours of the similar fate that has befallen them."

Morgaise looked up in alarm and a croak was all that came from her mouth.

"My noble kings," Arthur said, returning to his side, "our prospects have changed for the worst, and you must surely agree that our whole island is in peril. Now that Mordred is working in league with the South Saxons, it will not be long before they are at the gates of Caer Badon and Caer Gloui, barely three days ride from here. I believe we must form a council of war."

The kings looked at each other for a moment, trying to read each other's thoughts. King Caradog coughed and spoke quietly. "I would have a moment with my fellow kings, my western neighbours." With that he grabbed Vortipor of Dyfed and Cyngar of Demetia by the sleeves and guided them out of earshot.

"We can guess what is coming," Owain said, looking at his cousin, Cadwallon, with disappointed eyes.

Cadwallon grunted and merely stood with his great arms folded across his barrel chest. Arthur felt it best to keep his thoughts to himself until the three kings returned. In the meantime, Anne guided her sister and Isolde to a table in a corner, where Gunamara was organising refreshments for their weary and distressed guests.

"We are of a mind to stay out of this gathering storm," Caradog announced after a short while, to no one's surprise. Vortipor looked smug and defiant at his side, but Cyngar looked down to his shoes and would make eye contact with no one.

"Then will you help us with supplies of dried foodstuffs, arms and wagons?" Arthur asked.

After a brief silence, Cyngar the Wise broke ranks and said, "I shall send you what I can, Arthur, but only after some weeks as I must return to my fortress and take stock." His two neighbours shot him filthy looks.

The Head Dragon uncrossed his arms and with hands on hips boomed, "I too shall return to my home and take stock, dear cousin. I shall send you what support I can. These are trying times and we must assist each other as best we can." He looked with disdain at Caradog and Vortipor. "To this end, I will delay my departure no longer. Farewell, noble lords, and may the gods favour you."

The meeting broke up and Owain proposed that those remaining retire to his villa so that discussions could continue and the weary find respite.

"WE PASSED THROUGH northern Cornubia, once my father's stronghold, and I instructed them to send what fighting men they could muster north to Caer Badon and defend that fortress," Morgaise said, winding up her briefing. Arthur noted the sword belt at her waist and wondered how well his tall and broad-shouldered sister could fight.

"How many people have followed you from Dumnonia?" Owain asked, anxious to establish numbers of refugees.

"I would say, maybe, five hundred. Many more have fled to the coast to look for boats. The land will be empty, although much of the interior is already sparsely populated due to inhospitable moorlands."

"Then we must establish a camp for them, perhaps centred on the amphitheatre?" Owain replied. He looked to his steward who nodded and moved off to make arrangements. "Viroco, go to Cyngar and my cousin, Cadwallon, and ask if they might leave some tents and utensils for our refugee camp."

Arthur saw a chance for one final plea to the wavering Cyngar and took Viroco to one side as he made to leave. "Noble Viroco, tell King Cyngar that I implore him to send ships with men ready to fight to the port of Abona, that lies close to Caer Badon. We expect to be gathering our forces there at the new moon, and I fear a coastal attack by the Saxons."

"I will tell him, my lord," Viroco said, and then bowed and hurried away.

Queen Anne saw her moment to distract the fixated group by proposing a break for cakes and honeyed water. Gunamara had joined them, and the elderly Lady Isolde managed a smile as she took her seat. Arthur silently ate and drank, his mind a whirl of war preparations. Morgaise was keen to hear of recent events and the ever-boastful Peredur gave a dramatic account of the Coritani rescue and the fight with the giants.

"Oh, we also had a giant slain on the moors some years ago," Morgaise airily remarked. "Strange and mysterious creatures."

"They are but freaks of nature," Arthur said, snapping out of his reverie, "not devils who have passed through the Gates of Hades. They bleed human blood."

When the plates were cleared away, Arthur, Owain, Peredur, Bedwyr and Morgaise gathered around a parchment map showing Roman Britannia and its towns connected by a network of roads. Arthur pointed to Caer Gloui, once called Glevum, the former Roman fortress near the mouth of the River Severna, some eighty miles due south, where the descendants of mighty king Ambrosius Aurelianus held power over the surrounding lands.

"We must take our army to Caer Gloui to meet with the head of that noble family and garner support for our confrontation with the armies of Mordred and Cerdic."

Owain glumly remarked, "That would be Malachi, son of Gareth. I expect you will get little more than a pious sermon from him." He wrung his hands, betraying his lack of comfort at being in a council of war. "Must we act so swiftly, Arthur? It will take me two weeks to raise the levies and we might garner support from other quarters…"

Just then, they were distracted by a commotion at the gates, where Owain's guards had raised their voices in keeping someone out.

"I shall go," Arthur said, turning on his heels and marching towards the disturbance, causing Herrig to swiftly spring from the shadows and follow. At the gate, the two guards had barred someone from entering, with crossed spears, and angry voices could be heard beyond the creeping ivy.

"What is this disturbance?" Arthur shouted as he ducked under the bower above the gate. The guards half-turned towards him and Arthur could see the huge presence of Caratacus, champion of Gwynedd. Whilst Herrig's hand went to his sword hilt, Arthur merely barged past the guards and stood before the huge warrior. "Caratacus, what news?"

"May I speak with you, my lord?"

"Let him enter," Arthur commanded the guards.

The guards stood aside, and the big man turned sideways to enter through the narrow opening into the gardens, leaving his brooding men behind. His stern look soon melted to a roguish smile, something Arthur had seen before. The two men clasped forearms and Caratacus said, "Lord Arthur, my king has given me leave to come to your banner, and I bring thirty warriors."

Arthur's gratitude could not be contained and he stepped forward to hug the brute. "Am I right to think that you asked for this, noble Caratacus?"

"I was a flea in his helmet as we broke camp, my lord. Your captain, Viroco, did catch us just before we took to our road. He listened to Viroco's earnest entreaty and then agreed to release me and my men, together with some camp equipment. He sends you his best wishes for a successful campaign. I am at your service, and would relish the chance to measure myself in combat next to your own champion." He turned to Herrig and slapped him on the bicep. The hulking Jute broke into a grin, and both men clasped forearms.

Owain had now arrived behind Arthur to see the happy conclusion of events. "You are most welcome, noble lord," he said, bidding Caratacus to enter the courtyard with a sweeping gesture of his arm.

Caratacus shouted back to his men to wait for him by the stables and followed his hosts to the map table. Arthur introduced him to Morgaise and briefly outlined their plan to march south to Caer Gloui. "And from there we shall march the fifty miles to Caer Badon and unite with the garrison of Dumnonians and men of Cornubia to make out battle plans for meeting our enemy."

Morgaise clapped her hands and smiled for the first time since their meeting. "It is fitting, my noble brother, that we shall plan our defeat of the Saxons and that vile snake Mordred near Mount Badon, where ten years past your father, Uther, did unite the Britons in victory over the Saxons!"

"And will you also ride to war, Lady Morgaise?" Owain asked.

"You shall not stop me leading my people in defence of our lands," she replied, her hand on her sword hilt.

"Then we are in agreement," Arthur said. "By my estimation, we have close to a thousand men, and may yet gather more on our progress."

"I shall remain behind to raise the levies and coordinate the supplies that will follow," Owain said, having no appetite for battle. "Tonight, you are all welcome to my table in the great hall, and we shall toast the success of our alliance!"

BARINTHUS STOOD PATIENTLY in the portico of the king's villa, dabbing the sweat from his brow with a silk scarf, cap in hand.

"Enter merchant!" Anne's firm, regal voice floated out through an open doorway and he duly obliged, walking into a perfume-infused chamber where twin girls in colourful livery fixed him with twinkling hazel eyes, one moving to take his cloak and cap, the other offering him a silver goblet of honeyed water from a silver tray.

His expert eye floated from hand sewn tapestries of classical scenes hanging on the walls to exquisitely carved low couches and tables, silver and gold painted jugs and vases holding gay summer flowers, and to silver fox fur rugs between which a dolphin sprouted a jet of water on a worn mosaic floor.

"Ah, such an elegant room, my queen," he gushed, stepping down to the inner quadrant where three finely dressed ladies lolled on cushioned couches. "It is like a scene from imperial Rome itself," he added, bowing to left and right.

Queen Anne stood and offered a hand bearing a red ruby ring. "Then kiss it in the Roman fashion, dear Barinthus." He duly obliged, to the giggles of Morgaise and Gunamara. "Please sit; we wish to talk to you before you leave."

Barinthus was guided to a cushioned seat by one of the twins, and he squeezed his broad posterior gently between the arm rests. "I am at your service, dear ladies."

"Our army rides out this morning, taking our men to war. I hear that you will be following them to the courts of Malachi and Gareth?"

"Indeed, my lady. I intend to take orders from those most noble of chiefs before taking ship to Gaul. It has been a most enlightening visit."

"All the more so for being chased by pirates, I hear," Morgaise said, between sips.

"Ha! If it wasn't for your husband, my lady," he bowed to Gunamara, "I would be lying slaughtered on a rocky beach and my valuable cargo plundered."

"Then I am pleased he was on hand to save you and bring you to our service," she lightly replied.

"But we are short of time and both you and my lady Morgaise are to ride out soon," Anne said. "We wish for you to bring us some fine furnishings on your return, for our private chambers." She waved her arm at the walls, and his gaze followed, estimating the value of her finery. "When Arthur wins his war with Mordred, he will be undisputed King of Britannia, *Rex Brittonum*, as the Romans would say, and my sister Gunamara will be queen. They must have the best for their royal abode. Also, our sister, Queen Morgaise of Dumnonia, whose port you will use once the Saxons have been driven off, would welcome your expert eye for finery in her rooms." She paused and raised a querying brow. He nodded vigorously. "And do not forget me. I wish to refurnish this room and perhaps another for my little one." She patted her small bump and popped a cherry in her mouth.

Barinthus's mind was a whirl of possibilities and his eyes bulged at the prospect. "It will be MY pleasure and most solemn duty to collect the finest treasures of the Roman world and bring them to you ladies for YOUR pleasure," he gushed, slowly moving his sweaty palm from his knee to the purse on his belt in an involuntary act.

Anne noticed and said, "We shall send you on your way with a list we have prepared and a pouch of gold and silver coins. And you will be rewarded on your return should we be pleased with the treasures you bring." She signalled for one of the twins to come to her with a scroll tied with a ribbon and a leather money pouch on a silver tray. Anne pointed to the merchant and the tray was held before him.

"My ladies," Barinthus replied, struggling to his feet to take the scroll and pouch.

Anne smiled and said, "God's speed to you, Barinthus of Armorica. Our prayers shall follow you for a safe journey, and we hope to meet again in happier times."

Chapter Ten

ARTHUR CALLED A halt as their road passed through a glade. Around them, ash and oak trees thrust their green leaves upwards to the blue sky as a thrush chirped warnings at their coming. His commanders rode their horses to his side to receive their instructions.

"That track leads to the farm where my guardians raised me as if I were their own son," he said cheerfully. "Indeed, I thought I was Sir Hector's child, and gentle Gayle's, until the mysterious Merlyn came here. He told me of my true identity." He glanced at the smirking faces around him. "I caught rabbits in these woods, and when I grew to a youth I was trained with wooden sword and shield. My guard saw to that."

"You had a guard then?" Morgaise sounded surprised. She knew little of her half-brother's childhood.

"Two veteran warriors, Varden and Casius."

"They made a good job of it, my lord," Bedwyr remarked.

"And the gods favour you by returning you to your childhood place," Morgaise lightly remarked, her frisky white mare dancing in the dust.

Arthur laughed and said, "We are only five miles from Caer Gloui. If you continue at a steady pace, I shall catch you up in an hour. Let me indulge my memories by riding down this track to see what has become of their farm."

"Then take Herrig with you, my lord," Bedwyr said. "I shall lead our army onwards."

Arthur trotted along the single track, now overgrown with bushes and trees. He brushed past the last leaves and saw dilapidated barns on both sides, and the house before him. It was clearly occupied. As he entered the farmyard, a bare-legged little maid was pouring swill into a pig trough, and an old man sitting on a three-legged stool was peeling root vegetables into a bucket. The girl dropped her pail and ran inside at the appearance of the two horsemen.

Arthur dismounted, handed his reins to Herrig, then walked towards the white-haired old man, who stood and shuffled forwards with bent back.

"Is it you, Casius?" Arthur asked.

"Who are you, to know my name?" the old man croaked, looking up through rheumy eyes.

"I am Artorius, the boy you once taught to sword fight."

The old man's face lit up, "Can it be? Is it you, Master Artorius?"

"Yes, although I am now called 'Arthur', in the Briton manner. I was passing by and came to see who is here. Greetings, my old teacher." Arthur awkwardly hugged the old man. Casius was forced to retreat to his stool for support and Arthur squatted close by, the better to be seen and heard by his old fencing master. They regarded each other in a kind of wonder as familiarity and old affections wakened, until a shadow clouded Arthur's smile.

"I had news of the passing of my parents, some years ago." Arthur shook his head, their absence being starker to him in this yard than on the windy walls of Vindolanda. "Where are they buried?" he asked.

"They both met peaceful ends from old age, my lord. Their graves are at the back of the house behind the orchard. Come, I will take you there."

Casius led them into the gloomy interior of the kitchen, where an old woman bowed to them as the young girl hid behind her skirts. He muttered a few words to Arthur by way of introduction as they passed through. Outside, a mangy dog growled, and Casius waved it away with a curse. He hobbled along an avenue between fruit trees to a low wall. "Do you remember that I challenged you to jump over this wall? And with sword and shield in hand?" he asked.

Arthur *Rex Brittonum*

Arthur laughed at the memory, imagining a boy with a helmet too big for his head, struggling to scale the wall that was low enough for them to sit on and swing their legs over. "Yes, I remember it well, dear Casius. I was eager to learn the ways of the sword. And I longed to prove to my father that I was grown enough to hunt with him."

Casius led them to a family cemetery bounded by a low picket fence. Inside were a dozen tombstones crudely carved with Christian symbols and the names of the deceased. He apologised for the weeds that encroached here and there, but in all, it was a tidy patch made less lonely by the clucking of a couple of browsing hens. Arthur knelt before the graves of Gayle and Hector and offered a prayer for their souls. He touched Hector's headstone as he stood.

"It is a plain stone for a brave knight who once fought for Ambrosius and Uther. You were good folk and will be enjoying God's favours in Heaven," he murmured, half to himself, getting to his feet and dusting his knees. More clearly, he said, "I am pleased to have found you, Casius, and to see they were buried in a fitting manner."

They started back, both subdued at first, until Arthur brought them into the present.

"Tell me, who owns this place now?"

"It passed into the hands of a magistrate from Caer Gloui, my lord. Some of his family live here, but he rarely visits. We exist on a tithe of what we produce, the bulk of which goes to town by wagon after harvest. It's a simple life and one that is free of outside interference."

"Then long may it stay that way. I am riding to Caer Gloui now, with an army of Britons from many tribes. We are on a path to war with the Saxons."

Casius croaked his alarm at this news. "My lord! Are the Saxon wars starting again?"

"I'm afraid so. They have attacked Dumnonia and we must respond. Tell me, who is lord at Caer Gloui?"

"He is Malachi, son of Gareth and grandson of Ambrosius, my lord."

Arthur recalled a stringy youth attempting to pull Excalibur from Merlyn's stone. The healer and his aide, Varden, had slyly kept the sword trapped to thwart all comers, releasing it only for Arthur. He chuckled at the memory of the trick he had not been privy to, touching the hilt of Excalibur. It had once been Ambrosius's sword, thrown to the lady of the lake at his funeral, but recovered by Merlyn and saved until a time when his visions would guide his hand.

"Ah, the son of Gareth… What can you tell me of the nature of this Malachi?" Arthur asked, making ready to mount.

"He is a quiet, scholarly man, like his father, who shuns the way of the sword. There have only been years of peace here, since King Uther won his battle at Badon Hill. Only blessed peace, my lord."

"And I shall return the south lands to peace, dear Casius, once I have sent the Saxons packing to their ships. God's blessings and good day to you!" Arthur pressed a silver coin into the hand of his former guard before he mounted Mars. He wheeled around and then briskly led Herrig out by the concealed track. In no time, they were joining the rear wagons of the train, surprising his daydreaming cook, Derward, and waking the sleeping Ambrose.

CAER GLOUI WAS a well-maintained town – its Roman walls still intact, and its great double gatehouse manned by keen guards in green livery bearing a familiar emblem, that of Arthur's bear and dragon.

"They wear your emblem, my lord!" Caratacus exclaimed, as the riders passed through the archway into a lively marketplace.

"It is I who poached the emblem of Ambrosius," Arthur replied. "And it is they who might take exception."

Guards awaited them and asked them to dismount. Arthur introduced himself and asked to be taken to their master, Malachi.

"No more than half a dozen, my lord," a gruff guard replied, leading the way. They passed through busy streets to a great hall and mounted the steps. Malachi's steward led them to where a huddle of petitioners hemmed around a dais on which sat a lord dispensing rulings to plaintiffs. The royal party's arrival was announced without unusual ceremony, but at the mention of Arthur's name and rank, the babbling diminished and curious eyes were turned on the newcomers.

"Come forward, Arthur of the Britons!" Malachi called out, standing and waving dismissively to his minions.

Arthur, Peredur and Morgaise approached, leaving the other commanders in the background.

Arthur decided not to bow and said, "Greetings, noble lord Malachi, son of Gareth and grandson of Ambrosius. I am Arthur, son of Uther, and King of the Britons."

Malachi placed his hands in the generous sleeves of his handsome robe and looked down, unsmiling. "But these are merely claims, Arthur. You may be Uther's lost son, but I am only aware of one king of the Britons, and he is Mordred." He turned his attention to Morgaise and bowed slightly. "Welcome, Queen of the Dumnoni, our southern neighbours. I am sorely vexed to hear of your troubles and your loss."

Malachi stood examining his three guests for what seemed an age before his face cracked to a wan smile. "But where are my manners? You are my guests and have no doubt travelled far. Please, sit at my table and I will call for refreshments." He beckoned his steward and guided them to a trestle table beside his dais. Arthur noted his red and gold robe, the purple trim of his cloak, his long braccae and pointed slippers. The walls were draped with tapestries depicting the grisly martyrdoms of various saints.

Malachi followed Arthur's gaze and said, "The suffering of the saints reminds us of our faith and Christian duty, Lord Arthur."

"Indeed, Lord Malachi, but a man must also do his duty to his lord, or else those with evil intent will rule over us."

Malachi fixed him with a patronising look, and Arthur saw he was surrounded not by nobles or commanders, but a ring of tonsured priests.

"I have heard that the south regards me as a usurper and Mordred as their High King. But you should know that I have an army stiff with nobles and men from every other part of our island at my back, and I intend to deal with the Saxon threat, as my father and your grandfather did. The fact that Mordred has allied himself to the Saxons is convenient for me, for I shall deal with him also."

"Bold words, indeed. Then I wish you Godspeed, Arthur, and also our good neighbour, the Lady Morgaise. But do not look to us for warriors. We have no unit to spare, only a modest guard for our walls."

Arthur leaned too close to the cleric, unblinking and steely. "I have heard reports that your father has made a peace with the Saxons to stop them raiding his lands. Has he been handing over the riches amassed by Ambrosius? Does Gareth not know that they will keep returning for more until there is nothing remaining, and they will sweep you both aside? It is your land that they covet, my lord."

"Do not lecture me, 'king' Arthur!" Malachi growled, his knuckles glowing white on his arm rest. "We will secure our lands as we see fit. You must follow your own destiny."

As the men glared at each other, Morgaise spoke in a quiet voice. "Then, noble Malachi, in the spirit of friendship, will you give us provisions for our army? We have over a thousand mouths to feed and would welcome your Christian charity."

Malachi broke away from his staring match with Arthur and smiled sweetly at her, perhaps reminded that there was a huge and potentially hostile army camped outside his walls. "My lady, we are kin, perhaps in a distant manner. Yes, we shall aid you with grain and salted pork. Send your cook to my kitchens to see if we can assist with those items you may be lacking." He turned back to Arthur and said, "Let us not be enemies, Arthur. I shall pray for your victory, and shall bend my knee to you when you vanquish the cruel and troublesome Mordred and his unreasonable mother. But until that time, my father and I must remain neutral, due to our close proximity to your dread foes." He stood, bowing slightly, to take his leave. "And I trust you will honour the motif of my grandfather in your battles with the Saxons. Good day."

Arthur returned the gesture and the audience ended abruptly.

"It is good that I accompanied you, Arthur," Morgaise chided, pinching a foreign delicacy between her fingers, "otherwise you would have butted your head against his like a rutting ram. He has spoken plainly, and for that we should be grateful, and has offered victuals for our pots."

"You are wise, my lady," Arthur sheepishly replied, "and your addition to our campaign is most welcome and timely."

ATER TWO NIGHTS outside the walls of Caer Gloui, they set to marching southwest towards Dumnonia and Caer Badon. Two more wagons of foodstuff, together with cooks, and healers with medical supplies, joined them. Their road took them beside the widening River Severna estuary, and they could see across to the watchtowers of Gwent. Would Gwent remain neutral, Arthur wondered, or join the enemy?

They made camp on a plateau which bore the remains of a circle of carved stones, a sign that it had once been a place of the ancient people. As the camp was being set, Arthur walked with his commanders onto a rocky promontory to witness an orange sunset over the hills, before the band of gleaming water swallowed the light.

"My lord, riders' approach!" Viroco said, pointing back the way they had come. They watched the dust trail get closer as the last rays of the day gave way to twilight. In time, a group of three dusty riders made their way to the commanders.

Their leader sprung on his heels across the grass, his energy barely contained. His bow was another bounce. "Lord Arthur, I am Cadog, son of Cadern, and I am chief of the Silurian people. My father fought for King Uther at Badon Hill and I offer my sword and those of my sixty men to your cause."

"You come straight to the point, straight to your business. Well, I like that. You are most welcome, Cadog. Your lands are under the rule of King Caradog of Gwent, is that not so?"

"Indeed, it is so, my lord, and a source of great distress to our people. You are looking now upon our lands, across the wide estuary." He pointed to the right as shadows fell across his home. "We bridged the river at Caer Gloui, after a brief stand-off with Caradog's guards. We pray for a return to our own rule, if the God of Hosts favours us, my lord."

"Then you have risked the wrath of your king to join us, noble Cadog," Arthur replied, clasping his forearm, "and I am grateful."

Cadog grinned. "Except that our king has taken his army some few days ago to rally with Mordred and the Saxons. We know he has not left enough men to raid our land, and so we resolved to fight for you, in the hope that should you prevail, the yoke of tyranny will be lifted from us and we shall get our freedom back."

"Then we shall all pray to the God of Hosts that it shall be so. How many men did Caradog lead to the enemy roster?"

"About four hundred. Some of our own are in their ranks, and my hope is they will desert when they see our banner proudly raised next to yours, my lord!"

They shared a grim laugh at this, but the grief and misery of impending civil war was not lost on any of them. Arthur's mood was sombre that evening, as he now feared the enemy alliance might be double their number. After the meal he sent his squire, Dermot, to seek out Cadog.

"Ah, Cadog, come and sit. I wish to talk some more," Arthur said, on the Silurian's approach out of the darkness that hung over their camp. "I cannot be settled in my mind. You see, I suspect that the Saxons will sail their ships to the port of Abona, overcome the garrison there, and attack Caer Badon from the river. Are you familiar with that place?"

"Aye, my lord, I have been there. It is a dangerous crossing as the tides are treacherous."

"I wonder if fisherfolk travel down this coast to that place?"

"They do, my lord. The people here are what's left of the Dobunni tribe, and pay homage to the lord of Caer Gloui."

"And your people, the Silures, do they fish this mighty river and the sea beyond?"

"Yes, and our tribes enjoy a respect for each other, with many tales of rescue cementing our bond. It is one of fellowship against nature and the fickle will of water and its gods of old. Whether Sulis, Serverna or Coventina." He sucked on a reed and stared into the orange embers.

"Then before we leave these lands on our southward journey, will you help our cause by recruiting some of these Dobunni fishermen? We need them to ferry your men to the port of Abona, to warn them of imminent attack, Cadog, and to help bolster their defences. We have some Dobunni in our ranks – they can accompany you."

Cadog bowed his shaggy, brown mop of hair to Arthur. "If that is your will, my lord, it shall be done."

"Good," Arthur said, smiling and sitting upright. "I did send a message to King Cyngar of Demetia to aid us with ships of men and to sail on Abona, but I do not hold out much hope of his support. I did not approach Vortipor with the same request, thinking he may be an ally of Gwent. What can you tell me of these kings?"

Cadog frowned and gathered his thoughts. "I can tell you that my sister is married to King Vortipor of Dyfed. He is no friend of Gwent, although he gives Caradog the false impression. Because of that we have a secret alliance to support each other against the worst excesses of the White Stag, Caradog. Our alliance is as yet untested."

"Ah, that is of interest," Arthur replied, now leaning forward in a conspiratorial manner. A log cracked on the fire, causing an ember to settle on a sleeping dog, who yelped and slunk away. "Then, how do we petition your sister in Dyfed to add further weight to my entreaty? She must inform my lord Vortipor that you have joined with us, and that Gwent has sided with our enemy."

"I agree, my lord," Cadog replied, without hesitation. "That can best be done by sailing around the coast. If your scribe could write a missive, I will send my cousin to his favourite cousin, the Queen of Dyfed."

"Excellent!" Arthur cried, disturbing some of the men dozing nearby. He clasped forearms with his ally and called for Ambrose and a flagon of ale. The stars in the dark blue blanket above seemed to twinkle approval from the gods, and Arthur's mind once more turned to Merlyn, who understood the mysteries of the sun, the moon and the stars, of the natural world and how it related to the world of men, and pondered where his old friend might be.

Chapter Eleven

MORGANA WAS A bloodless, black-shrouded creature forever darning the old web of her dark influence. Her diplomacy had ever been thin, and in middle age her spider-like patience lapsed often, so that now she regarded her uncouth guests with barely concealed contempt. The Saxon kings, Cerdic of the South Seax and Octha of Ceint, hated each other and had to be separated by the wily King Icel of the Angliscs. These untamed warrior chiefs from across the Saxon Sea were now her allies and she was keenly aware that she must handle them with caution and tact. Her son, Mordred, now a pimply and restless young man of twenty summers, sat beside her on the throne where King Uther had once sat.

Because of the distrust between the Saxon kings, Cerdic had insisted on withdrawing his men after sacking the Dumnonian capital, Exisca. He feared that Octha would attack his southern holdings if they were left undefended. This had annoyed Morgana, who had wanted to press on into Dumnonia and capture more towns. Instead, they had fallen back, leaving a garrison to hold Exisca and its surrounding lands. They were now plotted their next move in the company of King Icel, who held a long sliver of land stretching up the east coast.

"It has not escaped my notice," Morgana drawled sardonically, "that in the lands you nest in you are quarrelsome neighbours."

Icel barked a dry laugh, glancing at his surly neighbours through his one good eye. "It is the truth, Morgana. Even the Jutes who fight under Saxon banners do not trust them. We have been raiding each other's villages across salty marshes and through pine forests since Woden was a boy." His rough command of the Briton tongue made him the translator between the allies. Icel had been growing his holdings in the east for ten years.

Morgana regarded him with shrewd eyes and replied, "I understand your desire for new lands, and you shall have them. The usurper Arthur is rallying an army to stand against us in the west. This is good, as we have the opportunity to destroy all opposition to both our causes."

"Can we go hunting now?" Mordred asked, twisting in his seat.

"Soon, my love," his mother replied, patting his arm. "Let us set our plans for marching west, then we can hunt boar and stag in the forest." She turned back to Icel. "I propose we march west, along the Portway, to Caer Badon, and capture that town. It will cut off our Dumnonian enemy from their northern allies."

Morgana's secret strategy relied on it doing more than this. She hoped it would also force Gareth and Malachi to join her, but there was no need to raise that possibility with these three barbarian kings. It was a delicate matter indeed, siding with the Saxons and Angliscs. She had allied with them to break the resistance of the remaining Britons, but such an alliance was, to her mind, temporary.

Icel had discussed the plan with his fellows and turned to her. "We agree, and Cerdic proposes that his ships sail around the coast to the port close by Caer Badon, and attack from the sea. Once the enemy is slain, we shall take our pick of their lands."

Morgana smiled. "Then it is settled. We shall prepare our armies to march in the coming days, and further cement our friendship tomorrow on a hunt in our royal forest. I shall leave you to return to your camps. Good day, noble kings of the south and east." She watched them leave with their guards, wrapped in wolf or bear skins, the floor reeds sticking in clumps to their muddy boots.

"And so it shall be for our luckless people," she crooned.

"What do you mean, Ma?" Mordred asked.

"Like reeds caught under the tread of their boots - those unfortunate enough to be in their way. They are like the wolves of the forest, my son - killers who hunt in packs without remorse, without any feelings for those they deem lesser than they are."

"But we are not lesser than them. We have courtly manners and can read and they cannot," Mordred retorted, jumping to his feet. "I do not understand why you entertain those brutes."

"Because we need them to clear our path, my ardent king."

"I am my own man – you should not talk down to me!" he shouted, glaring at her.

She smiled and stood before him, "Yes, you are now a man and must learn to read the hearts and minds of others. Be patient - watch and learn. That will come with experience, my love. You are the king who shall rule over all of this land, once we've overcome opposition from the rebels and reached a settlement with our allies. But for now, leave the delicate politics to me, Mordred, and do not speak of these matters to anyone, for I fear there may be spies amongst us.

MORGAISE RODE BESIDE Arthur at the head of the column, waving to people clustered in hopeful groups by the side of the road, as they crossed into her kingdom of Dumnonia. The buttercups were spent, and half-grown lambs gambolled on the hillsides unaware of the anxiety in the world of men.

By midday they had reached the hillock that marked the northern edge of the Abon river valley. Before them the valley walls grew progressively steeper to left and right, and a waterfall from a rocky crag fed the stream that was to become a raging torrent further ahead.

"Repast!" Arthur shouted, holding his arm up to signal to those behind. Riders dismounted, stretched, and sought bushes behind which to relieve themselves. Shepherds drove their flocks to graze away from the gathering warriors, up the valley side where clumps of hardy grass grew around boulders that made it suitable for little else.

Morgaise asked him the question that was on many minds. "How far away is our enemy?"

Arthur led her to two wooden stools brought by Dermot and replied wearily, "I hope to hear before nightfall from scouts I sent along the Portway road eastwards. We can only hope they are slow in their coming. We may need a week or so for levies from Powys and beyond to join us, for they must first reap their harvests."

They had seen the early shoots of barley, wheat and corn in fields beside the road on their progress, planted early in the year and now thriving on the modest rains and warm days.

"Aye, we are ahead of the fighting season," Bedwyr added, bringing his own stool to the group of commanders. Arthur had already seen off Cadog and his Silurian war band on their mission the day before, so his command group now consisted of Morgaise, Bedwyr, Peredur, Caratacus, Viroco of the Cornovi, and Brian of the Coritani. In addition, there were the four sub-commanders, who hovered on the fringe in conversation. Whilst Derward and the other cooks busied themselves with serving platters of flat bread and dried foods, pitchers of water and drinking pots, Arthur beckoned the four young men into the circle.

"It is time to match these sub-commanders, who have learned the theory, to four experienced leaders. They will train them in the practical ways of warfare. I think Agravane may partner with my lady." Morgaise smiled at the offer of a muscular young man to swell her ranks and welcomed him to her side.

"As my lord Peredur has his own able deputies, I shall offer Mador to the service of Brian, and Pinel to Viroco." He paused to consider Lucan and then said, "And Lucan may go to Caratacus, so that he might teach our rough lord of war some courtly manners!"

Caratacus guffawed and waved the uncertain youth to come to him. "I will find a use for him. I thank you, my lord Arthur!"

"This is merely a loan until our battle is won," Arthur laughed. "Look after them and return them to me in good health! Those who distinguish themselves in the battles ahead may gain the rank of knight, as initiated by Ambrosius."

The young men beamed their good fortune at each other with raised eyebrows, knowing the time would soon come when they would be tested in battle.

"A messenger has come, my lord!" shouted a guard, causing Arthur to turn as he prepared to mount Mars.

"Come forward," Arthur called to the bedraggled and dust-covered young man leading a foam-flecked horse towards him. As he came close, Arthur recognised him as the scout he had sent with Gerwyn to spy on King Caradog. "What news?"

The scout dropped to one knee before Arthur waved him to his feet. "My lord, I have ridden from Caer Legion north to Caer Cornovi, and was then directed south to follow you, passing Caer Gloui on the way…"

"…And you have done well to find us, good scout. What is your report?"

"Gerwyn sends his greeting, my lord. Our news is that King Caradog did receive a visitation from King Mordred…"

"He is not King Mordred," Arthur corrected, "Lord Mordred will suffice. Continue."

"Please accept my apologies, my lord. Lord Mordred sent his man to King Caradog to demand he join him and bring as many warriors as he can muster. They did ride out two days after, some four hundred in all. That is my report, my lord."

"Bring food and water for this fellow!" Arthur bawled, having seen the young man stutter through cracked lips. He slapped his scout on the shoulder, causing a cloud of dust to rise and drawing a wan smile. "You have done well to bring me this report. That I already know of this does not diminish the importance of your ride to find me. My thanks to you, and here is a coin for your purse. Now join your fellows and take a fresh horse from the rear."

LONG SHADOWS OF the dying day fell across the valley, as the column reached the walls of Caer Badon standing proudly on a wide plain beside a gushing river.

"The hot spring baths left us by the Romans are exceedingly restful and have restorative powers ascribed to the goddess Sulis," Morgaise remarked to Arthur.

"So I have heard, my lady. I shall try them if they are still functional, unlike the baths at Caer Cornovia, now filled with grain."

Their attention was drawn to activity on the far bank of the river, where a team of men were erecting a wicker structure around a frame of denuded tree trunks. Mules carrying dried branches brayed as they were forced up the steep slope, and their loads were added to the piles from which those tasked with building the structure took their materials. The far bank of the river was pebbly and patched with harsh tufts and thorn bushes, suited only to sheep and goat pasture, whereas the side on which the road traversed was a wide, grassy plain planted with crops at the fringes. Beyond the fields were gently rising green slopes that grew steeper until a band of rocky scree collared the impressive hilltop that appeared to have a wide, flat summit.

"That is the Mount Badon where Uther marshalled his army and swept down here to this plain to crush the Saxons," Morgaise informed Arthur.

Arthur looked up in wonder at the impressive natural feature and muttered, "Ah, long have I wished to see this special place." He pointed to a grassy mound in the distance and grimly added, "And that could be a burial mound."

Riders came out of the town's stone gatehouse to greet them. They bowed and fussed over their returning queen and invited the leaders to enter.

"There will be room for thirty or so within, Arthur, but the majority must make their camp here," Morgaise shouted over her shoulder, leading him at a trot towards a bridge over a muddy ditch.

A GREAT FOREST where Uther had once hunted ranged over the hills that surrounded Dunbulgar, the former Roman town of Venta Bulgarum. It was over the dank leaf mould of its shadowy paths that Morgana and Mordred led their Saxon allies in a boar hunt.

"Ma, I like that Saxon girl riding behind King Octha." Morgana followed Mordred's gaze to a young woman with long, yellow hair spilling over a red cloak. "Can you make a love potion so that she wilts readily into my arms?" Mordred whispered just loud enough for her to hear.

Morgana laughed and leaned towards him before replying. "My dear, Merlyn's recipes for love were always less reliable than his purgatives. And no doubt, she is betrothed to some dirty whelp of a Saxon lord. But I have my eye on a suitable match for you – the daughter of Lord Gareth, the last of Ambrosius's sons. It is a fitting match for the high king of Britannia. She is close to your age and they say she has her mother's famous beauty. Be patient, my young king."

A yell went up from the beaters, and the riders advanced cautiously towards a cluster of men armed only with sticks and baying hounds, who had surrounded a thicket ready to flush out the prey. But in a moment the orderly scene turned to one of peril.

Clods of earth and ground birds flew into the air, as a great tusked boar raced angrily past the beaters with their hounds straining on leashes, heading towards the riders. Morgana shrieked in alarm as the huge hairy-backed boar, its red eyes glowing, lowered its head ready to charge. Her panicked horse whinnied and reared up, threshing the air with its heavy hooves in a futile gesture towards the deadly beast. Morgana dropped her spear and clung desperately to the reins.

In a blur, a horse charged passed her and its rider planted his spear firmly between the boar's eyes, deep enough to enter its brain and kill it instantly. The boar crumpled in a cloud of dust before the prancing hooves of Morgana's mare and the rider hard-reined his horse by a wall of bushes and circled to trot back to survey the carcass. He jumped from his horse to retrieve his spear, and then took the reins of Morgana's frightened mare, breathing into her nostrils and patting her nose to calm her.

Morgana puffed to recover her breath and looked, wide-eyed, at her saviour, her gloved hands tightly gripping her reins. She had noticed him before, a guard of one of the kings, a handsome fellow with a confident air, with broad shoulders and bulging biceps. "Thank you," she gasped. "I could have been thrown, at the very least. What is your name, my noble saviour?"

"I am Beowulf, champion of King Icel, my lady."

Morgana smiled coquettishly at the muscular warrior; her cheeks flushed with colour. His blue eyes sparkled like jewels from under clean tawny locks. Unlike most of his fellows, his beard was trimmed, and his rugged frame was dressed to display thick forearms contained by bronze warrior bands bearing many scores. He stood tall and clearly enjoyed being looked at.

"Then I owe you my life, Beowulf. You must allow me to repay you in a fitting manner when we return to King Mordred's hall."

He bowed, mounted his horse, and then trotted to his master's side.

Morgana's eyes stayed on the mound of black bear fur across his shoulders as she muttered under her breath, "And perhaps a love potion will be needed after all."

"Are you alright, Mother?" Mordred asked her, trying to rein in his skittish mount.

"The boar is slain, and I have survived a goring thanks to the quick reactions of a Saxon guard. But where were our guards?" she growled, looking around and fixing her dark eyes on her dismayed followers. "Collect the boar and take it to the kitchen for roasting!" she shouted to the beaters. "We shall dine on it tonight and raise a cup in toast to our brave Saxon allies, for tomorrow we march!"

Arthur *Rex Brittonum*

The Saxon kings were laughing at the drama that had unfolded and chattered in their ugly, guttural language, causing Morgana to blush and grind her teeth in annoyance. She wheeled her mare around and dug her heels in, shooting past her fumbling followers out of the glade into bright sunlight, and leading her son and guards at a gallop back to the safety of Dunbulgar.

ARTHUR WALKED THROUGH the busy streets of Caer Badon, past a familiar jumble of dilapidated Roman structures and thatched wooden shacks built by the locals. Pigs grunted and cattle lowed in the pens squeezed into the spaces between buildings, as townsfolk hurried about their business. The impending war brought an air of urgency, and workshops and smithies were alive with men forging and fashioning weapons, shields and helmets. He was attracted to a crowd of noisy folk gathered around what looked like a Roman war engine, its great arm sticking up above their heads.

Arthur pushed his way through the crowd and let out a cry of surprise mixed with pleasure at the sight of a tall old man with long grey whiskers and unruly hair falling about his long black robe. "Merlyn!" he exclaimed, throwing his arms around the perturbed elder. "I had heard talk of a crazy old man fussing around an old engine of war, and here you are!"

"Ah Arthur," Merlyn grumbled, "and here you are. You took your time. I have been here a week waiting for you."

"My apologies for keeping you waiting, but an army moves slowly. What is this engine?"

Merlyn waved his sleeve with pride at the wooden monstrosity. "This is the only surviving Roman catapult from Uther's battle here some ten years ago. I have studied it and made some repairs. I think it is now ready to be tested."

"But what does it do?" Arthur asked.

"It throws a rock, or even a burning rock soaked in tar, in a high arc, some two hundred paces towards a terrified enemy. I have replaced the rope and some of the working parts… In truth, I think it is intended more to frighten than to kill. I have been told by one who remembers it that Uther assembled four of these at the top of Mount Badon, and they rained down burning rocks on the heads of the Saxons as they battled their way uphill. Now that must have been some sight!" he chuckled.

"Indeed it must," Arthur agreed, studying the great wooden frame. "I would like to see it throw a rock."

"Well, I sent some men to bring four harnessed horses some time ago… they will want to be paid, mind you." Merlyn's grey eyes peered at Arthur from under hairy brows.

"Everyone who gives service wants rewarding, Merlyn. But I am happy to part with some coin to see this beast come to life." He regarded his old friend with warmth and added, "It is good to see you again, and in good health."

"I have much to tell you, my boy, but that can wait till later. Ah, the horsemen come. Let us drag this thing outside the gates and see what it can do."

The Roman engineers who had made it had built the frame on two runners that allowed it to be dragged, with relative ease, by horses or oxen. An excited crowd followed them out of the town and onto the wide meadow beside the river. Merlyn supervised a team of four men who were instructed to turn two wheels and wind down the long arm with a bucket at its end. A group of boys had been sent to the riverbank to fetch the biggest stone they could carry or drag between them. In the end, they found a large rock that was round enough to roll, and presented it to Merlyn.

"Perfect. Now we need two strong men who can lift the rock into the basket." This was duly done, and Merlyn advised all to stand behind or beside the engine for their safety. He invited Arthur to assist him in releasing the stave that held the cogs in place. With a 'whoosh' the arm shot upwards and flung its load arcing in the direction of the river. The stone splashed into the water some one hundred and fifty paces away, to the delight of the hooting crowd.

Arthur *Rex Brittonum*

"It works!" Arthur shouted above the din, slapping his aged mentor on the back, adding, "And its very presence in our ranks will give confidence to our men."

"Of course it works," Merlyn replied with a smirk. "Now, I have made a drawing of this engine and can instruct a team of carpenters to build another, if it would help our cause?"

"Yes, it would help our cause, but how long would it take?"

"Let me think... The carpenters would have to source timber from the merchants' yards over there," he said, pointing to a row of shacks outside the town walls, "and then cut and fashion the pieces to scale. I have identified those who can do it. I would say, about three to four days once the materials are assembled."

"Good, then command your team and let me know of the costs. We will have at least one week, perhaps two, before the enemy shows itself, so maybe they can make two? Now, let me retire to my quarters and prepare for the evening. You shall join me at my table, Merlyn, to tell me of your adventures. I will hear your progress in uncovering and understanding the ancient mysteries of our land that I know is close to your heart."

THE SEA PORT of Abona had stood for more than four hundred years, its blackened sea wall offering shelter for a dozen sea-going galleys, their anchorage overlooked by a clifftop fortress that could house a thousand men. Arthur led a unit of one hundred of his best foot soldiers, all from the northlands and oath-sworn to him, to bolster the garrison there. He was keen to see how it was, experience the two-day march, and to meet both Cadog, his Silurian ally, and Cathan, the Dumnonian commander and trusted follower of Queen Morgaise.

"My instinct tells me the Saxons will attack here, and you must be ready to repel them," Arthur said to the eager commander and the Silurian chief. "To this end, I have brought one hundred of my best men to bolster your garrison. How many men do you have and how will you use them?"

Cathan sucked his teeth and replied, "I have two hundred from the Dumnonian guard, together with thirty Silurians and your one hundred. We have watch towers along the coast at half-mile intervals. Our defence plans are to block the entrance to our port and the river with a barrier of small boats linked with chains. That will force the enemy to beach their boats to the south of the estuary, and enable us to defend the bridge. We can set fire to the bridge as a last resort, lord."

Arthur nodded, looking below at a sturdy wooden bridge wide enough for an ox wagon, with stone foundations that spanned the estuary, linking the port and fort on the north side to the wide stony beach below a cliff on the south side. "Then I hope you have the time to deploy your defences," Arthur said, as he looked across the choppy waters to the grey skies beyond. "That may be enough to hold back a similar number of Saxons. But I still pray to God that aid will come from the west. Cadog, have you had a reply from your messengers?"

"I have not, my lord."

"Then have a messenger with a swift horse on standby, day and night, to ride to me at Caer Badon with news of Saxon sails and estimate of warriors. But also tell me if ships come to your aid from Dyfed or Demetia. And keep your beacon covered and in readiness to be lit. I shall eat at your table tonight and return to Caer Badon at first light. May the old gods and the new favour our cause."

Arthur *Rex Brittonum*

Chapter Twelve

ARTHUR WAS RESTING in his quarters in Caer Badon a few days later when he noticed a growing noise from the streets, gradually forming into the steady beat of hand drums accompanied by chanting. He hurried outside to the gate of the compound and joined dozens of curious men stretching to see what was happening.

"What is it, Herrig?" he asked of the tallest.

"My lord, your druid, Merlyn, is leading a procession through the streets, and many are following."

"He is neither mine, nor a druid," Arthur retorted, pushing through the crowd. "Come with me; let's find out what this is about."

They barged past curious onlookers who were spilling out of the townhouses to get to the head of the procession. Girls and boys had been clothed in white robes and were gaily decorated in necklaces of seashells and summer flowers. They threw dried petals on the ground from baskets and sang a song, familiar to Arthur, of the passing of spring to summer.

Merlyn marched at the head of the procession, flanked by two long-bearded fellows dressed in the manner of the druids, their woollen robes belted plainly, and with crowns of twisted ivy around their heads. Merlyn carried a dark-wood staff with a carved head staring out from the pommel.

"What is this festival?" Arthur asked, when he had drawn level.

Merlyn turned his head towards him but kept the same pace. "It is the festival of Litha, my lord Arthur, when we celebrate the longest of our days and call upon the sun god to drive out evil and to bring fertility and prosperity to men, crops and herds. As the sun goes down, we shall light the wicker man on the hillside and send burning wheels down the hill, so that the power of the sun is strengthened and the gods will bless our cause. Come and join us."

He grinned at his former pupil, knowing that Arthur would not, because the Christian priests would frown upon his participation.

"I… will join you anon, Merlyn. I have matters to attend to…" Arthur and Herrig stepped back into shadow against a wall and watched the procession leave the town through the west gate and make their way to the solitary bridge over the river Abon.

Arthur saw a group of priests gathered by the entrance to his quarters and spotted his chaplain, Father Asaph, as he attempted to slip past.

Asaph was the only man who could admonish Arthur with impunity, and he waylaid him now. "My lord Arthur, we are sorely vexed at this pagan ritual taking place, and have noted that most of our congregation have joined the procession. Can you put a stop to this?" His unshakable faith in his God gave him the boldness to publicly challenge his master, to Arthur's barely contained annoyance.

"Father Asaph, I was unaware of this festival and have only come to the street to find out its purpose. I see no harm in letting the people welcome in the summer and enjoy themselves on the eve of war…"

"No harm! There are three druids leading the procession and there will no doubt be blood sacrifices to their ancient gods, whom the Romans suppressed to light the way for the coming of the one true God. As a Christian believer, you must put an end to this…"

"Please do not shout at me in the street, Father Asaph," Arthur replied, cutting him off. "I have been advised that there will be no blood-letting, and I am of a mind to permit this harmless festival in the interest of good morale." He fixed his priest with a hard stare to show his will in the matter. Arthur was not entirely honest as he had witnessed baskets of clucking chickens and small pigs being carried along in the procession, their fate almost certainly to appease the gods.

After a moment, Arthur softened and took Asaph's arm, leading him aside. "Dear Asaph, allow our people this one indulgence, for soon many of them will lie slaughtered under Saxon knives and axes, and their families will weep in despair. Then your prayers and comfort will be most needed. I shall come to your church splendidly dressed, so that all the people will see me honour Jesus, the Christ. Now go and prepare your service and call the people who have remained, and I shall join you with the queen."

"You have spoken wisely, my lord," Asaph replied in a whisper, knowing this was the best he would get. He bowed and led the huddle of murmuring priests to the church, leaving Arthur and a smirking Herrig to return to the sanctuary of their quarters.

AFTER A DAY of sore heads and contentment, Arthur's scouts reported that a significant body of Saxons were marching on the Portway road, and had passed the turning to Calleva.

"This gives us two days to make ready," Arthur said with his characteristic grin of relish for battle. His white scar seemed to throb in anticipation as his commanders gathered around a roughly drawn map of the area. It was spread on a table in the magistrate's hall and illuminated by a shaft of morning sunlight from a high window. "My scouts estimate over a thousand men marching with shields and spears, and perhaps two or three hundred on horseback. Our numbers are similarly matched, although we have more horsemen, skilled in fighting from the saddle. We must make the most of our defensive position. Remember, they are coming to fight us on our ground, and they will not need too much goading to attack."

Morgaise caught her brother's eye and said, "Our men are restless and ready. They are fighting each other out of boredom."

"Then we shall occupy them with setting our defences." He pointed to a line on the map: "We shall draw them onto our shield wall here. Then our reserves from within the town can join once battle has commenced and form a second line behind them. On my command, once the enemy have committed all their men to the fray, I shall lead my cavalry down from Mount Badon and attack their left flank."

"The plan is simple and will play to our strengths, my lord," Bedwyr added.

"And we shall practise our plan today," Arthur said, smiling.

"How so, my lord?" Caratacus asked.

"Now that half of the men have shields made in the Roman fashion, let us line them up to face each other on this battle line, the first rank facing the reserves in a pushing contest. Also, the three catapults can be positioned here, behind our shield wall, where they can fire their rocks over the heads of the men and mark the range with painted stones. We shall dig a shallow gulley where the rocks will land and fill it with tar. Then, burning rocks dipped in tar can be fired during battle to make a fire in the enemy ranks. That will cause dismay, doubt and confusion. Viroco and Brian, supported by your deputies, Mador and Pinel, shall command the foot soldiers."

The two stood proudly to attention and slapped their forearms across their chests in a Roman salute. Arthur had found a skilled craftsman who had fashioned shoulder, elbow and knee pads of flexible, jointed leather strips for his commanders, in an imperial style. Thin strips of steel had been crafted for shoulder, shin and chest guards.

He returned the gesture and continued. "I shall take the riders out to scout Mount Badon and choose our hiding places. Caratacus and Peredur's riders, together with Lucan, will make camp up there from now onwards to remain hidden from enemy scouts and patrol the eastern approaches."

"What of other targets the enemy might attack?" Viroco asked.

Arthur pointed to Port Abona and replied, "They may attack our port from the sea. We have a modest force of three hundred and thirty there to repel them. If they are overcome, then we can expect to be attacked from the rear. The Dumnonians have men on the western cliffs, but I do not expect an attack from there, due to the steep drop to the river on that side."

"Then I shall lead my riders to face them, should they come from the south," Morgaise said, with grim determination.

"Yes, the lady Morgaise and her Dumnonian riders will remain within the town's walls as a mounted reserve. A relay of horn blasts from my position, summoning them to join the battle, will be heard from the towers. I shall be on the lower slopes of Mount Badon, with Bedwyr, where I can see both ways. That is our plan – a simpler plan than Uther's. He goaded them into attacking uphill. They will not fall for that again. Now, let us make use of this dry weather to drill our men."

MORGANA CALLED A halt at the junction where the road to Corinium forked from the Portway. They were one day's march from Caer Badon. Mordred, King Caradog of Gwent, the chiefs of other southern tribes and the Saxon kings gathered around as she explained her action. "An important ally of ours is based at a town half a day's ride north on this road. He is Chief Gareth of the Dobunni, a noble widely respected as a descendant of King Ambrosius Aurelianus. I will ride to gather him and his men for our army."

King Octha flinched at the mention of Ambrosius, who had beheaded his father, Hengist, on a northern battlefield at Maisbeli, when he was but a rush mat crawler. "Why would he join our cause if his father fought against my father?" Octha sourly asked.

"And why isn't he already in our midst if he is your ally?" the wily King Icel added, blinking at her with his one good eye.

Morgana nodded and replied, "You are ever wise, King Icel. He may need some convincing. Perhaps King Caradog and the chief of his eastern neighbours, the Catuvellauni, can join me to add their weight to our entreaty?"

Caradog bowed his assent, as did a woolly-braided chieftain to the rear.

"Good. Then can I propose that you make camp at the next meadow you reach along the road, and we shall join you or send word by dawn."

The kings briefly conferred and agreed to her ploy. "Then ride to your cautious ally and use your persuasion to good effect," Octha growled. "At the very least, we might prevent him from backing Arthur. We shall meet on the morrow."

"And take my personal guard, Beowulf, to watch over you, my lady," Icel added, waving his man forward before she could respond. He had approved of his lusty champion becoming the lover of Uther's widowed daughter, and had instructed him to underplay the extent of his understanding of the Briton tongue.

"My thanks for your concern for my welfare, noble king," she purred. "His presence will speak for the power of our alliance."

"SAXONS! THEY ARE coming!" a wide-eyed sentry shouted, running along the parapet of the fort at Abona. His mad dash came to an abrupt end before the solid figure of his garrison commander, Cathan.

"Stop your babbling and give me numbers," Cathan demanded.

"Twelve dragonhead ships, my lord!" he stammered.

"Blow the horns and light the beacon!" Cathan bellowed. "And call all men to report to their commanders!" He placed his huge hands on the stone wall and looked into the endless blanket of grey to the south – there was no discernible horizon as the calm sea appeared to merge with the sky. He narrowed his eyes and made out a line of striped sails emerging from the gloom, and then glanced at the clifftop where the yellow flames of a warning beacon had just become visible. "Caught them sleeping," he muttered.

Cadog joined him, buckling on his sword belt. "What number's our enemy?"

"Twelve ships reported. We can estimate up to fifty men per ship, so about six hundred, I expect," Cathan replied.

"Then I shall take my men to defend the bridge, as planned."

"Yes, and mine shall man the barrage and line up on the beach. Our battle has come, brother." The two commanders clasped forearms and ran to brief their subordinates.

The fort was alive with running men, and the gates opened for those tasked with manning the barrage across the estuary to take up their positions. Archers lined up on the harbour wall, each with a small brazier from which to light the rags on their arrowheads, ready to fire at any ships that came within range.

Cathan briefed two of his scouts to ride to Arthur with the news. "Our brothers in the west have not come to our aid, so it falls to us to keep the Saxons from marching on Caer Badon," he said, turning to his pale-faced sub-commanders, only two of whom had witnessed the Saxon looting and burning of the Dumnonian capital, Exisca. Cathan noted the look of dismay on their faces. "Be not afraid, my friends. We are fighting for our queen, for Arthur, and the very survival of our people. Our victory today will depend on the accuracy of your sword and spear thrusts, and your men will look to you for their courage."

They stood to attention and he slapped each of them on the shoulder, sending them to organise their men as they had practised in the days before. Cathan went to the parapet and then to the tower, kicking his negligent guards to find Arthur's bear and dragon banner and run it up the pole next to the black boar of Dumnonia and wolf's head of Siluria.

Thirty minutes was enough time to be in position just as the first ship attempted to ram the barrage blocking its entry to the river and harbour. Small boats, each with two or three spearmen, were joined together by a heavy chain that snared the Saxon ship. The chain bulged, but it held fast.

Cathan looked on in dismay as enraged Saxons jumped onto the small boats that had been dragged next to their hull.

Were they physically bigger or was it the effect of their high conical helmets and wolf fur cloaks over padded jerkins? They made short work of his men, hacking at them mercilessly with axes or stabbing with long knives, as if they were no more than sheep for the slaughter. If he had any doubts before about the callous and ferocious nature of his enemy, they were now dispelled.

"Reinforce the bridge head!" he yelled to a handful of men loitering outside the gate unsure of where they should be.

The Saxons rowed their ship backwards and their fleet clumsily turned, allowing the flow from the river to guide them out of the estuary. They had no choice but to beach to the south, as the north was a rocky place beneath high cliffs. The barrage had worked, forcing them to stage their assault on the shingle beach, where Cadog's Silurians and Arthur's men waited for them clustered in units.

As each ship beached, warriors yelling war cries jumped into the chilling surf. The defenders had decided to engage with them there, where they would be off balance and struggling against the slippery shingle. Fierce fighting ensued on the shoreline as the Britons threw their weight behind spear thrusts and sword swipes. Their early successes were soon overturned, though, by sheer weight of numbers. Cathan estimated that over four hundred Saxons had leapt into the water and were establishing a footing on the beach, from which position they were now driving back the one hundred and thirty defenders.

Soon, Cadog had formed his men behind a curved shield wall that was slowly retreating up the beach towards a path that led to the bridge. The air filled with curses and cries of pain when men on both sides were stabbed or hacked as the Saxons pressed forwards.

Cathan wrung his hands in anguish, but held fast to the plan not to send more men across the bridge. Men were dropping from the Briton shield wall, their wounded bodies trampled on and brutalised by the Saxon rear ranks. They were being pushed backwards and Saxon arms were thrusting between their failing shield wall at the men, inflicting

Arthur *Rex Brittonum*

grievous wounds on the arms and torsos of the retreating Britons. Those wounded men knew they must stay on their feet and hold their shields as best they could, for falling would lead to certain death.

Once on the path, Cadog hollered that they should run for the bridge. Those who chose to support a wounded comrade were easy pickings for the roaring, blood-thirsty Saxons, who hacked at the fleeing men. Only half of the men made it to the bridge, where the first comers turned to form a shield wall, through which their friends passed, before closing it on the furious Saxons. They retreated slowly onto the bridge, leaving a line of four brave men to take the onslaught of their enemy.

Cathan was also at the bridge and, seeing the size of the Saxon force, had decided the best ploy was to set the bridge alight. Tar-soaked faggots of dried sticks had been fixed along its underside, and he now ordered his two torch bearers to ignite them. Cathan and his men were still inching backwards across the bridge as flames started to lick around the edges and warm the planks underfoot. Smoke billowed to sting their eyes, and choke them. The Saxons pressed on, coughing, and so the defenders maintained their discipline and continued their slow, steady retreat, until the bridge was fully alight.

"Run for your lives!" Cathan roared, stepping aside as his men ran past him. He was the last and faced up to a huge Saxon with horns protruding from his helmet and the plaits of his forked beard swinging as he moved forward, his double-edged axe held above his head in readiness for a killing blow. Cathan surprised him by darting forward with outstretched arm, using his momentum to pierce his enemy's padded jerkin with the sharp tip of his sword. The Saxon's eyes bulged with pain, but his axe continued its downward arc, glancing off Cathan's metal shoulder guard that cushioned the force of the impact.

He still buckled under the force of the blow, causing gasps from his men as he staggered, flames snatching at his ankles. The Saxon slumped to his knees, and Cathan pulled his sword out of the bloody mess of the Saxon's guts. Cathan swayed backwards and then felt a pair of hands on his waist.

One of his men had risked the flames to grab him and spin him around, pushing him across the bridge that was now burning fiercely. The huge Saxon remained on his knees as flames engulfed him, then his burning body fell through the planks and hit the water with a hiss.

The other Saxons had fallen back and now stood on the opposite bank shouting curses and banging their weapons on their cow hide shields. Cheers went up from the Britons as Cathan was guided to safety, blood now running down his side where his left arm hung limp from a shoulder wound. He was taken to the fort, along with the other wounded men, while Cadog remained on the riverbank, staring at a huddle of half a dozen Saxon leaders deciding their next move. They pointed to the strip of riverbank where the barrage was anchored, then called their men back to their ships.

"They're going to try to beach their ships on this strip between the harbour wall and the barrage!" Cathan yelled, pointing.

"A difficult manoeuvre, my lord," the old harbour master at his side said, adding, "The current from the river is strong and the landing strip narrow. Only one ship at a time can line up there, and your spear-throwers and archers can pick them off."

"Aye, and they risk losing their boat to the rocks or fire," Cathan replied. "Bring forward the best spear throwers with braziers and rags to light the ends!" he yelled. Archers stood ready on the harbour wall, their small bows designed to fire arrows from horseback or chariots.

The Saxons' determination to land on their side was unnerving to the Britons who huddled in groups, discussing what they had witnessed of their savagery and willingness to risk all in getting at them. Soon, the entire fleet was lined up for an assault at the mouth of the river, and the Saxons seemed content to sacrifice the first of their ships to make a landing platform. Archers fired burning arrows at these vessels loaded with fierce warriors ready to jump off, and their gods seemed to favour them, as blustery winds filled the Saxon sails and blew them towards the sea wall. The first ship had run aground close to the barrage, and another was side on to the stone wall. Both their sails and hulls were aflame as eager warriors jumped on the wall or waded ashore to engage with the defenders. Archers fell back to be replaced by spearmen with shields.

The following ships came beside those first two, dragged to their sides with grappling hooks and ropes. A second wave of Saxons then joined the battle, jumping through fire to crash down on Briton shields with axes, and battering their enemy with sword blows.

Cathan ordered his archers to the walls of the fortress and stood with his shield men in a second rank, before the gates and blocking the road. He knew their main purpose was to stop the Saxons from marching on Caer Badon, so retreating into the fort and barring the gates would most likely cause the enemy to ignore them and march along the road that ran beside the fort.

The desperate battle at the port was now going the way of the Saxons, who had taken control of the shoreline and had released the barrage chain, causing the flotilla of small boats that supported the chain to be carried out to sea by the river. This allowed their ships access to the sheltered harbour, and one by one their skeleton crews entered, tying up to the orderly row of wooden piers.

Cathan could do little but watch and wait. He ordered his last scout to ride away with the news of their defeat to Caer Badon and then instructed his horn blower to sound a retreat. Those still able turned and ran to line up behind his solid shield wall.

"We defend the road to the last man!" he roared, and commenced his show of defiance by banging the hilt of his sword on his shield.

His men followed his lead, and they shouted war cries and curses at the advancing Saxons to give each other courage. Archers fired their remaining arrows over their heads at the Saxons, who held up their shields to swat them like angry wasps, and kept coming.

Outnumbered two to one, the Britons held firm for an hour, the front ranks taking the weight of the press, and the second rank looking for gaps to stab their spears at the feet and ankles or necks and heads of their persistent and powerful enemy. But soon tiredness took its toll and they were forced back off the road. With their backs to the wall and gate, they readied themselves for their last stand.

The shield wall broke and hand to hand fighting ranged before the fort. Fresher Saxons moved to the front to relieve their comrades, and their fierce blows shattered the shields of the Britons, cracking skulls and piercing leather jerkins. The cries of the dying filled the air and bodies were trampled underfoot as the Saxons moved in for the kill. Anguished defenders on the walls did their best to support their fellows below by throwing rocks and any items their women placed into their hands, but Cathan's orders to keep the gates shut were fulfilled, and he died alongside his fellow soldiers in a pile of bloody bodies outside the fort.

The Saxons, their work done, moved back onto the road, shouting insults and banging their shields in triumph at the devastated archers and wounded men on the parapet - all that remained of the ill-fated garrison. They spent an hour killing off the wounded and looting whatever they could before forming up in ranks and setting off on a march towards Caer Badon. Cadog, nursing his limp left arm and bandaged shoulder, counted three hundred Saxons on the march. There was little he could do except rally the remaining men and plot an attack on the few who had remained to guard their fleet in the night. They had lost the battle for the port, and Arthur would soon have to deal with an attack from the rear.

Arthur *Rex Brittonum*

Chapter Thirteen

LOUD, EARTHY BLASTS from the dragon-headed carnyces carried at the head of the army announced their arrival on the plain before the walls of Caer Badon. Close behind came a war chariot, in which the king stood beside his driver, proudly wearing Uther's crown of gold, with his mother behind him. Two pairs of prancing, shiny black horses were flanked by banner-bearers, who marched in time holding high their banners depicting an array of tribal motifs.

"Your time has come, my son," Morgana purred in the young king's ear. "All of Britannia will bend their knees to you after this day."

Mordred, resplendent in silver chest and shoulder armour, and plumed helmet to match them, lifted his chin and looked ahead at the row of rectangular Roman shields lined up before the walls of the town. "You are wise, my mother, and we must be grateful to Arthur for bringing all those who oppose me to this place."

The King of Britannia called a halt some two hundred paces short of the enemy shield wall. This prompted the smug Saxon kings to line their horses up to the left of the chariot, leaving the dour Briton chiefs to line up to the right on the softer ground close to the gushing river.

Meanwhile, halfway up Mount Badon, Arthur and Bedwyr sat, flanked by a hundred horsemen, watching the combined army of Mordred and the Saxons fan out from the road onto the wide plain. The sky was suitably grey, and a restless breeze ruffled Arthur's bear and dragon banners.

"It is a robust chariot, my lord," Bedwyr remarked.

"Indeed it is. This is Morgana's doing. She flatters herself if she thinks she compares with the noble warrior queens Cartimadua and Boudicca."

Arthur turned to his deputy and smirked. By doing so he noticed that the side flaps of his helmet were not tied, so he removed his gloves to tie them under his chin. His chaplain had surprised him a day earlier by presenting him with a round hide shield reinforced with a light metal plate, on which was painted a picture of the Virgin Mary with her Child. Arthur had warily accepted it and promised to carry it into battle.

"And yet she neither is, nor ever was, a queen," Bedwyr replied.

"A queen in all but title. Uther's first born has always had a thirst for power."

"It is hard to believe that sorceress is your half-sister, my lord," Bedwyr added.

As the enemy leaders conferred, Arthur noticed a dust cloud away to his left. A messenger riding hard had come from the port and pulled up before the gates of the town.

"I wonder if the news is good or bad," he murmured. He scanned the field below; from the catapult teams sitting on the grass behind their machines draped in canvas awnings, to the two lines of shield men, about three hundred wide and three deep, facing off silently; and finally to the group of kings who were sending a delegation of six riders towards him.

"They want to talk," Bedwyr said.

"A round of insults must precede the ire of battle." Arthur yawned.

Mordred himself had come with three Saxons and two Briton chiefs, one of whom Arthur recognised – Caradog of Gwent. They rode across compacted brown earth fields at the base of the hill, where stubble stalks told of a swift and perhaps premature harvest, then up the gently sloping lower reaches. Arthur, Bedwyr, and four deputies rode downhill to meet them.

Mordred was smiling broadly, like a child on his birthday. "Ah, my uncle, Arthur. We have not met since you escaped in rags from my dungeons!" He turned to encourage guffaws from his side.

"I see you have come out from behind your mother's skirts!" Arthur said, and one of Morgana's Saxons snorted.

"Do not mock me, rebel!" Mordred stormed, his cheeks a bright shade of red. "Our army is twice that of yours and we shall cut you to pieces before the day is through." He realised he was rocking with rage and steadied himself, adding, in a calmer tone, "Unless you submit to my authority."

"I see the weak and peevish youth is now a weak and peevish man," Arthur said. He turned to Bedwyr and asked, "Shall we surrender, Bedwyr?"

"I'm of a mind to test the sharpness of my blade on their milk-sop men, my lord."

"Many of whom do not want to be here, I'd wager," Arthur added, glaring at Caradog.

Arthur steadied Mars and turned to Mordred. "We are not here to follow you, Mordred, but to dethrone you, and right a wrong that has offended the gods. When I drew Excalibur…" Arthur paused to draw his sword and rest it gently across his pommel, unsettling the Saxons, "…from the stone, after your mother had failed on your behalf, it was the will of the old gods of the earth and air that I be king after my father, Uther. But your mother overturned their will, and a malodour has infected this land since that day. I have come to right that wrong and wrest Uther's crown off your unworthy head."

Mordred paled and seemed at a loss for words, and it was King Icel who jabbed his heels into his horse and moved forwards. "That is a nice speech Arthur, and invoking the gods is always a good way to rouse your men. But we come to this field with two thousand warriors and, even if you have some hidden from us, I suspect your numbers are barely half that. So, let us negotiate like kings and come to a settlement."

Arthur had met Icel before, and was still irked that he had let the king of the Angliscs escape from him in the north. "We meet again, King Icel, but this time you are clean and sitting in a saddle before your countrymen, and not grovelling in the filth of my prison. What is your idea of a settlement?"

Icel laughed and touched the hammer token that hung from his neck. "Thor was with me that day, Arthur, for he urges our people to make a new home in your lands. But there is enough land for us all, and we will let you return to the western bulge and the north west corner of this island with your followers if you swear an oath of fealty to King Mordred." He smiled and the black eye that saw everything blinked.

Arthur regarded the grizzled Anglisc with his hair fluttering against the black bear pelt protecting his broad shoulders. "I have never felt the hands of the gods on my shoulders more strongly than in this moment, looking upon you all. It is my purpose in this life to free this island from misrule and invasion. To this end, I decline your offer and call upon Mordred to bow to me, his true king, and plead for my mercy. I will give you and your pack one chance, Icel, to take to your boats and return to the lands from whence you came. Go now and free my people!" His final words echoed back to his men.

Mordred turned his horse, keen to get away from Arthur's confrontational stare and pulsing white scar. The Saxon kings seemed please at the prospect of a good fight.

King Octha had been itching for his moment and said, "I look forward to meeting you on the field, Arthur, and avenging my cousins who died here under Uther's sword."

Arthur just smiled and bowed. They returned to their positions and waited.

Arthur pointed towards the Saxon shield wall that was now four men deep. "Should we bring out our reserves now to bolster our shield wall?"

Bedwyr studied the field below, and could see that the Briton wall was but two deep and would easily be driven back. "Yes, my lord. We gain no advantage from surprise."

Arthur nodded and called for his squire, Dermot, who was a reliable messenger with a swift pony. "Ride to the town and to the Queen, and tell her that the reserves for the shield wall should go now to reinforce their comrades in the field. This is because the enemy outnumber us. Also, ask for news from the rider who came from the port and return to me in all haste. Also, tell her to make ready, as the battle will soon commence."

Dermot's face was set in a look of fiery determination, and, as he turned his pony and dug his heels in, Arthur remembered him as a trembling boy hiding behind his mother's skirts in the hall at Ebrauc, beside the body of his father, the Deiran chief slain by Icel's men.

"We all have loved ones to fight for," Arthur muttered as he guided Mars along the line of horsemen.

THE BRIEF LULL before battle is a time when men clutch their charms, whether pagan or Christian, and mutter their prayers, think of their loved ones for whom they fight, and draw courage from their comrades. Some are drunk and cavort around for the amusement of their fellows, but most are solemn and look to find a place to relieve their bowels or void their breakfast. These are the farmers and tradesmen, called upon by their lords to fulfil their oaths of allegiance. Warriors whose business is war will check their armour and weapons, chew a root for strength and conserve their energy.

It is a time for holy men to flex their influence and give their blessings and words of encouragement to men who fear death and ponder the afterlife. Father Asaph and his fellow priests now fell into step behind Bishop Aaron, who had come to lend his weight to such a great gathering of souls. They now processed before Arthur's men, most of whom dropping to one knee, as the sweet smell of incense wafted in the morning gloom. They planted their banners with the chi-rho symbol and cross beside Arthur's banners. Arthur and Bedwyr dismounted and also knelt, removing their helmets to receive the bishop's blessing.

Below Mount Badon, Saxon holy men, wearing animal pelts around their otherwise naked and dirty bodies, waved staffs topped with the carved heads or animal skulls and danced in front of their warriors, taunting and cursing the Britons who stared sullenly over the tops of their shields.

Arthur and Bedwyr mounted just in time to see Merlyn lead his two druid companions in front of the now-cheering Britons to confront their Saxon counterparts.

"Merlyn knows how to put on a show!" Arthur laughed, leaning forward on Mars and pointing.

The bishop and priests were not amused and watched in stony silence as Merlyn raised his staff above his head and shouted curses that carried in unintelligible snatches on the wind, pointing to the wretches before him. Arthur's men also stood and cheered, to the dismay of the priests. After ten minutes in which the Saxons danced, leapt and showed their naked buttocks, Merlyn waved his fist at them. Yellow lightning flashed from his palm when it sprung open, drawing gasps from both sides. He then turned on his heels and marched away, to the raucous cheers of the Britons.

"Merlyn has won the first duel!" Bedwyr laughed.

"And he distracted our men from those demons," Arthur replied. "They make my scalp creep."

Saxon horns, accompanied by high-pitched wails from the carnyces, sent the Saxon holy men scurrying and prompted the Saxon front ranks to lift their shields and chant a deep and ominous war song. Morgaise's Briton reserves had just arrived and swiftly lined up behind the second row, in readiness to resist the coming together of the shield walls. Drumbeats urged the two lines to march and meet with a resounding clash of shields, accompanied by angry cries from both sides, setting the battle in motion. The second ranks held their shields high over the heads of the men in front, and looked to stab their swords or spears into gaps above or below the opposing shield wall.

Arthur pointed to Mordred's cavalry, led by King Caradog, who were positioning themselves behind the left flank of the Saxon wall. "We must ride down there to counter their ploy to flank our shield wall. Send word to Peredur and Caratacus to be ready and move to a position where they can watch what is unfolding below."

Bedwyr bowed and rode to the rear to brief a messenger.

Arthur drew Excalibur and, holding it high above his head, rode before his men, shouting, "For Britannia and for Arthur! To battle!"

The men shouted, "For Arthur!" and banged their spears on their shields. They each had a quiver of a dozen short throwing spears, for additional use in battle, although the lance, sword and shield would be employed in fighting at close quarters. Their horses all had leather shin and chest guards, for they intended to break through shield walls.

Arthur led his men in a line down the hill, the signal for the catapult teams to commence their attacks, and cantered towards Caradog's static cavalry. Arthur knew Caradog was waiting for a command to attack and, ever the opportunist, took his chance to attack first. He cried out and led the charge, passing the shield walls locked in stalemate as the cries of men wounded with sword or spear thrusts filled the air.

The drumming sound of charging hooves, added to the war cries of their riders, caused dismay in the eyes of Caradog's horsemen, whose mounts wheeled and whinnied before Arthur and his men crashed into them. Horses and riders were speared on lances and many fell as Arthur drew Excalibur and flayed fiercely about him. The second battle of Mount Badon had begun.

MORGAISE, QUEEN OF Dumnonia, resplendent in her gold-edged armour and holding a crafted helmet under arm, watched the townsfolk scurry around her horse in mild alarm at the sounds of war without, relieved that her ten-year-old son and little daughter were with Queen Anne in the safety of Powys. She had received the distressed messenger from Port Abona and had briefed him not to spread alarm through the town. Next, she had received Dermot, Arthur's squire, and sent him back to Arthur with the terrible news that the port had fallen. Now, she had marshalled her troop of two hundred horsemen and had decided to wait no more and ride out to meet the Saxons approaching from the port.

She called for the south gates to be opened and led her riders out onto the road to the port. The road was empty as far as they could see, to a bend around a bluff. The scouts had noted where the road narrowed between high cliffs beside the fast-flowing river and she picked her spot to hide her riders from view.

They did not have to wait long, as the sound of marching men made them fix their helmets and clutch their spears tightly. Morgaise's commander, fearful for her safety, begged her to let him lead the charge. She saw determination in his eyes and prudently assented, moving back to lead the second rank of riders. The Saxons were marching four abreast and thirty of them had rounded a bend into a straight stretch of road when the cry of 'Charge!' echoed from the valley walls.

The Dumnonians swept through the startled front ranks, scattering and trampling warriors barely able to raise their shields in time. They thrust with their spears, as Arthur had trained them, then drew their swords and laid about the men beside them, using their shields to deflect blows from swords and axes. Some riders were dragged from their horses and soon a bloody battle raged across the narrow valley. Morgaise had trained alongside her men, and the widow speared a Saxon warrior on her lance before drawing her sword. The Dumnonians drew heart from her courage and ferocity, and her personal guards made sure she was not unseated.

Their surprise attack had given them the edge and the Saxons could not form a shield wall. Instead, the battle was fought in a series of duels, and the more skilful riders were able to stay mounted to slash down on their enemy. The two hundred Dumnonians in short time gained numerical advantage as the dead and dying littered the ground. A Saxon horn sounded the retreat, and those left standing, barely eighty, fell back to their commander and formed a shield wall.

Morgaise called on her men to rally to her banner, and they counted one hundred and twenty riders still mounted. In addition, thirty of her men who had been fighting on foot, some nursing injuries, moved to stand behind them or looked for horses. Her commander sat beside her and they briefly conferred. Between them and the Saxon shields were over a hundred fallen men and horses, the groans of the dying terrible to hear.

"We should pick our way cautiously through the field of battle," her commander said, "then line up and charge when we are close to them."

Morgaise patted her mare's neck to calm her and nodded. The horror of battle had assaulted her with terrible memories of the day her town was sacked and her husband killed. Her voice may have deserted her, but her sword arm was ready for another pass. "Lead on, my brave commander," she managed with a croak, then beckoned to young Agravane to come to her side.

The Saxons drew together into a tight group behind their shields as the Britons moved slowly towards them with quiet determination. At barely twenty paces, the Dumnonian riders lined up in two ranks of sixty, some with lances, others with swords. Those on foot picked up shields and weapons from the fallen as they moved through the scene of devastation, equipping the riders as needed. Each on the front rank was given a lance for the charge, and those behind held swords.

The afternoon sun was directly above them, and it reflected on their weapons and helmets, giving the Dumnonians the air of the justified, as the cry of 'Charge!' once more went up. The riders jabbed their heels into their mounts and gathered enough momentum to clatter through the shield wall, spearing as they went. The second rank joined in with swords and shields, hacking at the yellow-haired enemy as bitter battle resumed. The Britons, intent on revenging their comrades from the port, would not be denied their victory, and dispatched their enemy with ruthless determination. In half an hour it was all over, and Morgaise insisted on sparing the last two to take as prisoners.

"They will be my trophies to parade before my little brother, Arthur," she proudly declared to the grinning Agravane. "Take them into your care." The threat from the port had been eliminated, and she still had a hundred riders remaining.

BLAZING BALLS OF fire flew over the heads of the shield wall press, landing at the feet of the mounts of the Saxon and

Briton leaders. The horses hitched to Mordred's chariot reared up and bolted forwards as a burning rock bounced and rolled past. Morgana fell inelegantly from the back as Mordred and his driver clung on to the rail. Other horses had similarly bolted forwards into the cluster of reserves standing in front, causing men to be thrown to the ground and some trampled. The unnoticed shallow trench filled with tar caught fire, lighting up a curtain of yellow flames that separated the first group of reserves from their leaders and other reserves to the rear. Black smoke twisted to the sky as the holy men jumped and danced in the commotion, shouting spells to counter this unwelcome appearance of the Briton gods and cursing Merlyn's name.

Arthur broke off from his duelling to look up at the hillside and wave his sword above his head, hoping that Caratacus or Peredur would see him and join the battle. Seeing this, his bannermen waved their banners and horn blowers blew their horns. Despite being outnumbered, Arthur felt they should take advantage of the chaos caused by the burning rocks and throw their reserve riders into the battle. Midday had seen the grey clouds give way to sunshine, and Arthur smiled when he saw light glinting off helmets coming around the side of the hill.

Billowing banners depicting the red dragon of Gwynedd told Arthur that Caratacus was leading the charge down Mount Badon, giving heart to his men. The men of Gwynedd were ferocious in close combat, working out their frustration at being held back on their startled enemy. Much of the fighting on horseback was between Britons, and as much as it galled Arthur to be fighting his own people, he knew it was the only way to defeat Mordred and unite the Britons. Caratacus clearly did not mind who he was fighting, and the huge warrior, wrapped in a black cloak with an embroidered dragon's head motif, soon fought his way to Arthur's side.

"Greetings, my lord King!" he shouted, still panting.

"I am thankful to see you, my dragon lord. And the righteous blood lust in your warriors!" Arthur shouted in reply.

"They will vie each with the other for trophies, my king. But what is your plan?"

"We shall soon chase off this unhappy clutch of riders. Then we can attack the flanks of the Saxon shield wall. But where is Prince Peredur?"

"He has gone up to the summit of the hill and his men are watching the approaches from behind. He awaits your call to action."

Arthur noted one of the junior commanders, Lucan, lustily slashing at an enemy horseman with his sword, his purple-edged cloak dancing behind. He smiled and pointed, eliciting a laugh from Caratacus.

"For all his manners, the boy is fearless in combat!"

Bedwyr and Herrig were at the forefront of chasing off Caradog's dispirited cavalry and other minor chiefs under Mordred's rule. Arthur wondered how many were Silures fighting reluctantly under Gwent's banner, and pondered on the fate of Cadog and his men at Port Abona. He had not received any news from Dermot, his squire, nor was he aware of Queen Morgaise's entry onto the field of battle. He looked up at the sun, now moving to the west, and also wondered how the remainder of the day would unfold.

As if reading his mind, Bedwyr appeared at his side and said, "This battle is far from over and the Saxons do not like to fight at night. Something about their sun god."

"Aye," Arthur replied, snapping out of his reverie, "We had best push our advantage and slay as many of them as we can before they call a retreat and set their camp for the night."

He yelled a war cry and dug his heels into Mars, charging towards the left flank of what remained of the Saxon shield wall. His riders followed, and soon the wall was fragmenting as alarmed Saxons turned to face the new threat. Arthur's men marvelled at his enthusiasm and lack of tiredness in his sword arm so late in the day, and redoubled their own efforts. It was brutal work – slashing and hacking at screaming men, their mangled bodies littering the trampled grass, where horses now slipped on the slick blood and gore under hoof.

As the sun dipped behind the western cliffs and shadows covered the valley, Saxon horn blasts signalled their withdrawal. Arthur nodded to his own man to blow his horn and both sides stepped away from the carnage. Men so tired they could barely stand, their hands hanging limp by their sides, looked across at unfamiliar faces, and in that moment realised that many of their friends were no longer by their side. Men lifted wounded comrades from the field, and Arthur's cavalry covered the slow march of the weary soldiers back to the gates of the town. He looked about and was relieved to see that Viroco, Brian, Mador and Pinel had all survived the gruelling fight. He ordered men to bring teams of harnessed horses to drag the catapults to the safety of the walls.

Arthur handed the reins of Mars to Dermot, and only then received his news that the port had fallen. He ruffled the hair of the disconsolate youth and said, "I am not angry that you did not find me in the heat of battle, Dermot. After all, I instructed you to stay safe with the cooks and healers." Arthur looked about him and called Bedwyr and Caratacus to follow him to the hall, where he hoped to find Morgaise and the other commanders.

The magistrate's hall was alive with healers and their attendants helping the wounded in, and laying them on makeshift bedding along the side walls.

"I have instructed them to bring the wounded here, as it is the biggest space under roof in the town," Morgaise explained as she walked towards Arthur. She fell into his arms and they hugged with warmth.

"We guessed that the Saxons would fall back as the sun dipped, and it is a welcome relief for our men and horses. I hear it is bad news from the port?"

"Yes, my brother. A large Saxon force came by ship, as you predicted, and our garrison was not reinforced by men from the west. They fought to the last man, and those Saxon dogs, three hundred in number, did march on us." She paused to let her words sink in.

Arthur, his brow deeply furrowed, asked, "But what happened…?"

Morgaise smiled before replying. "I led my riders out to meet them, as we planned. They now lie dead in yonder river valley."

Arthur's face lit up and a cry of triumph escaped his lips, drawing disapproving looks from the healers who were attending to the wounded. He kissed his sister warmly. "This is the best news of an otherwise vexing day! My sister the warrior queen! They will sing songs about you!"

She pulled away and tutted. "Hush my brother. Songs are for victors, and we are still in much trouble. And you are disturbing the wounded. Come and share a drink with our commanders and let us review the day." She flashed her dark brown eyes at him and lightly added, "And your young commander, Agravane, did acquit himself well. His sword has been washed in the blood of the enemy."

Arthur followed Morgaise, mightily impressed and happy for her lifting his gloom. He greeted the commanders and they sat around a table where attendants poured ale into pewter mugs. They drank and waited for Arthur to speak first. He looked at them and then asked, "But where is Peredur?"

Caratacus replied, "He must still be in camp at the top of the hill, Lord Arthur. Shall I send for him?"

"No, leave him there. Whatever plan we agree tonight, Caratacus, you must send a rider to brief him."

Arthur gathered his thoughts. "We have fought well and bravely today, but we still have fewer men than our enemy. They have withdrawn for the night and we shall commence our fight with them in the morning. The queen has bloodied her sword and won an important battle with our enemy to the south, and we must now raise our mugs to her." They toasted the queen, and Arthur continued. "Our horsemen chased off theirs, but they will be back on the morrow. Our shield wall held well through the day, but they will throw more men to their wall tomorrow, and I doubt we shall hold them again."

He looked up at the dismayed faces around the table. "We must be realistic and introduce a new tactic."

"What do you have in mind, lord?" Bedwyr asked, draining his tankard.

"We have twice as many horsemen as they have, but they have twice as many foot warriors. So, I propose that our shield wall lines up as they will expect, but on our horn blast, the men part and let our cavalry through to charge their shield wall. Once our riders are amongst them, our foot warriors can join the battle. We may have more chance in broken combat."

Arthur sat back and looked around the table.

"It is a risky strategy, my lord," Caratacus said, "but I like your ambition."

"We shall all die quicker," Morgaise said, leaning forward. "If our strength is our cavalry, then should we not somehow get them to chase us, maybe thinking we are broken and in retreat? Then the cavalry can ride them down, as we did today."

Arthur sat back and looked at her. "My lady, you have changed much this day. You have become a tactician that Julius Caesar himself would be proud of. Your idea has merit. What do the rest of you think?"

After lengthy discussion and several barrels of ale, they were in agreement. Arthur called an end to the meeting and proposed that they eat together before retiring. The unnerving caws of ravens and crows circling above the battlefield assailed their ears as the commanders made their way through the streets of Caer Badon to their quarters, unhappy that the dead lay unburied, but weary and eager for their beds.

Chapter Fourteen

ARTHUR WAS RUDELY shaken awake by Dermot. He blinked at the oil lamp held by his squire and noted that it was still dark outside. "Why… why so early, Dermot?" he croaked, his head still thick from ale and his limbs aching from the exertions of the day before.

"My lord, the Saxons have come to the walls!" he cried, terror in his voice.

Arthur vaulted from his bed and dragged his woollen shift over his head. He sat whilst Dermot knelt to work his feet into his boots. Grabbing his sword belt and scabbard, he ran outside, shouting, "To arms, to arms! Saxons!"

Without waiting for Herrig or Bedwyr he ran to the main gatehouse and climbed the ladder to the parapet. In the pre-dawn gloom, lines of horsemen holding burning brands sat at about one hundred paces distance, whilst foot warriors ran behind them, taking up positions on three sides of the town, the fourth being a port to the river.

"Blow your horns!" he commanded the dumbstruck guards, who had clearly been caught sleeping. In a minute, Bedwyr, Herrig, Caratacus and the Dumnonian captain were by his side.

"So much for not offending the sun god," Bedwyr growled, buckling his belt.

"They have crept up in the night," Arthur replied, looking up to a blanket of dark clouds that obscured the stars and moon. "Now we are under siege."

Arthur noticed that Merlyn had also appeared on the parapet and he made his way to him. "Any thoughts on our predicament?" Arthur asked.

"It is not good, my boy. They are no doubt cutting and fashioning three battering rams from the forest and shall soon be at your gates. You could consider evacuating the women and children by boat to the port. And the wounded, of course."

Arthur nodded; the urgency now confirmed. "I am of a mind to ride out and fight them in the open."

"I know you are, Arthur. That is your nature. Are you expecting any help to arrive?"

"I petitioned the kings of the west, but I doubt they will come."

"You mean Vortipor and Cyngar? I share your doubt. They will sit and wait. It seems you have few options."

"I have some horsemen on the hill. I will send word to them to stay hidden and attack on my command," Arthur replied, staring out at the gathering force.

"The catapults can be employed to fire burning rocks at the rams once they assemble them," Merlyn said, offering a wan smile through his mass of beard.

"You and your toys, Merlyn. Yes, you can make arrangements for them to be dragged to the open spaces behind the south, east and north gates. If nothing else, it will give the impression to our people that we have a plan."

Merlyn leaned towards Arthur with a look of mischief in his grey eyes. "I have a small amount of saltpetre, sulphur and charcoal from which I made that lightning flash that so impressed the warriors. I can prepare some wrapped in leather pouches. Once lit, they will daze and confuse the enemy."

Arthur snorted. "It is not a time for magic tricks, my old friend."

"It may prove useful if you want to make a dash for it… bear it in mind, my boy. Now I shall go and organise the catapults."

Arthur marvelled at how nimbly the elderly healer moved, before he returned to his commanders to set their plans to defend the walls and be ready for an assault. When Queen Morgaise joined them, Arthur conveyed Merlyn's thoughts on non-combatants fleeing down river on the flat-bottomed trading boats that were tied to moorings.

"Yes, now the seaport is cleared of Saxons, that is a good idea," Morgaise agreed. "There will be fewer mouths to feed if the siege lasts long, and less to worry about if our defences are breached. I will arrange it."

The sun came up and a long wait set in. The Saxons and Mordred's Britons had nothing to say to them, and they simply set a camp behind their ranks of warriors, who could now be counted accurately. The Dumnonian captain came to Arthur after some time and reported that the defenders able to fight amounted to eight hundred, with three hundred horses. The enemy had one thousand and fifty, of whom two hundred were mounted. Arthur looked up to Mount Badon, knowing that Peredur's Rheged cavalry numbered about a hundred. He had already sent a messenger out by the river to make his way around the enemy and climb the hill to tell Peredur to hold his position. He was to wait until he saw Arthur's banner at the head of his riders coming through the gates.

By midday the enemy's battering rams appeared from the east, dragged by spans of oxen, to raucous cheers from their warriors. Three, as predicted by Merlyn. They were positioned opposite the three gates, each a mighty oak tree trunk on wheels of wood. Arthur watched on as their carpenters dug holes in the sides of the rams to fit wooden poles for warriors to push.

The catapults were in position and ready to fire rocks at the rams when they came into range. Merlyn had positioned a man on the gatehouse with a flag, whose job it was to estimate the correct distance and order the catapult to fire its shot. Clustered around the catapults were three squads of warriors whose job it was to defend the square should the enemy breach the gates. Saddled horses were held by stable boys in the main square by the great hall. The boats had gone, and were followed along the road to the port by roughly twenty enemy riders. What few archers they had, and javelin throwers, were on the walls, and the commanders had divided themselves into three groups, each on top of a gatehouse.

Arthur and Bedwyr, on top of the main gatehouse facing east, had sight of Mordred's chariot and the Saxon kings grouped to the rear of their men. Saxon drums and horns announced the start of the attack, and burly warriors took to their yokes and part-pushed and part-dragged the battering rams towards the gates. A young Dumnonian hesitated with his flag, uncertainty showing in his trembling lip.

"Be bold, and accurate," Arthur growled at him. The young man nodded his nut-brown hair and strained his eyes at the slowly rumbling ram as it aligned to the approach road and started to gather momentum. At about a hundred paces distance, he ran to the rear of the platform and waved his flag at his colleagues below.

A rock, wrapped in a cloth dipped in tar, was set alight and the huge arm released. With a 'whoosh' its load was flung into the air, arcing high over the gatehouse, landing just in front of the ram. Its momentum rolled it towards its target, and warriors were ordered by their commanders to stop it with their spears. A frantic effort was made to stop the burning rock from rolling to the ram, and one man's cloak caught alight, to the amusement of the men on the walls. But their efforts succeeded and the rock was pushed to one side of the road, allowing the ram to continue on its journey.

At the south gate a huge cheer went up, telling Arthur that a hit had been scored on the ram there. There was silence from the north gate. Merlyn ordered his teams to re-load their catapults, for he had made provision for three shots each. Further catapult shots sailed harmlessly over the two battering rams that had passed within their range and now approached the gates. The south gate ram was abandoned and left to burn. Those men moved around to reinforce the assaults on the north and east gates.

As the rams hit into the double-door wooden gates, Arthur ordered tar be tipped onto them from basins passed up the ladders. Then archers with blazing arrows fired down to set them alight. The enraged Saxons quickened their assault, seeing that the burning rams would soon be obsolete. But on the second push, the burning rams lodged into a gap in the gates, and the attackers withdrew to watch the gates go up in a great conflagration. The tactic had backfired, as the gatehouses above were also set alight. This had happened at both the north and east gatehouses.

Arthur ordered his men to the walls and went to consult his fellow commanders, as they waited for the attack to begin once the flames had died down. Black tendrils of smoke rose to air, filling the hearts of those in the town with dread fear. The enemy waited patiently, for up to an hour, for the fires to burn down, before sending their screaming warriors past the wrecks of the battering rams to kick the charred gates inwards and charge in.

They were greeted by burning catapults and yelping dogs that scurried for cover. The town was empty of people, apart from Merlyn and a couple of attendants, who threw down smoking pouches of leather from the parapet above onto the first of the Saxons to enter. The pouches fell at their feel and sizzled, before bursting into bright shafts of lightning, and then popping loudly as they exploded, showering the yelping Saxons with small stones. Merlyn laughed at his experiment and ordered his men to run along the platform to where their horses were tethered by the south gate and make their escape.

Arthur had already led his riders through the unattended south gate, followed by the warriors on foot, and set about attacking the Saxons from the rear. Their attack was so swift and unexpected that it caught Mordred and the kings and chiefs off guard. Morgana screamed at the driver to turn the chariot and head northwards to put distance between them and the hollering horsemen, taking a guard of a dozen riders with them. Arthur's pumped up men fell upon their static and dumfounded opponents with grim relish.

The Saxon kings rallied their Briton allies and turned to face the attack. From high on Mount Badon, Peredur saw Arthur's banner and ordered his men to charge downhill. The milling Saxon warriors outside the gatehouse did not know which way to face, but were soon rallied by their commanders and turned away from the town to form up a shield wall. Viroco and Brian led their Coritani and Cornovi foot warriors, with the remaining Dumnonian guard, in a charge on the Saxon's left flank, and fierce hand-to-hand combat broke out.

Arthur's blood was up and he drove Mars towards the Saxon and Briton leaders, hot for a high-born victim. He was rewarded with sight of King Caradog of Gwent's red and purple-edged cloak, beside his banner of the white stag. The king turned to see Arthur racing towards him, alarm in his eyes, too late to flee. Arthur hacked down on him, catching a glancing blow on his shoulder armour as he ducked. Caradog then bent forward and dug his heels into his mount, but his escape was blocked by another horse. Arthur reined hard and swivelled, then charged with sword arm outstretched at the static Caradog, running Excalibur into the Gwent king's side, where the straps held his chest plate. The blade entered between his ribs, causing Caradog to groan and rock in his saddle, dropping his shield and lance. Arthur pulled Excalibur out and slashed at his neck for good measure. Caradog tumbled to the ground, bloodied and dying.

Arthur found Bedwyr, Herrig and their closest guards by his side, and they looked at the men of Gwent, who lined up opposite them shocked at their king's death, but with lances poised for a charge. A horn blast away to the south, coming from the port road, announced the approach of warriors on foot, who could be seen in the distance jogging towards the fray.

"Men from the West have come to our aid!" one of Arthur's scouts shouted, riding to his side. Arthur narrowed his eyes and could make out Cadog's Silurian wolfhead banner, together with the banners of Dyfed and Demetia.

Arthur laughed and pointed, shouting, "The men of Siluria, Dyfed and Demetia have joined our cause!" A huge cheer went up and word carried through the throng of men, many of the Britons disengaging and stepping back from their opponents. Arthur remembered Cadog's words to him and edged Mars towards the line of Gwent horsemen, shouting, "Your brothers from Siluria have come to fight for their freedom! Join your brothers, those of you who would fight for your chief, the noble Cadog!"

This had the desired effect, and scuffles broke out as two dozen riders detached themselves from the Gwent ranks and rode towards the oncoming warriors. But the riders of Gwent had another more pressing problem to deal with, as they turned to face the sound of thundering hooves when Peredur's riders fell on them. Arthur's men also resumed the fight, and soon the remnants of Mordred's cavalry were overpowered. Many of Mordred's dispirited Britons surrendered and Arthur made his will known that they should be spared.

Now Arthur turned his men to face the Saxon shield wall, and the sporadic duels that were raging to their right and left flanks. He greeted Peredur and re-formed the line, with those men who still carried unbroken lances to the front. For once, Arthur, his lance discarded, moved to the rear with Queen Morgaise, deferring to Bedwyr and Peredur to lead the charge on the defiant Saxon shield wall.

With the arrival of what looked like, to Arthur, four or five hundred reinforcements who had come on the road from the seaport, the tide of battle turned in their favour, and the Saxon defensive position was gradually whittled away. After an hour's fighting, Arthur could see a circle of shields had formed around the Saxon kings, who sat impassively on their horses. The dead and dying littered the plain, trampled grass now slick with blood and bile, set against a backdrop of smoke trails rising from the town's shattered gates to the azure late afternoon sky.

With barely eighty Saxons warriors remaining on their feet, Arthur raised his arm and called for a truce.

"Let us desist from killing each other and make a settlement!" he yelled across the quietening battlefield. Tired arms hung by their sides as bloodied faces turned to him.

King Icel urged his horse forward, followed by Octha and Cerdic. "What do you have in mind, Arthur?" he growled.

"We could spend another hour killing you all, but I am of a mind to take you prisoner and negotiate a permanent settlement." Arthur knew there were thousands more of their fellow countrymen in coastal villages and more would come on spring tides to replace those who had fallen.

The kings spoke hurriedly in low voices. Icel turned to Arthur and threw down his sword. Octha and Cerdic followed his lead, and so did their warriors.

"We shall not dishonour you, but your warriors will be needed to dig burial pits," Arthur said, signalling his men to move in.

From what had seemed a losing position, Arthur's men had turned it around, aided by the late arrival of reinforcements. He now rode over to greet Cadog, who was still nursing a bandaged arm, and the leaders of the Dyfed and Demetian warriors, for kings Vortipor and Cyngar had not come in person.

"Let us secure our prisoners and attend to the dead, then retire to the great hall and drink a toast to our victory with our most noble and courageous host, Queen Morgaise," he said, mounting Mars and leading his men in a rousing victory song.

"WE SHALL RECOVER your home, dear sister," Arthur said, before slaking his thirst on a goblet of sour ale. The hall was once again employed as a place for the wounded to be treated and find respite. The commanders sat around their table, bruised and cut, but some seats were not filled. Arthur indicated that Cadog and his fellow commanders from Dyfed and Demetia should sit.

"My thanks, dearest brother, for knowing my thoughts in the flush of your victory," Morgaise replied, managing a tired smile. She had come through the battle unscathed, and glanced at Agravane by her side, knowing she owed him a debt of gratitude for watching over her in the madness of war.

"We have defeated Mordred's army and his Saxon allies, but our work is not done. Mordred and Morgana have escaped and will soon be plotting more mischief. We may thank Gareth and Malachi for not joining with our enemies, but they remain stubbornly neutral. And the Saxons will cling to their lands unless we drive them off…"

"And we shall!" Bedwyr interrupted, banging his goblet on the table and rousing a weary chorus of 'aye' from his comrades.

Arthur smiled and patted his loyal deputy's dusty arm. "But first, let us bury and honour our dead, then divide up the Saxon and Briton slaves between us and send some of our men to their homes." He paused to look around the table. "But I would ask some of you to stay on and march south with us." He paused again and made a slight bow to Queen Morgaise. "To take the town of Exisca from Cerdic's men, who hold it for the Saxons."

"I am with you!" Caratacus shouted, banging down his goblet.

"You are ever for a fight, my friend," Arthur laughed. He then turned to the newcomers and said, "But let us now thank our newest allies from Dyfed and Demetia to the far western edge of our island, and Cadog who survived the slaughter at Port Abona. Let them speak."

Cadog stood, bowed and said, "We fought bravely, my lord, and your men acquitted themselves well, next to my Silurian warriors and the noble Dumnonian guard. But they had the numbers on us and we left noble Cathan and his best men dead beside that fort. Then, as dawn broke, I took twenty men who had survived to the port with the aim of firing their ships. That was when we saw the sails of our western friends coming to help us. We cried tears of relief, but also wept for our fallen comrades who had given their lives the day before."

He paused to sniff at the vexing memory. "But let me introduce our saviours to you. This is Callan of Demetia and Morgan of Dyfed."

The two fresh and relatively clean commanders stood and bowed to the table.

"I bring you greetings from King Cyngar the Wise of Demetia, King Arthur," Callan said, taking his seat.

"And I bring greetings and good wishes for your victory from King Vortipor and Queen Alicia of Dyfed," Morgan said, then also sitting.

Arthur stood briefly and bowed to them. "And I send my heartfelt thanks to your noble kings for their most welcome support. Your coming to the plain of Badon was most timely and swung the battle in our favour. And I suspect that the entreaties of Queen Alicia to her husband on behalf of her people may have proven to be the key to this. Thank you, Cadog, for the suggestion. I would ask you to stay and secure this town before returning to your ships."

Arthur's eyes sparkled with joy, for he now knew he had powerful allies in the west, who would form the bedrock of his ambitions to rule over the entire island.

"But is it true that you slew King Caradog on the field?" Cadog asked, leaning forward.

"Aye, it is true. He had the misfortune to meet Excalibur." They laughed as attendants refilled their goblets and placed platters of hard cakes and summer fruits on the table. "I am resolved to move to Caer Legion and make my court there," Arthur lightly added.

"You are most welcome to pass through our lands," Cadog said, grinning at the prospect, adding, with raised voice, "and let no man on this island say you are not the King of Britannia!"

Laughter and the clashing of goblets drew disapproving glances from the healers and nurses who hurried between their patients carrying bowls, towels and bandages.

Arthur waited for the merriment to die down before saying, "But before we turn west, we must march south. So, who is with me?"

A PLAN WAS set, and after three days of rest and repairs, those who followed Arthur and Morgaise south to Exisca marched out of the town of Caer Badon, following the old Roman road that ran due south. Spirits were high and hope sang in the hearts of Britons from the many tribes who had united as friends and allies.

Arthur *Rex Brittonum*

A new dawn had come, and Arthur was hailed as a beacon of light shining across the land from east to west. The very mention of his name inspired a belief that the dark days of brutal invaders who killed at will and took their children into slavery were gone, and there would be peace between the quarrelling tribes.

Arthur *Rex Brittonum*

PART TWO

Caer Legion-on-Usk, Gwent, in the year 525

Arthur *Rex Brittonum*

Chapter One

A FEEBLE SPRING sun melted the last of the snow on the hillsides around Arthur's court at Caer Legion, beside the fast-flowing River Usk in the Kingdom of Gwent. Lambs frolicked on the southern slopes, calling to cautious ewes that shepherds had driven away from the snow line, and the wolf-ravaged carcass of the luckless member of their flock who had not survived the night.

Ambrose, Arthur's Chancellor, turned his head away from the pastoral scene at his window at the sound of the door to his study opening. This corner of the grey stone abbey dedicated to Saint Alban had become his favourite retreat, a space for books and manuscripts where his good friend Abbot Asaph had provided parchment, vellum, ink and a writing desk in a cosy chamber, now warmed by a roaring fire.

"Ah, Ambrose," Asaph said in greeting. "Are you keeping your numbers, or writing your story of Arthur?"

Ambrose smiled and put down his quill, rising to stretch his back and embrace his friend. "Dear Asaph, your loan of this room is greatly appreciated, as I can do little work in Arthur's smoky long barn, or my cramped and damp quarters. Please sit with me by the fire."

Asaph had grown fat in the ten years since Arthur's stunning victory at Mount Badon, his travelling days as Arthur's chaplain put to an end by Arthur's insistence that Bishop Aaron make him abbot of a newly built abbey with its own lands. "Dear Ambrose, you are a much-valued and learned friend, whom our Lord Jesus Christ has sent to keep me company and preserve my sanity."

Ambrose laughed and stoked the fire. "I am writing Arthur's story, whilst it's still clear in my mind. I have written an account of the terrible slaughter at Badon Hill, and Arthur's slaying of the treacherous King Caradog of Gwent, that led to our settling here at the fortress of the legion. Once the rump kingdom of Dumnonia was stabilised, and Queen Morgaise restored to her rule in Exisca, Arthur led his followers to this place, as you know. I have set down the detail of it, and how Arthur has settled where yonder Roman fortress stands between the river and the thriving settlement that has grown around the Roman arena we call Arthur's Roundel."

He sucked in a lungful of air and slowly exhaled. "I have recorded all of Arthur's battles, from the very first when I met him, at the River Glein close to Lindum, swiftly followed by a second battle at a black creek known as 'Dubglas'. He fought the Angliscs at Guinnion Fort, the Deirans at Ebrauc and, some years later, fought north of the Wall at Cambuslang and Celidon Forest. There are other minor ones, leading to his great victory at Mount Badon and the last battle, more of a raid really, when the remnants of Caradog's followers were chased off, here, at Caer Legion."

"Yes, as Arthur's chaplain, I also bore witness to the slaughter from the safety of the walls of Caer Badon," Asaph replied sombrely, as if recalling that day. "But do not forget to note that Arthur was presented with a shield by our holy bishop at Mount Badon, one that depicted the image of the Virgin Mary and baby Jesus; and that he fought for Christ against the pagans that day; and he himself slaughtered as many as nine hundred and sixty with his sword, Excalibur!" Asaph raised his voice along with his arm, pointing in triumph to the cobwebs on the beam above his head.

Ambrose laughed and nodded, "I shall, most holy Abbot, although it was not his first shield depicting the Virgin Mary, and the number of men killed by Arthur himself is greatly exaggerated by his followers, and is most likely the entire number of Saxons slain on that day…"

Asaph ignored the correction and continued, "…and this abbey, dedicated to our most holy martyr, Saint Alban, was built by him once Caradog's depraved followers had gone." He shivered at the memory. "It took us two years to convert these stubborn people to God's truth. Please record that."

"I shall, holy Abbot. And in time, I hope to record that you have been made a saint, for you deserve it."

"We are blessed to have this time of peace, thanks to Arthur's settlement with the avaricious Saxons. He has been gone some weeks, dear friend, and I am most vexed to hear he has once again travelled to the mountains to seek out that old druid, Merlyn."

Ambrose smiled benignly and said, "I first met Merlyn when a boy at Lindum. I remember cowering in fear and awe beneath his tall and fearsome frame, for he bore a look that intimated that the knowledge of the ancient world resided in his head. He was known as an adviser to kings and a healer of note at that time, but I have also heard he has the wisdom of druids, although I doubt that he practises their rituals."

"But we do not know," Asaph tetchily replied. "I worry and pray for Arthur's immortal soul, and question the wisdom of travelling to the dark interior of this land, where dragons and devilish faeries dwell in the rocky passes and caves. And what if Merlyn draws other druidic folk to him and revitalises that dread religion that the Romans all but extinguished?"

"You must not concern yourself with Arthur. He has come through many trials and remains true to the Christian faith. He seeks out Merlyn because they were once friends, and to ask his advice on the matter of Britannia. Merlyn can read Roman and Greek letters, and has many ancient manuscripts that contain much wisdom, no doubt."

"The Church has a list of banned texts that includes much of the writings of Greek and Arabic scribes. Those who read them are at risk of being named a heretic."

Ambrose laughed and put a fresh log on the fire. "Then do not tell our bishop that Arthur might be in the same room as ancient scripts! I too hope he returns soon and has not forgotten that the council of kings will gather this month-end at his roundel."

"Ah, but the Bishop does not share our benign view of Arthur. He feels his closeness to Merlyn, and Merlyn's druidic associations, undermines the Church and our holy mission to convert all to the Word of God. To this end, he has sent me a novice, Gildas, whom I feel is here to spy on us and report back. I'd wager he is outside with his ear pressed to that door," he whispered, leaning forward on his stool.

A faint knock at the door was followed by Gildas entering, as if he had indeed been listening. The short, wispy novice bowed to the Abbot, showing the white bald patch of his tonsure, and ignored Ambrose. "My lord Abbot, you are needed in the kitchen where our cooks are appraising foodstuffs brought by local farmers."

Asaph smiled and replied, "God's blessings on you, young Gildas. I shall be along shortly, but first, give me your views on our noble king, Arthur, whose history I am discussing with Brother Ambrose." He winked mischievously at his friend.

Gildas stiffened and, looking at Ambrose, replied, "I care not for your history of the sinner Arthur. He is part of the problem we face in converting our people to God's holy word. Should God plan for me to grow old in his service, I shall write my own history of these worrisome times, and I shall only mention the noble Ambrosius by name. He embodied the virtues of Roman times and was a true Christian, aiding Germanicus stamp out the Palagian heresy, not this Arthur who sways with the wind for his own devilish pleasure."

Gildas looked annoyed when Ambrose and Asaph shared a conspiratorial snigger.

Ambrose smiled and replied, "I have put up a defence of Arthur as a unifier and a man of deep faith, but who is also wise enough to be pragmatic in leadership. My history shall say that he fought for Christ against pagans, and won the day, so that God's holy word can cover this land."

"Here, here," Asaph added, standing. "And let us not forget that he founded this abbey that now supports a community of which you are a member, Gildas. Now I must take my leave, dear Ambrose, and bid you divine inspiration in your writings, for those who come after us must know the weighty matter of these days."

Gildas grunted in contempt and gave Ambrose an ill look as he followed his master from the chamber.

Arthur Rex Brittonum

Chapter Two

Three Years Earlier…

A LINE OF nine riders picked their way through a rocky landscape of harsh fescue grass lining high-side valleys, their compacted earthen track ever rising towards granite mountains that touched the sky. The last village was far behind; and they only encountered the occasional shepherd, with skinny dogs for company, watching over hardy sheep that hugged the sunny sides of the valleys. Skirting the top side of a wide, semi-circular quarry, they glanced down at the white cliff face once mined by Roman slaves for blocks and rock powder.

Winds buffeted the riders who did not speak, choosing to keep their cowls over their lolling heads. At the head of another valley, their guide stopped on a mound, facing the pale yellow sun in a gap between distant mountains. Above them, to their right, the road wound up to the walls and towers of a gleaming white castle.

"This is the castle of Dinas Brân, known as the White Castle, my lord," the guide said, turning to face his master.

Arthur pushed back his hood and stared up at the magnificent structure perched on a crag in a desolate but strangely beautiful landscape. Rain clouds had scudded east, leaving the walls shining white in the weak autumn sun.

"What a sight!" Bedwyr exclaimed, drawing level with Arthur. Peredur and Lucan also joined them as they gawped in wonder.

"It glows white after the rains have washed it," the guide explained, happy that his charges were impressed.

"Then lead on," Arthur said. "We shall arrive as the sun drops to the western sea."

Guards holding spears asked their business from a platform above the gatehouse. A banner bearing a white swan on a blue background fluttered above their heads.

"I am King Arthur, come to visit Merlyn."

Heavy bolts were drawn back and the twin wooden gates swung inwards. The line of weary riders filed into a cobblestone courtyard that faced a white-block hall with a high thatched roof. To their left was a stable block, and to the right crude huts were bordered by animal pens where hardy folk lined up to silently appraise the new arrivals. Stable boys came forward to take their horses, and then, leaving their squires and guide behind, they mounted the steps to the doors of the hall, where a steward in a white robe awaited them.

"Welcome to the White Castle," he announced, his outstretched hand indicating they should enter. "The Lady Guinevere awaits you."

Arthur led his followers across the dimly lit hall, past stone columns holding up roof beams beneath a thatch where birds fluttered, their droppings an obvious hazard as white patches patterned the floor rushes. At the far end a lady rose from her throne on a raised dais to greet them. Arthur marvelled at her long, braided copper-coloured hair falling over a shoulder. She was tall and was immaculately clothed in a pale blue gown edged with gold and belted with a golden sash. Her face was long and pale, her lips full and red, her eyes shining green between long lashes.

"Welcome, King Arthur of the Britons," she said in an assured voice. "I am Guinevere, lady of the castle, widow of Chief Madoc whose title has passed to our son, Elgan." A lad of no more than eight summers stood by her side, eying the visitors with suspicion.

"I thank you for your warm welcome, my lady. May I introduce my companions, Prince Peredur of Rheged and knights Bedwyr and Lucan. I have come to visit my old mentor, Merlyn, on his invitation."

"Ah yes, Merlyn is our good friend and guest. My steward shall direct you to his chamber without delay, and I will have my maids prepare your rooms. You must join us this evening for our meal, when I hope to hear of your many brave deeds, King Arthur."

Arthur's eyes locked onto hers, and he felt his heart beat more quickly. "I look forward to that, my lady," he replied, bowing low.

Merlyn's chamber was to the back of the rambling castle, an elongated room no doubt made for a feasting table. He was sitting at a desk amongst rolls of parchment and velum manuscripts, and rose with a cry of joy when Arthur entered.

"My boy! You have come at last!" he cried with a croak in his voice. "Come in, and your knights. Let me see you." Merlyn crossed the flagstones with deceptive speed, his black gown flapping in his wake, and held Arthur by his upper arms, peering into his face as if reading his past adventures. Arthur noticed movement by the hearth – a small figure in rags was stirring the streaming contents of an iron caldron suspended over a fire with a long wooden stick, muttering quietly.

"It is good to see you too, Merlyn, my mentor, my oldest friend," Arthur replied with a wide smile.

Merlyn waved Peredur, Bedwyr and Lucan to a bench and noticed Arthur looking at the bubbling cauldron. "Do you remember our encounter in the Celidon Forest, Arthur?" Arthur nodded. "That is where I acquired the cauldron of Dyrnwich, one of the Lost Treasures of Britain, now found, by me."

Arthur laughed, "Yes, I remember that night well. And what is the magical property of the cauldron?"

"You cook a portion for two, and it will feed twelve, so the legend says," Merlyn replied, his rheumy eyes twinkling with pleasure.

"And does that happen?"

"Oh yes, Nimue and I have been living off one cooked meal per week, but eating every day. But how remiss of me not to introduce my assistant." Merlyn pointed to her but she didn't approach. "She is shy and bad tempered at the best of times, but she is clever and has become my memory."

Arthur looked more closely at Merlyn's creature, barely recognisable as a girl, one on the cusp of womanhood. She looked around with a scowl at Merlyn's mention of her name, her unevenly cut shoulder length hair framing a face of pointy nose, chin and cheekbones that gave her the appearance of a rocky crag. Tiny black eyes sunk in deep cavities seemed to take in every detail of the visitors, as if appraising the suitability of their body parts for a potion.

"Nimue, ask the lady Guinevere for a pitcher of ale for our weary travellers," Merlyn asked, receiving a scowl in response. She skulked off towards a second doorway at the end of the long chamber, past tables and shelves bearing jars of small animals and human body parts floating in clear liquid. Bedwyr, Lucan and Peredur's attention was drawn to a table at the centre of the room. On it rested a large glass dome containing a human skull with strands of hair and rotten strips of flesh hanging from it and floating around it, that rested on a bronze base on which ancient runes were engraved.

Arthur approached the cauldron and looked disdainfully at the brown, viscous liquid inside. "And what of the other Treasures of Britain? You told me then that you were busy collecting them in your quest to understand the wisdom of the ancients."

"Indeed I am," Merlyn replied, lifting an unremarkable drinking horn from where it sat on the lid of a cedar chest strapped with leather and copper. "This is the horn of Brân Galed. Whoever drinks water from this will taste whatever they wish for. I tried to give it to you as a gift but you refused, no doubt afraid of its magical properties." Merlyn paused to fix Arthur with a disapproving look. "But I find it useful for enjoying the taste of the finest mead brewed by monks from their sweetest honey, whilst only drinking water."

Arthur laughed. "Aside from conjuror's tricks, what other value do they have?"

"Do not mock, my boy. They are a gateway into the realm of ancient magic and belief that is now, sadly, lost to our people. By studying them I have deepened my understanding of the ancients and..." his voice trailed away and he turned to point at the table. "Come and look upon the legendary Head of Brân, the most beguiling of the Treasures of Britain."

"Certainly the most gruesome," Bedwyr remarked, as the five men gathered around the glass dome.

"Legend has it that Brân the Hunter was the builder of this castle in a time long before the Romans. He outlived his peers by many lifetimes, but finally succumbed to a wounded foot whilst hunting – perhaps a malicious deity of the forest – and died of infection. His head was removed from his body and preserved in this jar, so that those of noble birth can converse with him and receive his wisdom."

"Ah, would I qualify?" Arthur lightly asked.

"Do not dabble with the forces of evil, my lord," Peredur cautioned.

Merlyn ignored the dark looks of Arthur's companions and replied, "Yes indeed, King Arthur of the Britons. It is my hope that you will consult with the Head of Brân and gain an insight into the uncertain future of this island."

"This is nonsense, my lord," Bedwyr said, tugging Arthur's sleeve.

Arthur pulled away and replied, "It was Merlyn's visions of the future that led to my being conducted to safety as a child, to my drawing of Excalibur from the stone and my rise to be king, finally defeating Mordred and the Saxon kings at Badon. There is more to this life of ours than comes from the mouths of Christian priests."

Bedwyr and Peredur looked shocked and regarded their king as if he were a stranger.

Merlyn gave a little chuckle and said, "There is no harm in trying, and indeed, Prince Peredur, being of royal blood, will you not also attempt to glean some wisdom from the Head of Brân?"

"I will not! This witchcraft is not for me, Merlyn," Peredur replied, taking a step back.

"Then I propose that you return to your seats and let Arthur try." Nimue had silently re-entered the room and now stood at the side of the bench, where she poured ale for them. Merlyn picked up a silver tin from the table and lifted the lid. He leaned towards Arthur and whispered, "The experience works better in a darkened room and after inhaling this powder, my lord Arthur."

Nimue moved swiftly to cover the windows with black drapes, leaving the only light source the orange glow from the hearth fire and some candles she now lit and set on an iron stand. Before Arthur could reply, Merlyn lifted a silver spoon of white powder and blew some into his face. Arthur coughed and took a step backwards, blinking his eyes. Merlyn took him firmly by the arm and positioned him beside the glass dome.

Arthur's head seemed to be full of clouds as his eyes struggled to focus on the hollow, dark sockets of the skull that now seemed to glow orange in the reflected fire and candlelight.

"Ask him a question, Arthur, in your mind," Merlyn quietly intoned.

Arthur swayed as he thought. Merlyn held him as he fell into a trance, muttering unintelligibly. Bedwyr and Peredur shifted uncomfortably, sipping from their goblets, but stayed silent. Lucan kept a close watch on Nimue, not trusting Merlyn's strange assistant. Arthur's head rolled and he gave soft shouts as if reliving past events. After fifteen minutes, he cried out and collapsed to his knees, Merlyn only partially breaking his fall.

"What have you done!" Bedwyr thundered angrily, lifting Arthur and carrying him to the bench. They laid him down and he muttered, white foam flecking at his lips.

"Lift his head and give him ale," Merlyn commanded. Peredur obliged, and Arthur came to, spluttering and fluttering his eyelids.

"What… what happened?" he asked, blinking and looking at the concerned faces above him.

"You talked to the Head of Brân," Merlyn replied. "Sit him up."

Bedwyr and Peredur took an arm each and pushed Arthur into a seated position on the bench, supporting him on either side. Arthur continued to blink and asked for more ale.

"What did you ask and what did you hear?" Merlyn asked, leaning forwards to Arthur.

"I… I asked about my future and that of my kingdom," Arthur slowly replied, coughing. They waited for him to continue as Nimue danced behind Merlyn, unsettling the watchful Lucan.

Arthur gathered his thoughts and whispered, "I heard his voice, Merlyn. I heard him say, 'a pestilence shall spread across the land, making the people sick and weak. Then the enemy shall rise again and swarm like bees, covering the land in a black shadow…"

"Go on," Merlyn urged, excitement in his voice.

"I saw a meadow in the hook of a river, shrouded in mist. The mist lifted slowly to reveal an army of knights on horseback, their faces black holes in helmets, crows sitting on their shoulders, black banners hanging limp, silently waiting…" Arthur's voice trailed away and his chin sank to his chest.

"Enough, Merlyn, he needs to rest and recover from the effects of that damn powder you blew in his face," Bedwyr growled.

Merlyn nodded in agreement. "Yes, that is enough for one day. He will remember more in his dreams. Take him to his room and we shall talk more this evening at table."

Arthur's companions lifted him by his arms and roused him enough for his feet to move in a slow stagger as they guided him to the door. Merlyn and Nimue exchanged grins as their visitors left the chamber.

"He has seen the moment of his death," Merlyn whispered to Nimue as the door closed. "I will find out more about his visions in good time."

ARTHUR AWOKE FROM a fitful sleep and sat upright, sweat beads on his forehead. He saw he was in an unfamiliar bed chamber and remembered he was in the White Castle. Bedwyr snored gently from a chair in the corner, a bear rug over his lap. It was dark outside and the chamber was lit by candles on two stands and a fire in the hearth, telling him that an attendant had been in the room whilst they slept. He shook his head as if to dispel wild dreams, and walked to a bowl and jug of water on a table next to a looking mirror.

Now approaching his fortieth winter, he studied his image critically. He ran a finger down the scar on his cheek and noticed how fleshier his face had become. Turning sideways, he patted his round stomach. "Less lean warrior and more comfortably padded king," he muttered in a low voice. He saw that he had been softened by six years of relative peace, only riding out from his hall at Caer Leon on brief missions to enforce the Saxon truce, quell disputes with recalcitrant chiefs, or chase off northern raiders. He was now more considered in his movements and weightier from nights of feasting in his hall.

And yet he had felt youthful and invigorated in the presence of Lady Guinevere.

"Wake up, Bedwyr," he said, kicking his companion's foot. "Let us go to the hall and see if the feast has begun."

"How do you feel, my lord?" Bedwyr asked, stretching and yawning.

"My head is thick as if I have already drunk a cask of ale. That powder Merlyn blew at me awoke something in my head and gave me vivid dreams, some good and some not so."

"That sort of trickery, or sorcery, is not good, my lord," Bedwyr chided, getting to his feet.

"I am ever curious, my friend. That can be both a blessing and a curse," Arthur replied, holding the door open.

They followed a trail of oil lamps glowing from the walls of the passage that led to the great hall.

There they found Peredur at table, and Arthur was shown to the seat next to him and beside a vacant chair at the head of the table. Merlyn sat opposite and, after formal greetings, indicated that this was not the place to discuss the afternoon's events. A fanfare from a single horn announced the arrival of Lady Guinevere and her son. They took their places at the head of the table, and Arthur was pleased that he had been seated next to her. He inhaled her heady perfume of rose and lilac and drank in her unusual beauty at close quarters as she laid a dainty hand on his.

She clearly intended to impress her royal guest, and several courses of roasted birds, meats and pastries were brought to the table. The wine was to Arthur's taste and he drank and ate heartily, exchanging anecdotes with the enchanting Guinevere, enveloped in her company. It had not gone unnoticed by the other guests who whispered and giggled at the seemingly besotted couple.

"The lady Guinevere is weaving a web and Arthur has been caught in it," Peredur whispered to Lucan, frowning.

The young knight was not interested, as he was making eyes at one of Guinevere's maids. "Our king is merely being a good guest and amusing the lady," he said dismissively, returning to chew meat off a bone and raise his eyebrows to the giggling maids opposite.

Peredur sat back and crossed his arms. He could not complain to Arthur's most trusted knight, Bedwyr, so he called an attendant to refill his goblet with wine.

Opposite him, Merlyn chuckled at the drama before him and picked at his food, enjoying a rare invitation to the lady's table. He would seek out Arthur in the morning to find out more of his dreams.

Arthur Rex Brittonum

Chapter Three

525 - three years have passed since Arthur's first visit to the White Castle

ARTHUR AWOKE AT the cockerel's first crow on the morning of the long-awaited council meeting. He hurriedly dressed and made his way out through the gates of the stockade that enclosed the royal buildings, past the tents and banners of visiting chiefs, towards the stone walls of the abbey. He paused to draw his cloak more tightly about him, distracted by the shouts of children. They were driving goats and sheep to pasture outside the crumbling Roman fort that had given up its granite blocks to the building of this abbey by the rushing River Usk.

He woke a dozing guard at the Abbey's gate and crossed a courtyard to the chapel. Once his eyes had adjusted to the gloomy interior, lit by fragrant candles, he saw the portly figure of Abbot Asaph kneeling at the altar rail, offering up morning prayers.

"Father, may I speak with you?" Arthur asked in a loud whisper, sitting on the front bench.

Father Asaph looked up in surprise – he was used to having the chapel to himself in the early morning, a time to thank God for his blessings and compose his list of the day's duties. Arthur's unexpected appearance had wrenched his mind away from thoughts of schooling the choir of novices, who would chant at the coming baptisms because this audible and visible sanctity pleased the king and queen. Now Arthur sat hunched by him, wrapped in his cloak, like a sinner waiting for absolution.

"Are you troubled, my lord?"

Arthur sighed and gestured for Asaph to sit beside him. "While I was out riding yesterday with my hound, we killed a fox, Asaph," he said in a distant voice.

"Was he near the chicken coup? Better dead than putting the hens off their laying."

"Not a 'he', a vixen, and she was by the roadside. She led us a dance, and I knew she was leading us away from her cubs. We found them wandering about, still blue eyed and mewling for her. I was struck by regret. Can you believe I rode on and left my squire to finish them off?"

"We need the eggs, my lord. Foxes are vermin."

"But it set me to thinking, Asaph. Of all the things I have been and might yet become, I will never be a mother. Hector's wife lavished a mother's love on me when her natural son was killed in battle. And I have watched my own wife devote herself to the comfort and welfare of our three. She schools them in map-making herself."

"You are blessed to be their father and their king, my lord." It was not the first time, of late, that Asaph had found himself called on to reassure Arthur.

"You say that so surely, Asaph. You know, living as I have done, surrounded by friends and old allies of Uther, I have believed myself to be king because it is my right. I believed that I had our Lord's blessing when I was a harsh adversary, but I never sought to cause suffering for its own sake. Now the fox has made me think of Morgana."

"Aye. I have heard she is a wily one." Asaph made as if to stand. There were things he needed to do, and this was not on his list.

But Arthur gripped his wrist to stay him. "I do not mean that. I mean her determination to put her son Mordred before all else, and I thought this: what if she is right? What if his claim to the crown is just?"

"You are speaking in riddles, my lord. Maybe we should pray together."

"You must have heard the rumours about Uther and Ygerne. Even if I am Uther's son, my claim is stained if Uther took his noble's wife by force. Morgana may have reason to feel aggrieved. She believes her mother, Jessica, was Uther's best loved wife and true queen, and Ygerne was merely an old man's infatuation."

Asaph's sandals seemed a subject of great fascination to him. He looked up then and stood, determined to be about his business, for he did not believe that Arthur had developed a bad conscience. It was more likely that he was about to recruit his chaplain for some jaunt, to evade the routine duties which seemed increasingly tedious to him. But he answered the king, all the same. "She has no cause to be aggrieved."

"I killed her husband, Mordred's father, Velocatus."

"That was in battle, a matter of self-defence. And have you forgotten she tried to poison your sisters?" Asaph knew the history of this family feud.

"A wicked act, but Merlyn tells me she was not always so. She was his pupil, a nurse in his dispensary and a loyal daughter who ran her widowed father's household."

Asaph bridled and crossed himself at the mention of Merlyn. "My lord, it is not my place to say whose counsel is worthy, but the druid is not a wholesome man."

"Possibly, he is not wholesome, but he is not a druid. And he saved my life, you know."

"Arthur, I think you know that we were all innocent in our cradle, but Morgana has not rocked Mordred's cradle for many a year. Though she has nourished a bitter and callous nature in her son. And she has been no friend to Merlyn, by all accounts. Without a doubt, I believe they are not and never have been justified in their ambitions to usurp you, Uther's only son, my lord."

Arthur smiled at his chaplain and outside a smithy's hammer began a rhythmic clanging, a sign that the working day had begun. "You are right, Asaph. My thanks for your good counsel. There is no room for doubt when I am sworn to preserve my people from malign influences. And I should not forget that. Well, I must about my business in preparing for the Council of Chiefs, so I will wish a good day to you."

But having said that, Arthur rose and stood in front of the crucifix, as if he was not quite convinced by his own words. Asaph remembered his nosy novice, Gildas, telling him that Arthur was a king who merely 'deliberated', and decided to extend his devotions and pray that Arthur would regain his lost vigour.

THE SUN HAD reached its highest point when Arthur took his seat on a raised dais, beneath a shaded awning, in the centre of the amphitheatre. His throne was mounted on a horizontal wheel that his squire could swivel, allowing him to look directly at whoever was speaking from the floor of the gravel arena. Above the kings, chiefs and knights, their followers and some locals sat on the stone terraces, for Arthur had decreed that council meetings should be open to public scrutiny. He saw Ambrose looking with satisfaction at the full complement of delegates from the tribal territories augmenting the local crowd, for this was the first such council meeting in more than two years.

A herald stood forth to hush the chatter and announce the King's Council was in session. Herrig, once his bodyguard but now his steward, strode around the pit, staff in hand, ready to quell any arguments, and Ambrose sat beside Arthur, furnished with quill, ink and parchment.

Arthur slowly rose to his feet and eyed the gathering before him. "You are all welcome to our Spring Council Meeting in this year of Our Lord, five hundred and twenty-five. I call upon Abbot Asaph to give us his blessing." Arthur returned to his seat and muttering began.

"I expected some words on the security of his kingdom and the subjugation of our enemies. It has been the way in previous councils," Peredur remarked to an aide.

Elsewhere, King Cado of Dumnonia noted to a smirking Agravane, "That was a brief and tired welcome after two years of neglect."

The wan and frowning king beckoned to Herrig and bade him to summon, in turn, those with the authority to speak and then sent his squire for honeyed water to assuage his dry throat.

Over the next two hours, tribal leaders or their ambassadors gave their submissions on matters pertaining to their territories, reporting on security, food stocks, the numbers who had died during the summer plague and, most importantly, tax revenue collected. Arthur nodded and recited the customary greetings and thanks, but twice Ambrose urged him to speak louder. Alert at last, he leaned forward and gripped the arms of his throne when the chief of the Catuvellauni tribe, an earnest young man named Adminius, the son of his once-enemy, Caradoc, stood to speak.

"My lord and king, we are still manning the great dykes dug in the time of Ambrosius that mark the boundary of the lost lands of Lloegyr, beyond which the Angliscs and Saxons hold sway. But we have noticed more armed opposition, and have suffered increasing raids on our villages as they test our strength. I appeal to you, Arthur of the Britons, to send knights and men to curb the raids." He remained standing, jutting his sharp chin forward in expectation.

Murmurs surged through the roundel as Arthur pushed himself to his feet. "My noble Adminius, I knew your father in my youth." He smiled. "These complex matters of security cannot be addressed here. I invite you to come to my hall after this meeting to discuss the matter in the detail it warrants." The murmurs continued, edged with anger, at Arthur's apparent dismissal.

Herrig prowled the dirt where gladiators had once fought, fixing the delegates with a stern look to quell the dissent. He pointed his staff at a chief, inviting him to speak next.

Arthur stood and smiled, spreading his arms wide in welcoming the next speaker. "Ah, Dermot! My former squire, now a sturdy fellow - I congratulate you on coming of age and succeeding your father as Chief of the Deiran people!"

Dermot, blushing at the special attention, bowed to his king. "My noble king, and my second father, my thanks for the faith you have shown in me and for your encouragement…" He looked about him before continuing. "I have sad tidings to report, my lord. Our tribal fortress, Ebrauc, has again fallen into Anglisc hands." Concerned grumblings rippled around him and he paused, nodding in acknowledgement to left and right. "I have led my people northwards to Catteric, where we have sanctuary, but it is not our home. Noble Arthur, my father, I also appeal to you for help to once again rebuff this vile enemy."

Arthur stood, shaking his head in sorrow. "Since your father died, I have taken you to my side, and now to see you standing before me as your people's chief fills me with pride, but your plight is intolerable to me. Dermot, you must also come to my hall after this meeting to discuss these issues of great import to us all."

Peredur was next, the queen's brother and King of the Rheged, and he was warmly applauded as he took to his feet, having served loyally at Arthur's side since Badon. He reported that he had kept the Scotti and the Hibernians in check, but his affirmation of loyalty to Arthur was the briefest of courtesies and he looked ill at ease.

Next, Gawain's son, Gwyar, reported for the Goddodin tribe, northeast of the Great Wall. "My lord, I have been chief these past two years, since the peaceful passing of my noble father. We have sent men to reinforce Percival's Wall watchers on the eastern part of the Great Wall, where Anglisc raiders now menace the Brigante lands where you yourself are tribal chief."

This may not have been intended as a rebuke to Arthur for his negligence, but it was taken as one by the grumbling councillors. Herrig strode the floor, holding his staff above his head for silence.

Arthur pushed himself up once again and spoke with sorrow in his voice. "I still lament the passing of my great friend and mentor, Gawain, the best of warriors, and I regret that I have not travelled north of the wall in these past ten years, as I pledged to do. But I have not forgotten my oath to the Brigante people to protect them, and shall also welcome the north-eastern chiefs to my hall."

Arthur *Rex Brittonum*

Cadog the Silurian chief, King Owain of Powys, and representatives from Dyfed, Demetia all made brief reports. Then Gwynedd's new king, Maelgwyn, robust son of a mighty father, delivered a fulsome report.

"Ah, I see the dragon's fire in your manner, Maelgwyn, very like your father," Arthur said with a chuckle. "But what of your kinsman, Caratacus, who fought so fiercely at my side at Badon Hill?"

Maelgwyn let forth a deep, rich laugh. "Caratacus is well, my lord king, and sends you his good wishes. He says he is ready to fight under your banner again, as Badon was the best time of his life!"

Arthur clapped his hands in pleasure and joined in the laughter that rang around the arena, lightening the mood. "If you will release him, Head Dragon of Gwynedd, I shall be pleased to see him rally to my banner once again. We shall talk more of this in my hall after all have spoken."

Then Malachi, dressed in the finest clothing on display, spoke eloquently for the Dobunni and his elderly father, Gareth, who was bedridden with gout. Arthur nodded the while, but the finger tapping his chair arm told of his desire to be away. The prospect of another campaign had energised him, and his face wore a thin smile as the sun began to set over the western mountains.

Finally, Morgaise's son, King Cado of Dumnonia, stood and pushed back his sleeves. "My noble uncle and king, I can report an uneasy peace on our border with the West Saxons. My mother, the lady Morgaise, sends her warmest love to you and your family. She wishes me to inform you that she has founded an order of healers on an isle in the Lake of Avalon, in the marsh lands near Glastonbury, where she spends much of her time." He smiled at the cheers and applause before sitting.

Arthur drew himself up in his chair a little and grinned at his nephew. "I am glad to hear my sister has dedicated her island to the noble and holy cause of healing, and that the southlands are quiet. Although your borders are secure, Cado, I invite you to join us in my hall."

Arthur *Rex Brittonum*

Arthur looked expectantly at Ambrose, gripping the arms of his chair in readiness to rise, but was stayed by his chancellor rising to his feet and stepping down from the dais to speak from the gravel floor.

"My noble king knows I have held the position of chief of the Coritani since Maddox's death in the summer plague," Ambrose began, turning to address the delegates. He paused to bow his head in acknowledgement of the sympathetic groans that rumbled through the roundel. "I must add my voice to those appeals to my master, King Arthur, to honour his oath to my departed father and take Lindum back from the Angliscs. For although our long-standing enemy, King Icel, has died, his sons and his ruthless champion, Beowulf, do menace our lands."

Arthur nodded yet again and replied, "I solemnly acknowledge my pledge in this matter, and you must also join us at our hall, together with your fellow eastern chiefs. After you have collected the taxes, of course." The caveat on the end of his invitation was not gallant, reminding his chancellor of his duties before the whole gathering. He knew it and silently chided himself.

Arthur paused before introducing his knights – Bedwyr, Agravane, Lucan, Pinel and Mador - to call for a moment of silent prayer for the souls of their departed chiefs and all those who had perished in the pestilence of the last hot summer. His forehead was creased with worry as he called upon those with taxes to be paid to remain behind and see Ambrose, and those with security concerns to follow him and his knights to his hall for further deliberation.

A SYMBOLIC WICKER fence enclosed the cluster of buildings where Arthur, his family, and his closest supporters lived. Paved walkways connected the stone foundations on which sat timber-framed houses with thatched roofs. Arthur's queen, Gunamara, had insisted on only flower, herb and vegetable gardens within the compound, banishing animal enclosures with their attendant smells to a discreet distance beyond the stockade.

During the council meeting, Gunamara and her sons, Llacheu and Amhar, and daughter, little Gwen, sat in the garden with her visitors, Queen Anne of Powys, Arthur's sister, and other wives of chiefs with their children.

Anne took Gunamara by the arm and led her away from prying ears. "It sorely vexes me to see you so unhappy, my sister," Anne said, concerned and coming straight to her point.

"My husband has had his head turned by another lady, and in these past three years he is a changed man," Gunamara answered. Her answer was blunt and this was the first time she had been disloyal to Arthur, a heavy burden to unload on her sister-in-law.

"But who is this mysterious 'lady' and how did this come about?"

"You are diplomatic, but I know you will have heard about my husband's obsession with the lady called Guinevere. He speaks of her to me as the poor widow with a plucky outlook. It was Merlyn who led him to her, as he lives in that enchanted White Castle on the western borders of your lands. It is said that Merlyn has placed a spell on Arthur and that is why he looks distracted and uninterested in what is said to him. I feel invisible in his presence, dear sister."

She stifled a sob and let Anne hug her briefly, blinking tears from her eyes before continuing. "Arthur has visited that wicked place many times since he first went there three years ago, lying to me about where he is riding to. The knights he drags with him are angry and unhappy that he is distracted from the business of ruling this land. They are the source of gossip about my husband in our town. Arthur denies to himself that his name is taken in jest and the loyalty of his followers has waned. I fear for him and this land, dear sister. And I am angry and sad. I left behind all I held dear for him. And I feel the absence of my father so keenly that only my children preserve me." She turned and stared into Anne's green eyes, seeing Arthur's look there and hoping for a clue to a solution.

"I… I do not know what to say, dear Gunamara. This is terrible news, and much worse than I had thought. We must talk to him together and try to get to the crux of the matter. His first duty must be to his family and his kingdom. Perhaps he needs reminding."

Anne took Gunamara's arm and they walked past calming beds of lavender and sweet-smelling basil, waving a hand at dancing bees and butterflies. Before long, they heard the commotion of the men coming to the longhouse and broke off from their unhappy reflections to order attendants to the hall with firewood and refreshments.

They were too far from the roundel to see Peredur hold back from the line of chiefs filing through the gate to take Bedwyr by the arm. "Hail, friend, it has been a long year since we rode together. How are matters at court?"

Bedwyr stopped to look at him and gave a slight tilt of the head, knowing what he was being asked. "Hail to you, lord King. No longer the wilful prince, eager to ride at the enemy with no thought for your safety." They shared a laugh until the last had passed through the gate, then Bedwyr continued in a low voice. "It is good to see you, Peredur, and I wish my news of Arthur was better. Since we first went to that evil place, he has returned more than ten times, courting the lady Guinevere in an unseemly way, oblivious to the looks of her courtiers and his knights. Lucan and I usually accompany him, and have vowed not to besmirch his good name, but others are not so loyal."

Peredur shook his head in sadness. "This is not good for the kingdom, nor for my sister, his wife and queen. I will speak with her anon, but what can we do to separate him from these ne'er do wells?"

Bedwyr sucked in air and looked to the sky. "I have tried, but he rebuked me with angry words. He said it is on a matter of importance that he consults Merlyn, and brushes aside any suggestion of betrayal with the lady Guinevere. I do not want him to drive me away, for there are others who would whisper mischief in his ear and lead him further astray."

"Who would do that?" Peredur asked in alarm, gripping Bedwyr's arm.

"I have heard that Mordred is amassing an army across the Narrow Sea in Armorica, and is looking for an opportunity to raid this place. I have also heard that he has spies here, but I know not who."

"This is heavy news, my old friend. We must be vigilant and set our own spies to uncover the traitors who are close to the king. Now we must join the war council before we are missed, come."

ARTHUR LISTENED PATIENTLY to the troubles and pleas of his eastern chiefs before standing and spreading his arms for silence. "Some of you have chided me, more so with your eyes than tongues, for not patrolling the boundaries of Lloegyr these past few years and ignoring the growing threat from the Saxons and Angliscs."

He paused to blink through the smoky haze to the sombre faces before him. "Some say I was foolish not to have cut the heads off their kings at Badon Field…" His voice fell away and he tugged at his sleeves. "I… have also dwelt on that and wondered if our land would now be safer if I had done so, and visited their villages with terrible slaughter." He pulled a rag from his sleeve and wiped his nose and then blinked about him, his train of thought apparently lost.

Ambrose stepped forward from the gathering and said, "My king, we have enjoyed ten years of peace because of your victory at Badon. Those of us who were there remember that we had fought ourselves to a standstill and won by the narrowest of margins. We cannot blame you for your mercy, given in the belief that it would buy this very peace we have enjoyed." He turned to face his fellow chiefs with raised tone and eyebrows, drawing some grunts of agreement.

Turning back to Arthur he added, "But I must add my voice to those of my fellow chiefs in imploring you to ride out at the head of an army and show yourself to your people. You have gone unseen for too long."

Arthur Rex Brittonum

A chorus of 'aye' rang out around the dimly lit hall.

Arthur turned and moved slowly to his throne, his back hunched, as fatigue caught him at the end of a long day. Once seated, he slowly intoned, "You are ever wise and loyal, Ambrose." He exhaled deeply and drew in a lungful of air, adding, "I shall answer your call and lead my army to the east."

Cheers rang around the hall, causing Arthur to smile and nod at his followers. He felt his sinews tighten and a sudden surge of energy course through his body as he pushed himself to his feet and raised his arms. "But you must first return to your lands to gather your harvests and raise your fighting men. Then, we shall assemble on the plain before the gates of the Coritani town of Lindum three months from now. Gather supply wagons with food, and send a messenger to me when you are ready to march."

He paused to enjoy the mood of expectancy, noting that those loitering at the back had joined the press of bodies before him. "A month before that, I will lead my men to Verulamium to meet with the Catuvellauni and inspect the defensive ditches dug in the time of Ambrosius. We shall chase off any Saxons in that part. Then we ride north to take back Lindum, and north again to liberate Ebrauc. This is my vow to you, as your king!"

Raucous cheering and calls for ale rang out, and the mood of the hitherto sullen day was lifted to one of rejoicing. Outside, the women lifted their babies and made ready to return to their quarters, knowing that the men would be carousing and feasting long into the night.

Long shadows across the garden prompted a game for Arthur and Gunamara's children who jumped in and out of the leafy shapes, laughing and shouting as they evaded their mother's attempt to round them up.

"Perhaps I can be of assistance, my lady?" the deep voice of Agravane boomed out, contrasting with the playful cries of the children. He stooped and lifted up the wriggling toddler Gwen, and she kicked and screamed in his arms.

"Thank you, lord Agravane," Gunamara said, grabbing her daughter from the huge man with a smile. "You are welcome to help bring my children to heel. It is time for their wash before evening prayers and supper. But why are you not carousing with your fellow knights?"

"My lady, I would speak with you a moment if I may," he replied in a coarse whisper.

She saw a serious expression cross his face, and called for her maid to come and take the children to their house. "What is the matter?" she asked, leading him along the path into the shadows.

"I… I know not how to say this, but my fellows have charged me with speaking to you about a very vexing matter, my lady…"

"Then speak freely, sir knight. I will hold nothing against you."

"It is a delicate matter, for it relates to the king and… a certain lady." He stopped and looked into her eyes; his clean-shaven jaw set like a granite block.

Gunamara knew what was coming, but still held her breath. "Speak freely," she managed, sighing.

He spoke with urgency, glancing about for any signs of movement. "Some rumours may have come to your ears, and being a lady of virtue and a royal queen, you have dispelled them. But I must tell you that the rumours have substance, and that your husband, the king, is in love with the lady Guinevere and intends to bring her here to this place and his bed…"

Gunamara let out a little cry of anguish, causing Agravane to look about. "So, faithlessness worse than I ever imagined!" she cried out, and then was quiet.

Agravane leaned towards her and lightly held her arm. "I am sorry to be the bearer of such ill tidings, my lady, but you deserve to know that you will soon be replaced by a woman who is little more than a witch. Even the cause of the pestilence in which many died has been placed at their door.

You can see how the king wanders about in a lacklustre fashion, as if under a spell. Believe it, my lady, for it is true. I… we, fear for your safety and urge you to leave this place before the witch's curse falls on you and your…" His words trailed off; the meaning conveyed.

Gunamara breathed deeply and remained composed. "I cannot blame you for the doings of Arthur. He has brought this on himself and now we shall suffer the consequences. I thank you for your briefing, good knight, but I must be alone now to dwell on these matters." She turned and stumbled away from him, blinded by tears, and hurried along the path to the garden where earlier she had walked with Anne.

Agravane turned and followed the path back behind the longhouse to where Mador was waiting for him. "It is done, my brother," he reported with a smirk. "Now she is beside herself with fright and worry. She will confront Arthur and add to his woes, further weakening him in the eyes of his followers. Let us return to the feast before we are missed."

Chapter Four

SIX YOUTHS WAILED and protested, looking in terror at the men surrounding them, their bodies bound tightly with cords over sack cloth and jerking wildly under the oak branch from which they were suspended. Mordred, clean shaven, expensively dressed and sitting on a fine mount, tossed back the long black hair so much like his mother's and laughed at them.

"Bring me my crossbow," he demanded of an attendant. He turned to the twitching figures and addressed them. "You have been convicted of poaching deer from this royal forest of Armorica, and will now receive the punishment devised by myself and my host, Prince Catocus." He turned and grinned at Catocus, who was already armed with a crossbow.

"The most hits before the last one stops wriggling wins a purse of gold," Mordred said, taking aim.

He lifted the ingenious weapon to his shoulder and put light pressure on the release, sending a bolt flying through the air. It thudded into the chest of the nearest youth, silencing him. The target fell still as his fellows swung themselves more desperately, triggering nervous laughter from the watching attendants. The pair exchanged crossbow shots until their six victims were dead. Then they calmly rode away, debating who had won the bet and remarking on what an effective weapon of war the crossbow was.

"I shall send a unit of crossbow men with you, dear cousin, when you sail to Britannia to reclaim your kingdom," Catocus said, throwing a pouch of gold coins to his smiling guest.

"It shall not be long," Mordred replied, his black stallion keeping pace with his host. "I have turned two of Arthur's knights to my service and they will soon inform me of his movements. They grew tired of Arthur's empty promises of lands and wealth, but soon turned their ears to my own promises of the same!" Mordred let out a guffaw that startled his horse into tossing its head. "They are brothers and have a cousin in my service, and juicy missives sail between them. When Arthur next rides out from Caer Legion with his men, I shall take ship to the coast of Gwent and capture that place."

Catocus guffawed and flicked his reins to free his mount's neck of blood-sucking flies. "You have thought of everything, my cunning cousin. And I have heard your gold has added six hundred mercenaries to the exiled Britons who have flocked to your banner seeking a return to their homeland."

"Yes, and I am grateful that you allow me to assemble a fleet of ships in your harbour, Catocus. I have been away too long and yearn to meet my uncle on the field of battle."

"His power is waning as yours rises, like a blood moon over an enchanted forest. Your mother's magic will no doubt calm the seas before the bows of your ships!"

Mordred laughed and replied, "Yes, the old witch has her uses. She has also vowed to poison Arthur and his entire family. But I would prefer to separate Arthur's head from his body on a bloody field and parade it on a spike before his cowering knights. It will not be long."

WHEN THE SHOUTING started, the attendants scuttled to the dark corners of the great hall, far enough to be unnoticed but close enough to hear when summoned.

Gunamara, her face stained by dried tears, but set in fury, rounded on Arthur, whom she had cornered on his throne. "So, you are shameless enough to admit that this Guinevere is your whore!" She paced back and forth in agitation, having drawn the admission from her husband. "You have shamed me and your children, Arthur, and I shall never forgive you! You forget I am the daughter of the once-most powerful lord in this land! At least he has not lived to see this betrayal…"

"My lady, be calm," Arthur said in as soothing a voice as he could muster, "I have wronged you and enough know of it to make my denial… without point."

"Without point?" she screamed. "I had come here to ask you to give her up, but I can tell from your mumbling indifference that she has beguiled you completely, and little more remains than for me to leave with the children. I have made up my mind to go with King Owain and Queen Anne to Caer Cornovia." She glared at him with hands on hips.

Arthur knew she was a king's daughter with a will of hard oak, and would not be talked into remaining. He did not want to lose his family, but he had fallen so deeply in love with Guinevere that he longed to be with her every moment they were apart, and knew he would be unable to resist riding to the pleasures of her bed chamber again, as soon as he rid himself of his over-bearing wife.

"Then go to Powys and be at peace there. You always complained of this smoky hall and the rush mats underfoot. Go to the Roman luxuries of my sister's chambers and be at peace. I have seen that merchant, Barinthus, creeping about the place. I regret saving him from the clutch of pirates, for he has drained my purse these past years like a lamb suckling on a ewe's tit. Take him with you as you go. I can find no more words to say."

Gunamara shouted, "Foolish King! Have a care for your people or all shall be lost in that sorceress's lair!" She turned with a swish of her skirts and stormed out of the hall, leaving Arthur alone with his thoughts.

Arthur waved away attendants who meekly offered him food and drink, instead calling for his chancellor, Ambrose.

Ambrose strode lightly and with purpose across the empty hall towards Arthur, who noted, sourly, that his close friend and age-mate was still in the manly flush of good health and outward contentment that had deserted him.

"My dear Ambrose, I seek the wisdom of your counsel, as my head is a swirl of mist and I cannot see my way through it."

Concern creased Ambrose's face and he stepped onto the dais to place a hand on Arthur's arm, something few would dare to do. "I am most sorry to hear that you are troubled, my lord."

Arthur looked up to him and tried to smile, "But not here, my friend. Let us go to the abbey where I may also talk with my confessor, Asaph, for my soul is afflicted."

Ambrose bowed and waited for the king to rise and lead him from the hall. Arthur had decided to remain in the abbey until the queen and their guests were gone, for he could not face them without appearing weak, caught in a faithless act that stripped him of regal authority. He thought of Gerwyn who played at being kings, but with an air of foolishness intended to elicit laughter, and then shook his head to rid himself of these spinning torments as they approached the gate of the walled abbey in the manner of road-weary pilgrims.

A LOW MIST rolled off the River Usk at dawn and crept up green and dewy meadows, engulfing the feet of grazing cattle whose bodies seemed to float above it, stretching its fingers towards the walls of the abbey and the old Roman fort, where women and children busied themselves with fetching water, lighting fires or feeding their livestock.

The fields surrounding Arthur's Roundel were alive with visitors packing their goods onto carts, fitting yokes to the necks of lowing oxen or snorting horses, and saying their farewells to friends old and new met during the three days of the council.

Arthur looked on from a high window in the abbey, wringing his hands in worry and regret. He had done the right thing to commit himself to a military campaign that would settle the unease of his chiefs, but he felt wretched that his love for Guinevere, more like the addiction of excess of poppy oil that vexed wounded warriors, had destroyed his marriage, and threatened the peace of his kingdom. He had dreamed of Uther, the king he had seen only fleetingly in a victory parade as a boy, and his obsession with the wife of a noble that almost brought his kingdom to civil war. That union, between Uther and Ygerne, had led to his birth, and it now seemed that it was being repeated, like a curse from the gods of mischief. Perhaps that was part of the problem – his reluctance to wholly separate himself from the old gods and fully embrace the new, leaving him without focus and exposed to unsolicited influence.

"I must not have a child with Guinevere," he muttered under his breath.

A knock on the door pulled him from his reflection. "Come in," he said.

Ambrose entered and bowed, as if his king was a strange and distant figure to him. "My lord, King Owain has sent an attendant to inform you that he is leaving and asks if you will come to give your blessing for a safe journey."

Arthur stared at him for a moment, unsure of what to do.

"It must be these walls, Ambrose, that cause a man to turn on his inner thoughts, and implore God's forgiveness for errors made and offence given - and seek guidance."

Ambrose noted his distracted manner and dishevelled look and said, "Shall I tell him you are unwell with fever and under instruction from your healer to remain in your chamber to keep warm, my lord?"

"Erm… yes, and add that I send my blessings for a safe journey to them and to Queen Gunamara and our children… and I shall soon come to visit…" his words fell away and Ambrose stood, not yet ready to take his leave.

"There is another matter, my lord," Ambrose said after a brief silence. "King Peredur, the queen's brother, is also taking his leave, and with him all the men from Rheged who were in your service…"

"Then let them go," Arthur said softly, looking out of the window at a kestrel hovering above the mist.

Ambrose bowed to his back and hurriedly left.

MORGANA TURNED AN hourglass and set the sand falling, before turning her attention to the writhing body on the stone floor of her dispensary in the castle of Budic, the Armorican king. She leaned forward and studied the dying girl, who groaned and clutched her stomach. Morgana's assistant, a bony young woman wearing a beaked mask, rubbed her hands together in satisfaction at every jerky motion of the unlucky peasant girl. As the sands of life ran out, their victim shuddered and then she lay still.

"Five minutes from eating the poisoned apple to death, my lady," the assistant said, prodding the body with her finger to make sure.

"Are you sure no one will miss her?" Morgana asked.

"She is from the forest and came alone to the kitchen door selling sprigs of parsley, my lady."

"Well, we never saw her, did we? This poison is potent and will serve my purpose."

"Are we going on a ship to the old country, my lady?" the beaky assistant asked, dragging the dead girl by her feet towards an alcove.

"You are too curious!" Morgana snapped, cradling her jar of poison in her hands. Then her voice softened. "Yes, we shall be sailing in a few weeks from now. But before then, you must bring me a box of the juiciest apples you can find, picked the day before we depart. I intend to take a gift to my brother Arthur's court, one that they shall choke on for their last five minutes in this life."

Chapter Five

AN UNEASE FELL over Caer Legion in the days after the queen's leaving. She was much loved by the townsfolk and a source of great encouragement and livelihood to the craftsmen and women and traders who frequently visited the thriving town. The two hundred remaining men of Arthur's retinue trod lightly and spoke quietly for fear of being given impossible commands, as he continually changed his mind when giving them instructions and his moodiness kept them all on edge.

"Mador, where is your cousin, Agravane?" Arthur demanded of the young knight. His commanders had gathered in his hall for a briefing prior to his riding to the White Castle and stood in a line before the throne.

"My lord, if you recall, he asked your permission to accompany King Cado to Dumnonia, and you gave it."

Arthur blinked as he tried to recall if he had done so or not. "Ah, yes. That's right. They shall raise their men and meet us at Verulamium. Then you shall accompany me, Bedwyr and Lucan on our visit to the White Castle of Dinas Brân. Make preparations, for we leave at first light."

Mador bowed and stepped back into line.

Arthur turned to Cador, chief of the neighbouring tribe, the Silures. "Noble Cador, you shall make use of these summer days to raise no less than one hundred men and provide horses and training for them in the next three weeks, for they shall accompany us on our campaign to the east."

Cador bowed and replied, "My lord king, I have sixty Silurian horsemen at the ready, and will scour the outlying areas for as many again who can be trained for your service."

"Good. And make use of my captain of the guard in my absence to find these new recruits and see to their training. Herrig, see to it that more barrack blocks are prepared for the new arrivals."

Arthur *Rex Brittonum*

The tall Jute stepped forward and bowed, saying, "It shall be done, my lord. And I shall speak with your chancellor about supplies we shall need for the campaign."

"And you will be joining me, noble Herrig, for you are my good luck charm," Arthur replied with warmth. "Now let us all get to our tasks, for the crops will soon be ready for harvest, and after we shall ride out once more to secure our kingdom."

THE WALLS OF Dinas Brân were a dirty grey, and the grass beside the trail had turned brown, as there had been little rain. Arthur was welcomed like a returning hero by his lover, Guinevere, and she fussed over him in her gaily decorated hall.

Guinevere was in many ways similar in appearance to Gunamara, and no more than five years her junior. She was as tall as Arthur, and had long hair that hung to her waist when brushed, but hers had a reddish tint, whereas Gunamara's was of soft brown. Softness of word and movement allied to modesty and plain speaking were Gunamara's features, whereas Guinevere moved like a cat with a sway of the hips and had a habit of fixing her alluring green eyes with disturbing boldness on all those who crossed her path, making it plain that she was of a higher value. Even Arthur was subdued in her presence, and she most often guided the conversation, sitting at the head of her table, where once her husband had sat.

Guinevere reached out her long fingers and gripped Arthur's hand tightly at table, drawing dark looks from her son and smiles from her attendants. Arthur's knights tried their best to keep straight faces and show no opinion, fearful of the lady's withering look and sharp tongue.

She waited until those around her were locked in conversation before leaning close to Arthur and purred, "How is the lady Gunamara, my lord?"

Arthur looked at her helplessly, like a penitent sinner ready to confess. "The queen has gone, with the children, to my sister at Caer Cornovia, and we shall not be reconciled."

He felt a dryness in his throat and drank deeply from his goblet.

A smile briefly played across Guinevere's face, but was swiftly replaced by pursed lips and a frown, and concern tinged her carefully chosen words: "I am sorry to hear of your troubles, dear Arthur. But let us speak no more of this now for fear of prying ears." She sat back and looked along the table to see if she could catch any interested gazes, but all were consumed by conversation. From that moment Guinevere was impatient to curtail the evening, and whispered to an attendant to not bring any more from the kitchen.

After Arthur had finished his plate, she announced that the meal was over and stood to take her leave. Arthur would go to his room, as was the agreed protocol, and wait for Guinevere's handmaid to knock lightly on his door and escort him to Guinevere's chamber.

Arthur could feel his heart beating fast, like a lovesick youth, as he inhaled the sweet fragrance of sandalwood, and drank in the sight of his lover reclined on her bed in a thin gauze shift, surrounded by rose petals. She giggled as he almost fell over removing his leggings, and once his nightshirt was thrown off, he lay beside her on her bed. She allowed him a brief kiss on the lips before the questions came.

"Are you well, my lord?"

"I am full of fire for your love, my Guinevere," he panted, running his hand over the curves of her body.

"But will you take me to your hearth, Arthur?" she teased.

"You shall return with me to my royal enclosure, as my lady."

"But I will not be your mistress, Arthur. I would be your queen," she purred, stroking his hair.

"And you shall, my love," Arthur panted, moving closer to her.

She pushed his head from her breast and locked her eyes on his. "Then we shall return together to Caer Legion and I shall make our home there a warm and loving den. Give me a

Arthur *Rex Brittonum*

day to make ready. My son shall remain here with his uncle to rule over this stony and unproductive land."

"You have already given the matter some thought," Arthur murmured, kissing her neck.

"I can think of little else than being with you, Arthur, my love." With that, she wriggled out of her shift and enveloped him in her warm embrace.

As the first fingers of dawn crept to the shutters, Guinevere's maid knocked gently on the door and roused the sleeping Arthur, indicating she would wait outside until he dressed. Arthur left his lover sleeping and returned in a haze of mellow contentment to his chamber. He washed and dressed, and before long Bedwyr knocked on his door.

Arthur spent the morning with Merlyn. Wandering around his dispensary, he looked with unease at the Head of Brân.

Merlyn noticed and said, "It will not harm or enchant you, Arthur. The dreams you had were merely drawn from your spirit by a combination of ground poppy seeds, nutmeg and dried mushrooms – all perfectly natural plants. Together with the suggestion that the preserved head of Brân could commune with you, it was enough to stimulate the imagination that is the window of the spirit. In your case, you carry the essence of your parents, both of whom were guided by the gods of old in their plans for this ancient island of Albion. You are a part of that, Arthur, and I was naturally curious to know what visions you had had. Have you had any more dreams since that time?"

"I am sure I dreamt of my death, Merlyn, on a misty meadow beside a wandering river, where a line of faceless riders in black await me."

"Do you recognise the place?" Merlyn asked.

"I do not, but may do so if I ever come there. There was a line of trees before that bare meadow, and a white tree next to a woodman's hut in a glade with acorns strewn about it. That is all…" his voice faded as he tried to remember more.

Merlyn patted his arm and said, "Do not force it, Arthur. Perhaps that is all the gods wish to reveal to you. It is your destiny to face your fears at that dread place, and it may not be your end but that of your enemy."

"I pray to the God of Christ that it may be so, and that I will vanquish my enemies once again."

"I also pray for that outcome, dear boy. I feel both our fates are intertwined, like ivy creeping up a wall, and to that end I shall do all I can to aid you."

"Then you will accompany me to Caer Legion?" Arthur asked, sitting on the stool next to his old adviser.

"Oh yes, I have already instructed Nimue and my attendants to prepare our things. You must provide me with a new dispensary, and quarters for us four."

Arthur laughed, knowing he was somehow part of Merlyn's journey, and felt strangely comforted by that thought. "I am happy for it, dear Merlyn."

"But I am too old to sit astride a horse or even a mule," Merlyn chuckled, "so must lie on a straw mattress in a wagon. I will ask the lady for two wagons to carry my things." He looked about his room as if already calculating how he would pack. "I look forward to being of service again, my boy," he puffed, patting Arthur on the arm and stroking his long beard.

Arthur wondered at the age of Merlyn, studying his beard and ring of white hair around a bald patch, but felt it rude to ask and risk a sharp rebuke. "Then take the rest of day to make ready, for we may leave in the morning if the lady Guinevere is ready."

GUINEVERE AND HER maids inspected Arthur's adapted Roman villa with ill-concealed disdain, picking up the unwanted items that Gunamara had left behind and casting critical eyes over the sparsely furnished rooms.

"It is as Queen Gunamara left it," Arthur said. He glanced at the head of a wooden horse that protruded from under a low couch, left by his youngest child, and then quickly averted his gaze upwards at a cobweb on a beam in the abandoned family chamber.

"Then we have much to do," Guinevere said firmly. "It is as well that I brought some furnishings with me." She gathered her maids and Arthur's house attendants and gave out her instructions whilst Arthur stood in the courtyard, watching water spill from the mouth of a sea creature and trickle down the into the fountain's basin. Small birds jabbered and ducked their heads into the water in the warmth of the afternoon.

Guinevere appeared at Arthur's side, smiling as she took him by the arm. "My love, this villa shall soon be transformed into a home befitting the king of this island our ancestors called Albion. We shall do away with the conceits of Rome and make a new fashion that is appropriate for our Briton people."

"You are both wise and beautiful, my love," Arthur replied, admiring her unblemished white skin and the reddish waves of hair cascading over her shoulder.

"And tomorrow you shall send for the bishop of this place and instruct him to annul your marriage to Gunamara so that we can be wed," she said, lightly.

Arthur felt a shudder run through his body at his new love's mention of his wife's name. "As… as you wish, my dear. There is little to be gained from delays, particularly as I must ride out when the leaves fall to patrol with the eastern chiefs on their borders with the enemy."

Guinevere stopped their walk around the shaded portico and faced Arthur. "My love, do you not think that it is too soon to be leaving your new wife? Surely it would be better to delay your campaign until the buds of springtime sprout on the trees? Winter is no time to be laying siege to towns, and you are no longer a sprightly young man…"

"I am not yet an old man either, Guinevere!" He blurted it, raising his voice.

She put a soothing hand on his arm and quickly replied, "I did not mean to say you are old, my lord. Just that you have seen forty winters, by your own admission, and must choose your battles wisely. Autumn is but a brief season and the rains may turn the roads to mud. I feel you would be wise to see out the winter here with me in our new home. Then take to the road with brightly coloured blossoms, birdsong and the favour of the sun god to bless your cause." She leaned forward and kissed his cracked lips, and then stood back with eyebrows arched, waiting for his inevitable acquiescence.

"I... I suppose I could send messengers out to postpone the rally. Though I gave my solemn oath..."

"...And you will not be breaking it, my love. It is more prudent to wait for better weather and to give more time to amass a bigger army that is well-supplied," she purred.

Arthur grunted and took her arm again, guiding her around the enclosed space. As they approached the gate, he said, "Well, you have given me much to ponder, my dear. I shall take my leave to attend to petitioners in the hall. We shall talk this over in the evening."

THE NEWS OF Arthur's marriage to Guinevere and his delayed campaign reached the ears of Mordred and Morgana in Armorica.

"This delay is intolerable!" Mordred raged, throwing a goblet of wine at an attendant. He had gotten used to treating his host's castle and his attendants as his own, unaware that the elderly King Budic and his queen longed for him to leave and release their son from his cruel influence.

Prince Catocus smiled and said, "Be patient, my cousin, for Neptune is restless and the Narrow Sea is beset by storms. I fear winter has come early, and the time for warfare is past. We shall have more time to practise with our crossbows, and you shall have more of our men for your cause after the darkness gives way to light."

Mordred grunted and took to his feet, restlessly pacing the floor. "Arthur has a new queen, one younger and fairer, so my spy reports, than the one he cast aside. He will be loath to leave her come springtime. We shall stick to our plan to raid

Caer Legion, and perhaps capture his new queen, should she be left behind. That will enrage him and make him come to me."

Mordred grinned and clapped, turning to his mother, Morgana, who was finally showing the wrinkles and grey strands that she had kept at bay for some years. "Dear mother, what do you think about spending the winter here? It will certainly be less cold for your aging bones!"

The young men laughed as Morgana scowled. "Do not call me old, my son. If Arthur can still ride to war at the head of an army, then I can also go forth to make my mischief." She wrapped her shawl about her, as if in readiness for the coming season, her mind turning to thoughts of what mischief she might conjure.

Chapter Six

"WE HAVE SEEN the evidence with our own eyes!" Gildas shouted in exasperation at his tormentors, Abbot Asaph and Ambrose, who derived amusement from provoking the over-zealous novice.

"The queen has been attending holy mass with our king, and she has taken a personal interest in organising baptism festivities," Asaph chided, trying his best to imbue his tone with gravitas, whilst creasing his wide forehead into an ill-suited frown.

"Guinevere was seen dancing with the pagans at their illicit Sah-wen orgy in the forest, half naked by all accounts, whilst we were celebrating the Feast of All Souls in the chapel," Gildas persisted, pulling at a loose strand of hair above his ear – a familiar mark of his agitation. "The bishop shall hear of it."

Ambrose and Asaph shared a sly smirk, before Asaph replied, "It is accepted that our people mark the old festivals whilst becoming accustomed to Christian observances. Even the bishop notes the need for patience and forbearance in this matter. Come now, Gildas, don't be so critical of our new queen – she merely wants to be accepted and loved by our people."

"She is working with Merlyn to turn Arthur's eyes and soul away from the Church," Gildas muttered, his eyes rolling in his head. "We should chase that old druid into the forest where he belongs."

"Merlyn's presence has raised Arthur's spirits, and we can all enjoy the benefits of that," Ambrose replied. "And he keeps his own counsel and rarely shows himself. Dear Gildas, he is an old man in the autumn of his life – please show a little charity."

Gildas's cheeks were flushed with colour as he rocked from foot to foot before his elders, suspecting he was being taunted like a blindfolded dog beaten with sticks by callous children. "I… shall pray for them, lord Abbot," he stammered.

Asaph saw they had gone too far in teasing the young man and stood, putting a paternal arm around his shoulder. "Come now Gildas, let us be thankful for these years of peace, and rejoice at a contented king. Now go and rouse the other novices and meet me at the kitchen, where I shall instruct you all to clear the snow from our doors and gatehouse. You must all earn your supper."

IN TIME, THE snows melted and birdsong returned to the warming skies. The growing days turned Arthur's mind towards his promise. "Summon the captain of the guards, my knights and my lord Cadoc," he shouted at a guard as he bustled through slush to his hall in readiness to discuss the day's business with Ambrose.

"Ah, Ambrose!" he called across the floor as he strode with purpose to his throne. "Before you surround me with quarrelling farmers, I want to send out messages to all chiefs to honour their pledges and raise their men in the coming weeks. We must set our plans for our campaign in the east. For just as we note the lengthening days, so does our enemy, in their smoky longhouses in the lost lands of Lloegyr."

"And our people are needful of hope, your majesty," Ambrose replied, bowing with a smile. "I shall instruct my Coritani captain in Powys to raise the men in readiness to reclaim our ancestral lands, my lord."

"This is a good day, Ambrose. We shall summon the spirit of Mount Badon and once more ride out to remind our unwelcome settlers that this is the land of our fathers!"

Arthur's unexpected exuberance put a spring in the steps of all his attendants, who went about their tasks with a new sense of purpose.

Throughout the morning Ambrose prepared royal summonses, to which Arthur affixed his seal before signing them with a flourish. The northern and westerly chiefs were to assemble at Caer Cornovi in Powys and make ready to march eastwards on the road Arthur had previously taken, through the mid-kingdom mountains into the lands of the Coritani. Ambrose would lead the expedition with his Coritani exiles. They would fight their way to the walls of Lindum, if necessary, and there set a siege in readiness for Arthur's arrival.

Seeing his hall fill with knights and assorted commanders of the guard, Arthur stood and declaimed in a loud voice: "You shall all accompany me eastwards on the Portway road to Lundein and there chase off the Saxons. Then we go north to Verulamium and join with Adminius and his Catuvellauni warriors to patrol the dykes of Ambrosius. Once they are cleared of enemy insurgence, we will ride northwards to join you at Lindum, dear Ambrose. We shall likely arrive at the time of the Beltane celebrations, when we will mark the spring festival with the just slaughter of our enemy!"

Arthur's knights and attendants cheered and stamped their feet at the news. They saw their king once again infused with energy and the gleam had returned to his green eyes, and they rejoiced at the prospect of another campaign against the hated and feared Saxons.

No sooner had the messengers been dispatched than Guinevere and her maids appeared by Arthur's side. "My lord, you awoke early this morning and I can see you are happy with your men," Guinevere crooned in his ear.

"The time has come after the long days of winter, dear Guinevere, for me to ride out with my men and honour my pledge to my chiefs," Arthur replied with gusto.

Guinevere shooed her companions away and bent and kissed his cheek, whispering, "But my lord, do not be in such haste to leave me unattended. What if this place is attacked by your enemies?"

Arthur looked at her and dragged his thoughts away from his campaign. "I do not expect any attacks here, unless from the Hibernian raiders from the western isle. But do not fear, for I shall leave a knight and the captain of the guard with a company of men to guard you and patrol these lands, my dearest."

"I would be happier if you were to stay with me, my love, and send your men to fight your enemies in the east. Can you not forgo the hardship of weeks in the saddle and let me care for your comforts?" She widened her alluring eyes and pouted her lips, hinting at the joys of her company.

Arthur smiled and held her hand. "My love, I will sorely miss you, but we have been together every day for six months, and I am king of this land and must be seen by my people. It has been too long, and I know the time has come for me to ride at the head of my army once again. My earnest hope is that this will be the last campaign, that I can vanquish those who would push us aside, so that we may grow old together in peace."

She pulled her hand away and smiled, knowing he had made up his mind and would not be persuaded otherwise. "Then let us spend as much time together as possible before you leave, my love. I shall prepare your favourite dish of roast partridge and garden vegetables for our evening repast. I will leave you now to your preparations and to make sacrifice in my temple for your success, my lord."

She turned abruptly and marched out, her maids trailing behind. The knights whispered that she seemed displeased, but Arthur appeared not to notice and called for ale to be served.

AGRAVANE AND MADOR joined in the toast to Arthur's success and then quietly took their leave from the hall.

"I must take to ship to tell Mordred of this news," Agravane whispered when they were away from others.

"And I shall ask Arthur to let me stay and guard the Queen," Mador replied. "Once Mordred has taken Caer Legion, he will draw Arthur into the battle that will decide the fate of this island."

"Aye, and we can only hope that Arthur's army is reduced in number by his war against the Saxons and Angliscs. Our lands and titles will follow once Mordred defeats him and takes the throne."

The brothers grinned and clasped arms, believing their time would soon come.

"Arthur is getting old and must make way for his younger nephew – it is the natural order of things," Mador added, glancing over his shoulder. "Time to re-join the throng before we are missed. We have much to do in the next few days."

CAER LEGION WAS alive with warriors sharpening their blades, attending to their quilted padding, knocking dents out of helmets, laughing and throwing out challenges for mock fights. Women fussed around simmering pots of broth over camp fires; children carried buckets of water from the river in the background as soldiers were put through their paces; and archers on horseback fired arrows from their small bows at targets set up on riverine meadows.

Bedwyr, Arthur's age-mate, pulled up sweating, his unit running ahead. Arthur broke off from supervising the archers to ride to his side.

"Bedwyr, you have a girth like mine after years of feasting. I blame myself for not sending you out more often on patrol!"

"We have enjoyed each other's company these past years, my lord," he puffed. "Now it is time to sharpen our blades and test our sword arms against younger men." Bedwyr drew himself up, holding his side.

"We have eight hundred, enough to start our march to the east," Arthur said, looking over his faithful knight's head to the units of fifty, at their training under noisy commanders eager to prove themselves.

"Aye, and with the men from the north set to join us at Lindum, we shall remind the Saxons whose country this is."

"Then instruct our commanders to brief their men that we shall march in two days, once the supply wagons are full." He looked down at his trusted adviser and added in a low voice, "Mador has asked if he might remain to guard the queen and command the garrison in my absence, whilst his brother, Agravane, has ridden south to raise the men of Dumnonia. I am reluctant to leave a trained knight behind – what think you of this?"

Bedwyr paused before giving his answer. "My lord, you need a commander with authority who has the respect of the men. Either a knight or Herrig should remain, together with fifty men, I think."

"Yes, it is important the queen feels safe and that I am not putting her at undue risk. Mador it is, for I want Herrig by my side. He has saved my life twice in battle, and I feel the need to have him with me. The men talk of me being invincible as if protected by the gods. If only they knew. I am sitting here because of the bravery and skills of Gawain, Varden and Herrig. Only Herrig remains."

"He would die for you ten times over my lord," Bedwyr replied with a grin, "and it is important that the men believe you cannot lose. As for Mador, we can only hope that he would die for our queen," he added wistfully.

Arthur glared at his oldest friend, sensing doubt. "I will tell Mador that he MUST protect the queen at all costs, even at the loss of his men and his own life!"

"They are Gawain's nephews and were admitted to knight's training on his say. They would not betray you, lord," Bedwyr replied softly, patting the flank of Arthur's stallion, Son of Mars. He bowed and jogged off to find his unit, leaving Arthur to kick his mount into a charge across the well-trodden grass, whooping and yelling at no one in particular but drawing cheers from those men who stood by.

Chapter Seven

MORGANA AND HER three attendants jostled past sailors, soldiers and slaves balancing boxes and bundles on their shoulders on the busy quayside. Ships were being loaded with arms and provisions for Mordred's invasion force, and Morgana was looking for the merchant vessel she had hired for her own crossing of the Narrow Sea. She spotted the ship's captain, a squat fellow who looked more pirate than honest man, shouting orders to his crew.

"Hail fellow!" she shouted from under her hood. "The day has come for my journey to the port of Gwent. How soon can you be ready?"

The black-eyed captain turned his thick neck, morning sunlight glinting off a silver earring, and fixed his stare on his latest customer. "My lady, we are set fair to leave on the next tide if you wish. The sea is calm and the wind freshening from the south. But shall we leave ahead of the fleet?"

"Yes, we shall leave ahead of the fleet, and you must go quietly about your business as I wish our exit to go unnoticed. They will most likely follow in a day or two, but I must lay the groundwork for their expedition." She held his stare until he looked away.

"As you wish, my lady. I estimate the tide will turn in two hours from now."

"Then we shall be here and ready." Morgana turned on her heels and marched away, pushing through the throng, trailed by her minions.

THE IMPERIAL WALLS of Caer Gloui rose before Arthur as he led his army over a well-kept bridge onto a wide plain. He marvelled at how flawless this Roman fortress remained, its flags flying proudly from the corner towers and gatehouse.

Turning to Bedwyr he remarked, "It is as if the gods have frozen time and Agricola's legions are now approaching. They have maintained it well."

"The grandson of Ambrosius is proud of his heritage, my lord," Bedwyr replied.

"Aye, and for all his distance from me, I would welcome his counsel."

Arthur detailed his commanders to set camp outside the walls and entered through the gatehouse with Bedwyr, Cador and Herrig. They were greeted by an elder and led into the great hall where they strode over polished paving slabs and tiled mosaics, noting the sweet smell of incense and the absence of soiled rush mats underfoot. Clods of earth dislodged from their boots, but slaves with reed brushes appeared from the shadows to sweep up after them.

Arthur felt strangely soothed at the sight of the imperially garbed Malachi, still thin but now balder and more wrinkled of face, unlike the last time he had come here in confrontational mood. Aside from his curt public report at the last council meeting, when Malachi's entourage was amongst the first to leave, they had not spoken since then.

"Ah, Arthur, welcome! And this time I can welcome you as king!" Malachi chirped in his reedy voice.

"Lord Malachi, we missed you at Badon, but were happy that your banner did not fly on the other side!" Arthur replied, clasping his host's forearm and grinning at him.

"You have a long memory, Cousin. I had received the Lady Morgana and her burly Saxon escort a few days before, in this very hall. They pleaded with me, then made their veiled threats, but I remained steadfast in my neutrality. I did send out my scouts to watch the battle and had my men at the ready, but for what outcome I knew not... I beg your forgiveness and pledge my support to your cause, for I now know you are the true heir of my grandfather."

Arthur leaned back and did not hide his surprise at this candid account and show of fealty. "You are ever known for your plain speaking, and you speak well, my lord. I bear you no grudge and understand your predicament at that time, and can only offer my thanks for holding fast in the face of my determined sister. By God's grace, we won the day."

"Praise be, and my prayers were answered, Arthur. You have brought peace and stability to this land these past ten years, and the people are grateful. But now I see you are once again dressed for war. Come to my table and tell me all."

Arthur ensured that Malachi was aware that his western neighbour, Cador, chief of the Silures, was now a trusted commander in his army, and that they would soon be joining with his eastern neighbours, the Catuvellauni. "I will not command you, noble Malachi, but entreat you to provision us for our expedition eastwards against the encroaching Saxons, and ask for whatever men you can spare."

Malachi sipped quietly from a jewel-encrusted golden goblet and eyed his king over the rim. "I would never dare to refuse you twice, King Arthur. I shall provide a wagon of healers, as before, and two wagons of food and ale. Following the council meeting, I have dwelt on this matter, and have prepared a company of men, led by my captain of the guards, a stout fellow named Gaheris, for your service."

He waved to the wings and a burly warrior with broad head and shoulders stepped from the shadows. His eyes were set deep beneath a single overhanging brow and his thin lips were firmly compressed, showing no opinion or emotion.

"Come forward, Gaheris, and meet your king," Malachi said, with a flourish of a purple sleeve. Arthur smiled and asked Herrig to stand next to him. The two captains seemed a match in height and bulk, although Herrig was the older.

"Welcome, Gaheris!" Arthur shouted eagerly, and stood to embrace his new commander. "I am pleased to have you ride at my side. How many men do you have? How many horses?"

"My company has one hundred riders and two hundred on foot, my king," Gaheris boomed in a deep voice that carried across the hall.

"Excellent! That swells our numbers to over a thousand – a match for any Saxon rabble who stand in our way!" Arthur sat, smiling broadly to show his pleasure at this unexpected gain. He must now rely on younger, stronger leaders on the field of battle, acknowledging the limitations of his age. He called for a goblet for Gaheris and proposed a toast to their success.

Malachi smiled and sipped quietly, ignoring the breach of protocol in his hall. Arthur was exuberant and behaving like a king in his own fortress, but Malachi was content to have played his hand well, for he would be the beneficiary of a successful campaign to keep the feared Saxons at bay.

"A feast this evening, in your honour, Arthur, King of the Britons!" Malachi squeaked; his words swallowed up in the din of the raucous warriors.

"MANANNON IS SLEEPING," the captain growled.

"We have made good time, as you said we would," Morgana replied, eying the waving marsh reeds to their sides as the single-mast vessel slipped into the narrowing river estuary.

Turning his thick body, the captain shouted to his crew. "Drop the sail and ship out the oars!"

A black cloud of birds marked their arrival at the seaport that once received Roman galleys to weathered piers that jutted into the river like a row of rotting teeth. The huge flock swooped overhead, forming shapes that held different meanings for the awe-struck sailors, passengers and folk milling about the quayside. Muddy paths radiated outwards towards warehouses and hostelries. It was towards an inn whose sign depicted a green dragon that Morgana went, lifting her skirts above the mud and glancing about from under her hood.

It was Mador who awaited her, sitting in a corner booth with two of his men for company. He rose to greet her, his lank black hair hanging about his leather jerkin, a wary smile cracking his dry skin.

"My lady, may I welcome you to the Kingdom of Gwent," he whispered, mindful of her desire for secrecy.

Morgana removed her leather gloves and pushed back her hood, eying his comrades with suspicion.

"My men will leave us to our business, my lady." He motioned them to vacate the table and Morgana took her seat.

"Some ale and cakes, my lord Mador, to assuage my dry throat and quiet my belly." She looked about her at the decrepit interior of what once was a Roman mansio where traders and other travellers would have stayed, its lime-washed walls now hosting patches of green mould and the running stains of spilt ale. The windows, a patchwork of glass and horn, were so dirty that oil lamps and candles on stands lit the gloomy room, even though it was still the day.

Mador signalled to a maid and then clasped his hands together to stop his inclination to fidget. "My lady, how was your passage from Armorica?"

Morgana fixed the younger man with a steely stare, causing him to shift uncomfortably. "The gods saw fit to speed me to my revenge. My son's fleet will follow in two days, so set your men at the ready to seize this port to ensure they disembark with ease. There will be horses and supplies."

"It shall be done, my lady."

"How many men do you have?"

"A dozen who owe their loyalty to me and my brother. We dare not widen the net of those who know our hearts…"

"Then it will have to do."

"I am the commander of the garrison, my lady, and will post my men to guard the port."

"And what of a dwelling for me and my maids? I need a place close to where the queen stays, but hidden from curious eyes." The cruel glint in her gaze betrayed her intentions.

"The… queen lives in a villa enclosed in a stockade of sharpened stakes, with a guarded gatehouse. Arthur has detailed six of his most trusted men to maintain a guard day and night."

"Then I must draw the lady out, or gain access to her kitchen…" Her voice trailed off as she thought of possibilities.

"One of my men has a daughter who is a kitchen maid there. She could take you. Do you have the power of invisibility, my lady?"

"I see my reputation precedes me," she said, and rolled her eyes.

His ears reddened. "A disguise, then?"

"Yes. I am prepared for that." She gulped two mouthfuls of ale and then asked, "And how is my brother, Arthur?" before biting down hard on an oatcake.

"The comforts of his hall have softened him these past years – he is not the warrior king he was up to the time of Badon. His knights live like beggars, travelling the land to seek out food and shelter. He has paid us little mind and our pleas for land have gone unheeded. Then his head was turned by a pagan sorceress from the dark interior of our land. She has cast a veil of gloom and despondency over his people, who did love the old queen he cast out."

Morgana's throaty cackle drew quizzical looks from other patrons. She glared at them and they looked away. "The day draws to an end, Mador. Lead us to our abode, and bring that kitchen girl to me. I am eager to meet with this Guinevere and be the cause of as much anguish to my little brother as is possible – to addle his brain with a grief that will lead him to act out of rage and make mistakes that will cause his downfall."

"Indeed, my lady," Mador agreed, "and so speed us to the final battle when Mordred will vanquish the old fool." With a sweep of their cloaks, the plotters departed the inn and strode on the paved pathway to where the unsuspecting town of Caer Legion lay on a bend in the fast-flowing River Usk.

Arthur Rex Brittonum

Chapter Eight

NEWS REACHED MERLYN in his cluster of huts on the forest's edge that an old woman accompanied by three attendants had been led by Mador's men to a woodcutters' dwelling close by.

"Bring my cloak, Nimue, we must investigate these new arrivals," he declared with sudden vigour. "This could be the moment I have seen in my visions."

"Why are you interested in these people, lord?" she asked.

"Because they were brought here by Mador's men, and I do not trust him. Something is afoot. Bring a basket of herbs and mushrooms for the lady Guinevere's kitchen, for I have a feeling our path may lead us there."

Merlyn fussed about his work bench, stuffing objects into a satchel, before fastening on his sword belt, donning his hat and cloak and gripping his staff of gnarled oak with its polished ball at the head. The morning was grey and a light drizzle greeted them as they hurried along a winding path that hugged the edge of the forest, passing turnip patches separated by hillocks of grazing sheep.

"Go ahead and search those huts for signs of people. If you find anyone say you are seeking shelter," Merlyn ordered his ragged followers, before climbing to the top of a hillock to sit and wait. Rainclouds scudded northwards and a shaft of pale sunlight fell on the old healer as he found a flat rock to sit on. He faced south, where he could smell the sea salt in the air and noted the cries of big white and grey sea birds bullying their smaller kind from the skies.

"It was ever the way," he muttered to himself.

In a short while, Nimue returned to him. "They are empty, but one has still warm embers in the fireplace, lord," she panted.

"Are there footprints?"

"Yes, lord. The prints of well-made boots, not the shoes of forest folk. Leading in the direction of the town."

"Then let us follow."

Their path sloped downwards, past ploughed fields and animal pens, towards the river that cut through the valley and the walls of the ruined fort and proud abbey. Their path reached a fork, and Merlyn carefully studied the muddy footprints before pointing away from the fortress towards Arthur's hall and private buildings hemmed into a wooden stockade.

Merlyn greeted the guard, a fellow known to him, and asked if any visitors had been admitted that morning.

"Yes, an old lady with a box of fresh, crisp apples she says have come from the orchards of Gaul," he replied with a smile, adding, "I have one here I'm saving for later."

Merlyn inspected the plump red and bright green apple, noting how unlike it was from the smaller dark green ones grown locally. He noticed a pin prick at the centre of a small circular bruise on the underside and raised his hairy eyebrows. "Do not bite this apple before I return, good friend. And do not let the visitors leave this place. Come Nimue, make haste to the kitchen."

They hurried along a boardwalk, displacing slaves and attendants carrying pots of water or bundles of firewood, who had to step into the mud. Reaching the whitewashed low stone wall of the villa, they moved around it to the rear entrance. Chickens clucked and fussed about their feet – something the previous queen had banished to beyond the stockade walls. Outside the kitchen door a group of three women huddled, their cloaks of fine burgundy wool marking them out from the servants going about their errands.

"Where is your mistress?" Merlyn demanded of one, towering over the crouching figures. She would not speak to him, but her glance flickered towards the kitchen door. The healer ducked to walk under its lintel, muttering to Nimue, "Follow me, with your basket."

Once inside the kitchen, he saw a hooded woman standing by the kitchen table with the cook, holding an apple in her hand. A box of apples stood on the table between them. "Ah, Morgana, it has been a long time," he said softly.

Morgana looked up in alarm, pushing back the hood from her lined and sallow face, her grey-streaked hair half-covering one eye. Her mouth screwed up in anger and she scraped her hair aside, glaring at Merlyn with fierce black eyes. "I did not expect to see you so soon on my visit, Merlyn," she growled through clenched teeth.

"Only after you had served poisoned apples to Queen Guinevere. You have come to settle old scores, I think, my unhappy apprentice."

The cook gasped and backed away as Morgana tilted the box towards Merlyn, spilling the fruit across the table. She moved around the table with surprising speed, drawing a dagger from her belt, as apples bounced on the stone tiles between them. Merlyn braced his staff in both hands before him, ready to parry any blows.

Morgana screamed in hateful rage and lunged forward, the point of her dagger aimed at Merlyn's midriff. He dodged to one side and brought his staff down hard on her wrist. With a cry of pain, she dropped the dagger to the floor, and Merlyn stepped forward, slamming the ball of his staff into the side of her head. Behind him, he could hear a commotion as Nimue fought with Morgana's maid, their snarls sending all others fleeing from the room, the contents of her basket adding to the mess on the floor.

Morgana fell onto the table and her hand grabbed the handle of a pot. Without pause for breath, she swung it towards Merlyn, connecting with his elbow. The old healer howled in pain and staggered backwards. Morgana quickly bent and picked up her dagger from the floor, and in one continuous movement threw herself at Merlyn, who was leaning away from her and off balance. Somehow, he managed to nudge his satchel to his front, and it took the force of the dagger's point. With his left hand, he brought his staff down onto the top her head, but the blow was weak and she shook it off, as if dismissing a persistent wasp, before renewing her attack.

Merlyn grabbed her wrist and pushed the point of the dagger away from him, whilst reaching for the handle of his short sword with the other, his staff now lying on the floor. The teacher's grey, watery eyes locked with those of his former pupil, feeling the strength of her arms and knowing he had no advantage there. Her breath was in his face and her black eyes shone with malice – this was no embrace of lovers, as once it might have been had he not scorned her. She fought with the ferocity expected of Uther's daughter, belying her age, snarling like a cornered wild cat, holding Merlyn's sword hand and slowly pressing downwards with her dagger.

"You… are… left-handed, I should have remembered…" Merlyn groaned as the point of her blade pricked his skin through his woollen garment. He pushed her hand with all the strength he could summon. "Arawyn, give me strength!" he muttered through clenched teeth.

She laughed in his face, and he wondered if the smell of oat bread and barley would be the last sense he would experience as his weakening arm gave way. "Your gods of the forest will not save you, Merlyn," she replied as she put all her weight behind her dagger thrust.

Prompting a hollow groan, the returning blade pierced his skin, scraping the chest bone whose purpose was to protect the heart. This Merlyn knew, and with his last morsel of strength, he twisted his body away from the knife, falling backwards and pulling down shelves of jars with his flailing arm, sending dried beans scattering across the floor. A falling jar hit Morgana and she stumbled, slipping on the dried beans beneath her boots. With a cry, she fell backwards, hitting her head on the edge of the table and knocking herself senseless.

Merlyn surveyed the scene of devastation in the kitchen, and saw Morgana's maid – her throat cut by Nimue, her lifeless eyes looking at him, her blood mixing with herbs, mushrooms, apples and beans on the worn flagstones.

"What is this madness?" Guinevere shrieked from the doorway, her maids cowering behind her skirts. "Merlyn, explain!"

The old healer, slumped against the wall, looked up, his white hair splayed across his shoulders, blood oozing between his fingers from the wound to his chest and staining the point of his beard. "My lady, you were visited by Morgana, who had brought you some… juicy, poisoned apples from Gaul. Please instruct your people to not… eat the apples…" his weakening voice drifted away and he sagged to his side, unconscious to the cries that filled the room.

ARTHUR AND HIS commanders were gathered under an awning on the field before the gates of Lindum when a messenger arrived.

Arthur received the panting youth with bulging eyes, noting the wolf's head emblem of Rheged on his tunic. "What news of King Peredur?" he asked.

"My lord king, my master, King Peredur, sends his love and God's blessings for your victory, and this missive." He handed Arthur a scroll on bended knee. Arthur slipped off the ribbon and noted the royal seal. He read with furrowed brow and then handed it to Ambrose, his expression showing discontent.

"Wait outside for my reply," Arthur curtly said in dismissing the messenger. He turned to his commanders and said, "So, Peredur will not join us here, and makes vague noises about reinforcing the Wall as his priority. I knew this would happen. I have lost a powerful ally through my faithless rejection of Gunamara."

Ambrose finished reading and looked up. "He has not broken faith with you, my lord. He will surely join your ranks once you reach Ebrauc in the north."

"You have high and sunny hopes of every situation, dear Ambrose," Arthur grumbled, rubbing his chin. "Yes, I shall send a rider for him when we reach the north, as you say. But for now, we must lay siege to this fortress with the men at our disposal. Let us wait no longer and bring up the rams to their gates."

Following a swift and successful series of skirmishes on the border between the Catuvellauni tribal lands and Lloegyr – the lost lands of the east – Arthur had moved northwards on the old Roman Ermine Street to the fortress of Lindum, now in the hands of the Angliscs. He had no choice but to risk losing men in an assault on their great oak gates, to fulfil his oath to his chancellor, Ambrose, now the chief of the local tribal, the Coritani.

Arthur gave orders to his commanders and chiefs, each commanding about two hundred men – Brian of the Coritani; Viroco or the Cornovi; Adminius of the Catuvellauni; Caratacus of Gwynedd; Gaheris of the Dobunni and Cadoc of Siluria. They would pair up and lead assaults on three gates, whilst Arthur and his knights – Bedwyr, Lucan and Pinel, would form the reserve and lead their mounted archers in peppering the defenders on the walls with their arrows. Some were veterans of Mount Badon, and some were young commanders eager for their first taste of battle.

They stood facing each other in a circle with the tips of their drawn swords touching. Arthur held Excalibur firmly and said, "May God bless us this day so we may drive out the pagans and reclaim this noble town for Christ and the Coritani once more."

"Amen," they responded.

"Then go to your men and make ready. Let the attack commence."

"A MODEST ROMAN villa was never going to be enough to contain Guinevere," Merlyn muttered, treading with caution from one flat stone to another, his left arm held by an attendant to steady him. He had remained in one of the guest rooms at Guinevere's insistence to be treated by her healer. His knife wound had been cleaned and stitched, and after two weeks he was strong enough to walk around the cluster of buildings that now surrounded the villa, inspecting the activity of Guinevere's people, and then resting in the temple she had had made to one of the more obscure gods of Western Cambria.

Merlyn had bonded with her druid, a young fellow who insisted on displaying his crooked teeth through his frequent grins, and he enjoyed their morning chats in the quiet glade behind the villa, a screen of trees enclosing the small stone building for privacy. He would also pay a visit to Morgana on his rounds, imprisoned in an outhouse but otherwise well treated.

"With the warming days, it will soon be time to celebrate the Festival of Light to honour our goddess Litha," Merlyn remarked to the attentive druid, inspecting the crudely painted murals of a druidic sacrifice on the walls.

"Yes, lord Merlyn, and I would welcome your leadership in that," the younger man replied, bowing and wringing his hands in anticipation.

"I have some ideas," Merlyn airily replied, rubbing his truncated beard – the bloodstained patches had been excised by the healer as he slept. "I last staged a huge festival in honour of Litha on the eve of the Battle of Badon…"

His words were cut short by a boy, summoning him to Guinevere. He stood slowly and stiffly made his exit into the warmth of the sun, muttering, "We shall talk more on this."

Guinevere waved an arm without rising and Merlyn hobbled to an armchair, avoiding the low couches.

"I am pleased to see you moving about, Merlyn," she said, fixing her bold green eyes on the old man whilst twisting her long plait of red hair.

"You are kind, my lady," he replied, lifting a goblet of berry juice from a tray and sniffing it. "Red currants and blackberries saved from last season."

"To speed your recovery." She waved to her hand maids and continued, "What do you think we should do with that old witch? Arthur will not return for at least two months."

"I fear that Mordred may come looking for her. We cannot help that," he replied, taking a sip. "Have you sent word to Arthur?"

"Yes. But I do not expect a reply soon. He may think this... incident trivial."

"Then we must keep her under your watchful eye. It is only you or the commander, Mador, who could make a decision on whether to move her."

"I do not trust that fellow," she replied tartly, popping a fig into her mouth.

"Nor I. It is not like Arthur to make an error in judgement. He has always seen into the hearts of men and determined their loyalty with remarkable accuracy. I remember the time..."

"Yes, yes. Spare me your stories of his days of glory. His judgement may not be what it once was."

Merlyn decided not to contradict her. "We all grow old, my lady, and old men can make fools of themselves..." He checked himself in alarm, but it was too late.

Guinevere's eyes flared in anger and she rose to her feet, jabbing a long finger at him. "...And he is a fool for taking me as his queen, you were about to add!"

"No, my lady, that thought did not cross my mind." Merlyn shrank back into his seat, fearing one of Guinevere's famed tantrums.

But she was distracted by her maids re-entering the room and checked herself, drawing in a sharp breath. "I shall let that pass, Merlyn. But you have spoiled my moment. However, I want to present to you a gift for saving my life from that evil witch and her poisoned apples." She beckoned her maids forward. They were holding a finely woven cloak of red wool, with an intricately carved neck clasp of silver and gold.

Merlyn stood and his eyes widened in amazement. "My lady, this a wondrous gift!"

"It shall replace the bloodied one we collected from the kitchen floor and duly burnt. Now that you can walk, perhaps you are well enough to return to your dwelling?"

"Oh yes, thank you, my lady. I shall collect my things and wear this in your honour." Merlyn bowed, his cheeks matching the colour of the cloak that the handmaids now fastened around his neck. He passed an attendant at the door, and the portly merchant, Barinthus, who was waiting outside. Bows were exchanged and Merlyn shuffled to his quarters, pleased with the cloak and glad to be leaving.

"Ah, Barinthus," Guinevere said, her mood lightening, "what beautiful wares have you brought for my perusal?"

Barinthus bowed with a flourish of his wrist that drew giggles from the maids. "My lady, I have listened to your heart's desire to decorate your rooms with treasured objects that speak more of our native values than that of our former masters. To this end, I have gathered these prized ornaments and carpet from my travels." He clapped his hands, silver bracelets jangling, and pushed back his sleeves. Two attendants entered with a rolled carpet and placed it at his feet.

The portly merchant moved as daintily as his curved satin slippers would permit, indicating that the carpet should be unrolled before the feet of the queen. Guinevere and her maids gasped in wonder at the dozen-or-so objects, and she bent to pick up a stag's head fashioned in bronze, with sparkling blue jewels for eyes.

"My lady has good taste," Barinthus gushed, rocking on the balls of his feet, his podgy fingers clutching his purse.

Her maids dropped to their knees to inspect the objects – golden goblets; ornate silver candlesticks; a wood carving depicting the four seasons; a miniature cauldron streaked with different coloured metals. The carpet depicted a hunting scene.

"You have excelled yourself, Barinthus," Guinevere purred, caressing the objects. "Now let us agree a price." She clapped her hands and a male entered carrying a wooden chest. He placed it on a low table and she sat to open the lid. "I have bags of silver coins, and even a small amount of gold aurei, and some bars of lead and silver. Name your price."

Barinthus smiled and signalled to his attendant to bring his scales. "I value all these items at ten Roman libra, my lady. I have scales here for your lead and silver ingots."

"Ten libra sounds rather a lot," she growled in a low voice laced with menace.

"But for you, gracious queen, and for the noble King Arthur… let me weigh your bars and I shall see about a reduction." He took her lead and silver ingots and weighed them, sucking his cheeks and pouting. "May I see your coins, please?"

Guinevere threw three leather pouches at him, and he sat in the armchair that Merlyn had vacated before pouring the silver coins into his palm. He studied the emperors' faces and made two piles. This he repeated with the second bag, and in the third was delighted to see gold coins.

"I will only take what I feel is fair, my lady. These few silver coins from the time of Claudius or earlier, and ten gold aurei, in addition to two ingots each of lead and silver." He smiled and awaited her response.

"Why do I feel you are cheating me, Barinthus?" she said, standing. She was taller than him and approached him like a lioness about to pounce. He flinched as she grabbed the bag of gold coins. "Shall we agree on five gold aurei and ten silver coins with the higher silver content from the reign of Claudius, plus two lead ingots and one of silver?" Her green eyes bore into the brown pin pricks in his puffy face, as beads of sweat stood out on his forehead.

"That would be most acceptable, Your Highness," he stuttered, grinning as he mopped his brow. He had obtained these unwanted items in exchange for modestly valued Roman goods with Malachi and other chiefs, so this was a bonus deal for him.

Guinevere stood and smiled. "Good. Now leave me in peace to enjoy my new treasures."

Arthur *Rex Brittonum*

Barinthus took his payment and hurried to the doorway, turning to bow briefly on his way out. He almost toppled the bard, Gerwyn, who was also waiting his turn to see the queen.

Two hours later, Barinthus was at the port. He had sold his horse and six mules to a horse trader and now searched the taverns for a ship's captain. He found one and negotiated his passage to the port of Dinan in Armorica, due to sail on the morning tide. That done, he negotiated stable space for his goods and attendants, and a room in the former Roman mansio for himself. He had no sooner ordered a platter of bread, cheese and cold meats and a flagon of ale than a boy ran in and shouted, "Sails approaching! Twenty, at least!"

MADOR AND HIS guard of twelve marched to the quayside on the news that many sails had been sighted approaching the port. Barefoot boys lolled around on packing boxes, waiting for the opportunity to earn some coins offloading ships. They threw stones at stray dogs, who ran from them with tails between their legs, and eyed the soldiers with a mix of curiosity and admiration.

The fleet from Gaul glided into the estuary one by one and berthed at the creaking and treacherous piers. Sea gulls wheeled overhead as sailors leapt ashore, mindful of the gaps where feet had gone through the rotting planks, and tied their ships to blackened stakes. Soldiers and sailors formed lines along the piers and passed their cargo from hand to hand, ignoring the boys who pleaded for work.

Finally, Mador spotted his brother, Agravane, and pushed through the crowds to get to him. "Well met, dear brother!" he said, hugging his bigger sibling.

"How is it here, Mador? Have you had any trouble securing the port?"

Mador laughed and replied, "None. I persuaded Arthur to make me garrison commander before he left, and in addition to my twelve followers, there are just forty guards from the local tribe who know nothing of our plans. We will have little trouble taking the town, but the most pressing matter is to capture the queen before she hears of your coming."

Agravane stared at him and asked, "Have you not captured her yet? Then let me inform King Mordred at once. He will want her captured before she can flee…" he turned and pushed his way back to the royal ship, jumping on and seeking out his new master.

Mordred stood by the central hold clothed in a black tunic overlaid with silver armour and a purple cloak edged with gold. A thin gold crown encrusted with blue and green jewels contained his shining black locks. He looked down his hawk nose at Agravane, his look cold and predatory.

"Is our landing opposed?" Mordred asked.

"No, my lord. Mador has secured the port with his men."

"Good, then we shall proceed to Arthur's stockade with all haste."

"Mador informs me that Queen Guinevere is there, but still protected by Arthur's guard. With your permission, I will ride there with Mador and his men to prevent her fleeing."

Mordred studied him before giving his reply. "Yes, but go with my captain and a dozen riders, in case you meet resistance. I shall follow with the remaining riders and the men on foot. Mador should leave me a guide. Did he bring supply wagons?"

"Yes, more than will meet our need, my lord." Agravane bowed and had turned to leave when Mordred shouted after him, "…And ask him where my mother is!" The hulking knight twisted and slightly inclined his head, then hurried back to Mador to brief him.

Mador led his two dozen riders at a gallop along the paved road to the fort, passing unhappy villagers who hugged their children by the roadside. Rounding the final bend, they gained a clear sight of the field before the old fort. Mador sat upright in his saddle and pulled hard on the reins of his horse, signalling a halt. Agravane and Mordred's man joined him at the head of the troop. In front, at some one hundred paces, the road was barricaded with overturned wagons and tree branches.

"What is this treachery?" Mordred's captain asked, eying the brothers with suspicion.

"Some misguided youth is rousing the remaining garrison against us," Mador replied. "I shall ride forward and discover who has done this."

"We will go together," Agravane growled, digging his heels into his horse.

"Stop there!" Merlyn yelled as the three leaders approached to within twenty paces of where he stood on the bed of a wagon. He leaned on his staff for support, as other soldiers climbed up beside him.

Mador grinned and shouted back, "Ah, Merlyn! I heard you had been skewered on Morgana's dagger and carried off to die in your hovel. Yet here you are rallying Arthur's rabble!"

"The wound was not deep, and I live to thwart your plans, treacherous brothers from beyond the Wall!" Merlyn replied in a powerful voice that surprised many. "I see the black swan of Mordred on the livery of those warriors behind you. I take it he has landed at the port?"

Agravane's voice boomed across the meadow, "King Mordred has come to reclaim this land from Arthur. Throw down your weapons and plead for his mercy, or we will kill you all!"

"We shall not give way, and will fight to protect the queen!" Merlyn shouted, drawing his sword in a slow, jerky motion and raising it above his head. Behind him, the garrison of forty and at least as many more townsfolk cheered their defiance, waving pitch forks and knives in the air.

"They are buying time to spirit the queen away, I think," Mador said, looking to his older brother for guidance.

"They are twice our number," the captain growled. "I shall request a company of riders with crossbows and others with lances come to our side so we can overpower them."

Agravane nodded and ground his teeth, annoyed at the unexpected setback. They trotted back to their men and waited as two riders galloped back to the main army. Turning to Mador, he said, "You have been careless, little brother. Merlyn has been Arthur's creature since he was born, and his loyalty is unshakable. He will have made a plan to send Guinevere to safety. You should have captured the queen before riding to the port."

Mador squirmed under his brother's stern look and rebuke. "I am sorry, my brother, I did not think…"

"You did not think and now will draw Mordred's anger. Let us hope that we quickly overpower them and find the queen and the lady Morgana."

Arthur *Rex Brittonum*

Chapter Nine

INSIDE THE WALLS of Lindum, Arthur and his battle-scarred commanders faced off against the army of Anglisc warriors who stood hunched with axes and swords in hand before the steps and columns of the imposing magistrate's hall. The Britons had battered their way in and fought through the streets to the forum, and now Arthur had called a halt to take stock of the enemy before deciding his next move.

Arthur sent Bedwyr and Herrig forward with upturned shields to ask their leaders to talk, and then instructed the local Coritani commander to send his soldiers to collect up surviving townsfolk and lead them to safety outside the walls. Captured Angliscs were herded by their guards into a corner of the forum and sat on the ground with their hands bound.

Before long, Herrig, with his knowledge of the Anglisc tongue, had convened a meeting of leaders, six on each side. They handed their weapons to deputies and strode into the space between the two armies. Arthur, flanked by Ambrose, Bedwyr, Cadoc, Caratacus and Adminius, stood ten feet from their Anglisc counterparts, with Herrig standing between them as interpreter.

"Where is your one-eyed king?" Arthur asked.

"King Icel is dead this past year, and now drinks in the Great Hall of Valhalla with his ancestors. I am his son, Cnebba, king of the Angliscs," Herrig translated for their burly leader.

"We have reclaimed this town for its rightful owners, the Coritani, and shall march you to the coast and send you to your homeland." Arthur waited patiently for Herrig to translate, seeing nothing but defiance in their eyes.

After a sneering and snappish response from the Anglisc king, Herrig turned to Arthur and said, "Cnebba says that the women and children from the town and surrounding farms are in the hall, with hay bales covered in tar. He will instruct his men to burn it if you do not leave this town."

The Briton leaders looked up at the top of the steps and saw a dozen men holding burning torches. Arthur turned to Brian and Ambrose and asked in a hushed tone how many townsfolk their men had found on their search. They broke away and marched back to the ranks to make enquiries.

Arthur briefly conferred with his fellows before turning back to the negotiation. "You are prepared to die by our swords, but will commit this crime of murder against our people as your parting gift. You should know, Cnebba, that we will not leave, nor will we leave you here. There must be another way. This is not how men of honour behave."

Herrig's translation seemed longer than Arthur's words, and Arthur surmised that he had made his own additions to appeal to their warrior code. More words were exchanged between the Jute and the Angliscs before Herrig turned to Arthur. By now, Ambrose and Brian had returned to the group and confirmed that hardly any townsfolk had been found, dead or alive, concluding that their threat must be believed.

"What do they say, Herrig?" Arthur asked.

"My lord, they say that they will release the captives and leave for their ships if your champion kills their champion in single combat. But if your champion is slain, then they will know their gods are more powerful, and they will burn the hall and fight to the last man, believing they will die a warrior's death and go to Valhalla to be with their ancestors. This way they are giving your Christian God a chance to better their gods, but if he fails, then they are justified in killing the women and children. It is their belief, their way of thinking, lord."

"Is this a trick?" Arthur asked Herrig in a whisper. "Who will be their champion?"

Herrig's wide mouth cracked in a rare smile. "He is the one next to Cnebba, dressed in fine clothing and arm bands with many notches. He is Beowulf, a fighter of great repute, a slayer of monsters and giants in their homeland. He wishes to fight me, Herrig the Jute, Arthur's champion, and so steal my warrior's soul."

Arthur's eyes widened in horror at the proposal. "I will not allow it! You are my bodyguard and like a brother in my household, Herrig. Since the time we were rescued from prison, we have stayed together, fought together and vanquished many enemies together... I cannot risk you in this..."

Herrig held up a hand, something no man had ever dared to do to Arthur. "My lord, king and master. I feel the hand of my ancestors on my shoulder, calling me to take up this challenge. When I was a boy, the Angliscs raided my village, forcing my mother to flee to the marshes with her children. They killed my father, our men, and burnt our village, taking our cattle and pigs. I have heard of this Beowulf, and now is my chance to kill him, lord, and avenge my father. Do not doubt me, and do not deny me, for I shall win."

Arthur looked up at the granite jaw and steely blue eyes of the taller man, at a loss. After a brief moment when the world seemed to stand still, Arthur replied, "Then so be it, my friend. I have come to believe that you are the immortal force that has surrounded me and kept me safe all these years. Now I must believe in you, and I do. Kill this Beowulf, avenge your family, destroy his legend, and we shall march them back to their ships and be rid of them." He reached out his arms and patted the giant's biceps, then stood back and shouted, "I accept your challenge!"

BARINTHUS HAD HIDDEN in the upper-most room in the mansio before the fleet berthed, listening to the noise of the army passing through the port on their way to the town. A sleepless night had passed, and he then cautiously emerged and crept though the quiet streets to the stable, where he was much relieved to find his attendants and goods undiscovered. He now wandered down to the quayside to find his captain.

"Come to the furthest pier and I shall pick you up in my ship," the captain whispered, looking to see if he was being watched by Mordred's lolling guards. They appeared not to be interested, and so Barinthus returned to the stables where his attendants waited with his bundles of goods.

Following a circuitous route behind the buildings, they arrived at the farthest-most pier, disused, dilapidated and overgrown on both sides with bull rushes. They gingerly picked their way past rotting boards to the end and waited.

"Soldiers approaching!" one of his attendants said in a gruff whisper, pointing to the path. Just then the ship appeared from out of the rushes, and tied up to the end of the pier. Barinthus threw his bundles in and jumped in afterwards, followed by his attendants.

The soldiers shouted and started to run, but they only reached the pier as the ship cast off and its crew of twelve expertly shipped their oars and started to row. By the time the soldiers had cautiously picked their way to the end of the pier, the ship's bow was beyond throwing distance, the current hurrying them out to the wide embrace of the sea. Behind the port, trails of black smoke rose ominously to the sky above the town.

"Much as I love your wild land and its people, good captain, I shall not be returning," Barinthus puffed, mopping his brow, as the soldiers became distant specks. "My days of trading across the Narrow Sea are at an end; only retirement to my estate in Gaul remains."

MORDRED STOOD ABOVE the gatehouse of the abbey, the only structure left beside the smouldering ruins of the buildings in the old fortress and in Arthur's stockade. Twists of black and grey smoke rose up from the buildings in and around the fort as Mordred's soldiers looted bodies, raped captured women or chased livestock across the desolate landscape.

"Well, Abbot Asaph," he said with a smirk, "your congregation has been somewhat reduced in number."

"God sees everything, Mordred, and your soul will be damned for this."

"It was damned a long time ago, and it's 'King' Mordred to you." He slapped the feisty priest's face with his leather gauntlet, drawing a trickle of blood from Asaph's lip. "It is lucky for you and your abbey that I need somewhere to quarter my commanders and my dear old mother, once they have found her."

"What will you do with Merlyn?" Asaph asked. "The old man instructed Morgana in the so-called healing arts. I would have a care where he is concerned, my lord. Unless you are sure she has done with him."

Mordred laughed. "Bring the old sorcerer out!" he shouted to his men in the courtyard below. Merlyn, his black and grey robes torn, was dragged out, blood and dirt soiling his white hair and beard, one eye blackened, his hands tied with rope. "I have a mind to burn him, but for now, he can share a cell with you, Abbot. Take them away."

Mordred climbed down the ladder and marched out towards Agravane, Mador and his captain. "Why are you three still here? We established some time ago that Guinevere took my mother hostage and fled to her mountain castle."

"We are waiting for your command, my lord." Agravane replied, with the slightest of bows.

Mordred glared at him and shouted, "Then I command you now! Take a troop of a hundred men and burn that castle down if you must. She has only a handful of followers. Mador shall remain here with me to await your return, but do not take more than one cycle of the moon, or you may find your brother hanging from a gibbet. I expect to see my mother and Guinevere alive, but for the others, I care not. Now go!"

ARTHUR COULD SEE the number of Anglisc warriors was close to five hundred, and his own force was now only seven hundred strong after the losses sustained in the assault on the town's gates. He had lost one of the young knights, Pinel, and two commanders, slain by spear or war axe. It would be a close and bloody fight if it came to it, so perhaps the single combat option was the best way to break the stalemate. As he watched the two muscular warriors circle each other and trade blows onto shields with battle axes, he put the word out that in the unlikely event of Herrig losing, the men should be ready to rush the Angliscs and a rescue team should enter the rear of the hall.

The enemy would not have time to gloat, or to make a peaceful retreat. Arthur had made up his mind - if Herrig triumphed, he would keep his end of the bargain and allow Cnebba to leave in peace, provided the women and children were unharmed. If Herrig were to lose, then Excalibur would sing his requiem, sending as many of them to Valhalla as came before him.

Beowulf was about ten years younger than Herrig, and he circled like a wolf looking for a sign of weakness in its prey, goading him with insults in their language. Herrig, for his part, remained silent and fully focussed on his enemy's movements. This was not going to be quick. Beowulf, supremely confident, was now getting impatient. He charged at Herrig and threw his axe at his head, causing him to duck and swerve. Beowulf had drawn his sword before reaching his opponent and sparks flew from their shield bosses when they crashed together. Herrig stood up to the shield thrust and blocked Beowulf's sword slash with the shaft of his axe. Their faces were close and they glared into each other's eyes, pushing with all their might.

The men around the circle roared on their champion, the noise filling the forum where market stall traders had sold their wares for over four hundred years. Herrig was slowly being pushed backwards, his boots leaving trails in the dust, something Arthur thought he would never see. Herrig had never lost an arm wrestle.

Arthur was sitting on his stallion, Son of Mars, behind the front row of his men, drawing his gaze away from Herrig's plight as cold dread crawled up his spine. The Angliscs stood in rows on the steps of the hall and along its portico, between carved Greek columns they would surely pull down should they remain custodians of the town. Brian was nowhere to be seen, as he was leading a unit armed with daggers and short swords through the streets to the back of the hall, where there was a walled garden and a rear entrance.

Arthur's attention returned to the duel. Herrig had broken free of the shield push, and now both men had discarded their broken shields and had swords in their hands. They circled each other, jabbing and slashing like gladiators. Beowulf had clearly decided to try and trip Herrig, and occasionally dropped in a squat and swung a leg to try and hook his opponent's leg. Herrig seemed to be slowing down, and he threw off his helmet to wipe sweat from his eyes. Beowulf seized his chance and charged at him, slashing at his sword arm and drawing blood from a deep cut. When Herrig staggered, the Angliscs screamed at the sight of his blood and then started a rhythmic chant, as if it were already a funeral procession.

Herrig's shoulders were hunched and his sword was down, swaying heavily away from Beowulf's jabs and slashes. Now Beowulf tried his squat and swing of the leg, this time connecting with Herrig's ankle, as if the previous attempts had been for practice. The big jute staggered and fell on his behind, one arm on the ground supporting him, the other waving his sword in front of him as if warding off an evil goblin. But Beowulf, like his spirit animal, knew his prey was wounded and moved in for the kill. With a flick of his wrist, he sent Herrig's sword spinning from his hand, and without delay he stepped forward and drove the tip of his sword into Herrig's throat, pulling it out and stepping back to watch his foe's life blood pour out.

The Angliscs jumped and cheered as Beowulf held his arms out to them still holding his bloody sword.

Arthur drew Excalibur and its blade flashed in the late afternoon sun. "Attack!" he yelled, and jabbed his heels into Son of Mars, scattering the men in front of him and entering the circle, where he charged at Beowulf. The nimble warrior ducked Arthur's swipe and ran into the crowd, disappearing from sight. Arthur flayed about him with his sword, cutting down those Angliscs who were foolish enough to seek their chance of a famous kill. The last thing they saw was a broad sword they assumed to be heavy, in the hands of an aging man, but that was their downfall, as Excalibur had a sublime lightness and Arthur wielded it with seemingly unnatural speed.

The whole forum was alive with duels as men battered and slashed each other. Arthur was afforded a pause by the close presence of Caratacus and his new commander, Gaheris, who both fought with a ferocity that was needed to vanquish the stubborn and hardy Angliscs who did not fear death. The doors of the hall burst open and Brian and his men stood in triumph on the step, yelling encouragement to their comrades. The tide of the battle was ever in the Britons' favour, and soon there was a mass of dead bodies, mostly Angliscs, littering the forum, their blood and gore mingling with the yellow dust. Few threw down their weapons, but those that did were spared.

Arthur mounted the steps and slapped Brian on the arm in thanks for his bravery in rescuing the captured women and children. His valiant commanders joined them on the step and took a weary and subdued cheer from the survivors of the bitter fight. The women and children, spared the scene of death and misery in the forum, were led from the rear of the hall to be reunited with their surviving menfolk, a consolation for their hard-won victory. At the final reckoning, it was noted that Cnebba and Beowulf were amongst a small band who had escaped, taking flight on horses tethered by the river gate.

Churches had been looted and burnt, and the charred bodies of priests nailed to beams in a crude simulation of crucifixion left a bitter aftertaste to their victory. But Ambrose was restored to his town, the town and surrounding lands he had known from childhood, the lands his father, Maddox, had ruled over at the head of a council for many years. Arthur agreed to release him from his service so that he might remain to rebuild and provide the leadership needed by the hard-pressed and much depleted Coritani.

Burial details set to work, and cleaning of the streets went on until nightfall as the commanders supped ale in the hall and chewed on their enemy's salt pork. Plans were made to ride northwards towards Ebrauc and another confrontation with the Angliscs.

"That is no doubt where we shall find King Cnebba and Beowulf," Arthur said, swilling his sour ale, his furrowed brow casting a shadow over his face.

"Then we shall have our revenge for Herrig, my lord, for he was our friend also," Caratacus remarked, his dark eyes gleaming in the lamp light.

"And now I must believe that you and Bedwyr are my invincible guardians," Arthur glumly remarked.

The normally silent Lucan stood and raised his pewter tankard and proposed a toast. "To Herrig. A mighty warrior, a Jute saved from Uther's prison, who showed us that loyalty and friendship can overcome tribal difference. We shall remember him."

Bedwyr was next to raise his tankard. "And we have found a new warrior in Gaheris, who showed his qualities today on the battlefield." They drank in weary silence to the mighty Gaheris, but in their hearts they knew that Arthur was inconsolable at the death of his dour and loyal flaxen-haired guardian.

Ambrose, seeing the fatigue in his comrades, rose to conclude the day. "I must thank our noble, and once more victorious, King Arthur for permitting me to remain here to serve my Coritani tribe as their chief, and rebuild our shattered lives and town. You are all welcome to find respite with us as you travel this land."

Slowly they took their leave, one by one, to find their bed rolls.

Arthur *Rex Brittonum*

Chapter Ten

CAER LEGION WAS a desolate place. Surly children and silent women fetched water and served food for the encamped army, mainly composed of returned Briton exiles and mercenaries from the wars in Gaul, who occupied the grassy river meadows under canvas awnings where Arthur's army had once trained. Mordred was more feared than loved, and none could feel at ease in his company.

He looked over the scene of destruction from the Abbey walls, a smirk of satisfaction playing across his face. A cry of complaint caused him to turn to his left, his smirk transforming to forthright laughter.

"My lord, we found him hiding in the queen's quarters," a bulky soldier shouted, dragging an old man in a torn, silken gown, through the mud.

"Ha ha! If I'm not mistaken, it's the court jester!" Mordred bellowed.

The short, round figure of Gerwyn was unceremoniously thrown to the ground before the abbey gates. The dishevelled actor looked up from his knees and his sausage fingers came together in a theatrical plea beneath a white, pointed beard. "Your Imperial Majesty, King Mordred of Britannia, it is I, Gerwyn, who did perform a play for you and your wise and noble mother at Dunbulgar some years past…"

"Yes, I remember. I was never so bored in my entire life. You did not please us, Gerwyn, with your tiresome celebration of the life of Ambrosius. I sincerely hope, for your sake, that your act has improved since then."

Mordred leaned forward over the parapet wall and stared down at the trembling bard. "You shall entertain me this eve in the abbot's hall, and you will have to give the performance of your life to avoid the fate of your fellow traitors." Mordred pointed to a row of bodies hanging from a workmen's scaffold beside the fort. "Lock him in a monk's cell."

AFTER SOME WEEKS, Agravane returned to camp, leading the men in a weary line. He was welcomed by his brother, Mador, and they marched to the abbey to meet with Mordred.

"I see you, Agravane, but not my mother," Mordred said, more as a challenge than a welcome.

"My king, I have unhappy news. We did find the body of Morgana and her maids lying dead at the bottom of a vast quarry of white stones. I believe they were thrown to their deaths, my lord." He bowed his head and waited.

Mordred screamed in wide-eyed rage and ran at Agravane, shaking his fist at the big knight, spittle dribbling down his chin. Agravane merely stood his ground and waited for the storm to blow itself out.

"I would have you flogged, Agravane, if I did not need your services," Mordred growled through gritted teeth. He turned and prowled around the room, trying to catch the eyes of his attendants. But they were too well practised in looking above his head. Reaching the abbot's throne, he sat and smiled. "Well, she was getting old and was too fond of telling me what to do. Perhaps it's for the best. I am my own man now."

"There is more, my king," Agravane said in a flat tone.

"Then speak."

"We came to the White Castle in the mountains and found the gates open and the place deserted. Guinevere had led her people on a trail that went deeper into those accursed mountains, on a westward path that entered the kingdom of Demetia, where she has allies, my lord. I felt it best that we return to you and report."

"So, my mother was murdered and Guinevere escaped. This is a black mark on your record, Agravane. Your reward is that you will lead the vanguard when we meet Arthur in battle. Now go and tell the men we break camp in the morning."

Nimue, Merlyn's wiry assistant, had evade capture by hiding in the woods and was watching from a rock above the camp. She had noted the return of Agravane without any captives and sniggered quietly to herself. She had already shown her willingness to kill in defence of her master, and now looked for an opportunity to rescue the old healer, whom she knew was being fed and kept in a monk's cell in the abbey. Nimue had recruited two soldiers who had fled the fighting to her small community in the huts by the edge of the forest, and she raced there to brief them that Mordred's army was about to break camp.

THE FOLLOWING MORNING, Nimue's band waited in the shadows as the army prepared to leave. She saw Merlyn and Abbot Asaph dragged through the abbey gates and tied by their bound wrists to the back of an ox wagon.

"We shall follow them and look for our chance to cut him free and escape to a dark forest where they will not want to follow," she said with grim relish, flicking her lank hair from her ever-watchful brown eyes.

Merlyn nudged Asaph and moved his eyes to his left. The abbot followed his line of sight and shuddered. At the end of a row of rotting corpses hanging from a scaffold was the familiar gaudy costume of the bard Gerwyn, his remains sagging in the silk like a gory scarecrow. A trio of ravens tore at his flesh with the strong hooks of their beaks.

"Poor Gerwyn; he has given his last performance and his soul is now in the care of our Lord God," Asaph whispered through dry lips. A whip cracked the air and their wagon lurched into a steady, walking pace. The two elderly companions stumbled forward, silently reflecting on the fate of Mordred's enemies, wondering if the same awaited them.

Mordred, looking out of place in his fine clothes, rode to the head of his army as it moved away, crossing the Usk and following the old Roman road that would take them to the bridge over the Severna.

Arthur *Rex Brittonum*

"I am looking forward to a reunion with Malachi in his hall at Caer Gloui," Mordred remarked to Agravane. His commanders following behind glanced at each other, pondering what mischief he had in mind, but thankful that he was in better spirits. The abbey was left standing beside the ruins of the fort on the far river bank as the horsemen, marching soldiers and lines of wagons followed in a slow procession to the east.

After three hours, the wagon train had strung out and the road had started to wind on an uphill gradient through a forest. The two prisoners were stumbling and encouraging each other to keep going behind the last wagon, forced to keep up with the pace of the great beasts in front.

"Now is our chance," Nimue said, drawing her dagger as she led her band through the trees, coming level with the two prisoners. Two guards with spears resting on their shoulders were marching on either side of the wagon, chatting to the cooks sitting on the bench seat.

She detailed the two young women to cut Merlyn free and guide him into the trees, whilst she and the two men would attack the guards. The ambush started well, with one of the guards taken by surprise, having his throat cut before he knew anything was amiss. The other guard called for help and faced Nimue and one of the men, thrusting his spear at them. Nimue circled to one side, and soon they had wounded him with enough slashes of their knives to bring him to his knees. Nimue saw other soldiers were running towards them from ahead, and swiftly cut his throat before running to the back of the wagon. She found Merlyn making a fuss and refusing to be led away.

"Hurry Merlyn!" Nimue shouted.

"You must free Asaph!" he yelled, wriggling out of the grip of the two women.

"He is a Christian – leave him to his fate," she said, and turned, dismissive.

"No! Cut him free, he is my friend!" Merlyn cried.

Nimue could see they had no time to waste and approached Asaph with her knife. He recoiled in alarm, seeing blood on the blade and a killer's look in her eyes. She sighed and sawed at the rope.

"Bless you, my sister…" the tonsured abbot gushed, but Nimue was already running away from him, up the grass bank, urging Merlyn into the trees. Asaph grimaced as he struggled up the bank and hurried after her, grateful, despite his stiff limbs, that he was somewhat slimmer after his internment.

ARTHUR'S ARMY WAS arrayed on the plain before Lindum, ready to leave, when a messenger arrived in a cloud of dust before the group of commanders.

"What news?" Arthur asked, jumping from his saddle to face the boy.

"Grim news, my king," the thin lad wailed, shaking the dust from his hair and trying to catch his breath.

"Then tell it. Bring water and cakes for this boy!" Arthur yelled.

"Your fortress of Caer Legion has been captured by Mordred's army…" He paused to suck in more air.

"What? And what has happened to Queen Guinevere and my men?"

"The queen did escape, my lord, but your men were betrayed by your captain, Mador, who has joined the enemy. The guards were led by Merlyn, but were soon overcome. And I fear all were killed. I saw the town burn as I rode away. It was lord Merlyn who sent me to find you."

Arthur groaned and appeared to stagger, reaching out a hand for the rump of his horse. He shook his head, raking his hand through the grizzled hair that once was nut brown, and then looked to the heavens. "This is heavy news that must now change our plans. Come, let us convene a council away from the others." Arthur took the reins of his horse and led him to one side, followed by his commanders.

Bedwyr noted that Arthur appeared more confused and distraught than angry, and took it on himself to address the group. "We had feared the return of Mordred to our land for some years, and now it has happened."

They all looked to Arthur for his thoughts. Arthur was staring at Bedwyr as if he were a stranger, trying to make sense of what he had said. The pause was long before Arthur spoke. "Mordred, my nephew, has come to kill me and take the throne. I fear that Herrig and Merlyn's deaths are bad omens and signal an end…" His voice trailed away to silence and he looked to the blue skies, as if searching for a shape in the clouds that would offer him a solution.

"Then we must ride to meet him, lord king," Caratacus said, his deep voice demanding attention.

Arthur looked at him, blinked and smiled. "Yes, noble Caratacus, we must ride to meet him." Arthur staggered slightly, then abruptly righted himself and puffed out his chest. "And we shall meet him in a battle that will decide the fate of our island. We have been here before, and must do so once again."

Arthur had snapped out of his reverie and looked at each of his commanders. "Our journey northwards must be curtailed, and we shall take the road to Caer Gloui that cuts across our land." His slow sweep settled on Gaheris and he patted his arm. "Yes, Gaheris, you shall see your home soon. We will go to your master, Malachi, for shelter and supplies whilst we gain news of Mordred."

Then Arthur turned to Adminius and said, "You shall ride south to your people, Adminius, and raise as many men as you can and join us at Caer Gloui without delay. Go now."

Adminius bowed and jumped on his horse, calling to his troop of followers to leave with him on the south road.

"Tell the men we march for Caer Gloui," Arthur said to his remaining commanders. "I will speak with Ambrose and then follow you."

MALACHI QUAKED WHEN he saw Mordred's banners at the head of the approaching army. He thought about barring the gates, but knew that would make matters worse and result in the destruction of his town. The gates of Caer Gloui remained open and Mordred led his retinue in.

"Ah, Malachi, we meet again!" Mordred quipped with a laugh.

"You are most welcome, King Mordred," Malachi gushed, indicating he should sit at the long table with his retinue.

Mordred ignored the gesture and walked to the dais, sitting on Malachi's throne. "Bring wine – the finest. Do not keep your best from me."

"Of course!" Malachi clapped his hands and his servants went scurrying to the kitchens. The aging grandson of the mighty king Ambrosius Aurelianus stood unsettled in his own hall, not sure what to say to his unwelcome visitor.

"So, this is where you hid after you ignored my command to bring your men to swell my ranks at Badon Field?"

"I… explained to the lady Morgana that we are a peaceful people and do not keep a standing army, only guards for our gates and walls…"

"Enough! Your lies and the smell of your fear disgust me." Mordred was served a golden goblet of wine from a liveried attendant. "Serve my men, they are thirsty."

Malachi's face had gone white and he waved away a goblet, instead, wringing his hands in agitation.

Mordred saw his fear and laughed, his black eyes dancing with mischief. "My spies tell me that you sent a troop of men to Arthur's rally. That does not sound like you have no warriors at your call, Malachi." He drained his goblet and threw it across the floor, causing Malachi to stifle a cry. "Tell your guards to place their weapons on the table."

Malachi sensed his doom and motioned his guards to come forward, instructing them to place their spears and swords on the table and withdraw. Mordred sent two of his men to bar and guard the great oak door.

"I have a new weapon that I brought with me from Gaul. I'd like to show it to you, Lord Malachi." He called his squire and took a crossbow from him. Mordred pulled back the string and set an arrow in the groove. "It's called a crossbow. Please, sit on your throne."

Mordred motioned two of his men to grab Malachi by his thin arms and place him on his throne. He did not wriggle, knowing resistance would only increase Mordred's pleasure. He swallowed and faced his tormentor, determined to die with the dignity befitting his noble house.

Mordred grinned and pointed the weapon at him, then released the spring. The bolt flew swiftly, piercing Malachi's right shoulder and pinning him to the back of the throne. His screams of pain were accompanied by Mordred's laughter. He called for another bolt and re-loaded. "Oh, my aim is not so good, my apologies. I'm still getting used to it."

He fired again, this time at his guts. "Was it the five wounds of Christ?" he asked, jauntily, gazing at the biblical scenes hanging on the walls before re-loading. Malachi lost consciousness with the fourth bolt, his balding head lolling forwards on his chest, his purple and gold robe stained with dark red patches. The fun had gone from the game, and Mordred's fifth bolt entered Malachi's chest, piercing his heart and killing him.

"This is perhaps the best-kept place in my kingdom," Mordred remarked to his commanders as a terrified steward took them on a tour of the royal quarters and storerooms.

"I shall move here and make this my capital, once I have dealt with Arthur. Tell the men not to abuse the locals. This town is to be our new home."

MORDRED'S SCOUTS HAD informed him of the approach of Arthur's army a few days later. Arthur's scouts had informed their king that Mordred's army had left Caer Gloui and taken the south road. Arthur rode ahead with his commanders and Gaheris's troop of riders to see what had happened in the town, fearing some sort of mischief. They were greeted warmly by the townsfolk, who were preparing to bury their dead lord. Arthur raged at the murder of Malachi and vowed his vengeance to the elders of the Dobunni tribe who had gathered to give Malachi a fitting burial.

"He wants to pick his field of battle," Arthur said to his men as they dined in the great hall. "We shall leave at dawn and catch up with our marching men. There can be only one way to end this. Gaheris, can you raise more men?"

"The townsfolk are angry, my king. Many farmers have come forward, and the gate guards have asked to join us. The people know their fate if… Mordred were to return."

Arthur laughed, unexpectedly, lightening the mood. "Yes, if he defeats us, he will come here with his pox-ridden mercenaries to infest this place, like a plague of rats!"

"He will not defeat us," Bedwyr said, banging his mug on the table. "You are Arthur, King of the Britons, undefeated on the field of battle!" They ate and drank heartily, exchanging tales of bravery, knowing that come the morning they would pursue Mordred relentlessly until they drew him to battle, for good or ill.

Chapter Eleven

AFTER THREE DAYS they had crossed into Dumnonia, and were approaching the low lands that were wont to flood in the winter months. Arthur's scouts gave him regular updates and it seemed Mordred was camped and waiting for him.

"Riders approach, my lord!" a scout yelled, disturbing Arthur's quiet reflection. He was thinking of Guinevere and wondering if she had made good her escape. She would be in the far west, where her people lived, safe from the clutches of Mordred. He had sent a scout to find her before he had left Caer Gloui, and report on the state of Caer Legion.

"From which direction and how many?" Bedwyr demanded.

"From the south, carrying the banner of Dumnonia. More than a hundred, my lord."

Arthur saw they were on a wide meadow and called a halt, allowing their horses to graze on the green grass whilst they stood in the shade of a large ash tree.

"Ah, it is my nephew, Cado," Arthur said, walking into the sunlight to greet the approaching rider with a broad smile on his face. "Welcome, nephew, I am most pleased to see you and your men."

Cado jumped from his horse and embraced his uncle. "I came when news reached me of Mordred's attack on Caer Legion. But I see you are well, uncle. Tell me, what has passed?"

Arthur led him to the shade, reacquainted him with his commanders and introduced him to a newcomer. "This is Gaheris, captain of the Dobunni guard. He is a fierce and valiant warrior and I have made him knight after his bravery at our battle at Lindum where we defeated the Angliscs."

Cado raised his eyebrows and shook Gaheris's hand. "Our king needs brave leaders whom men will follow – you are a welcome sight, Gaheris."

Arthur continued, "But there is mischief about in our land, now Mordred has returned. He has sacked my town, slain my guards and, we think, killed Merlyn. I had a report that Queen Guinevere escaped, and I have sent a scout to find her. But that is not all. Mordred moved his army to Glevum and there did kill in a most cruel way the lord Malachi, and the Dobunni people are now mourning his loss."

"And I shall avenge my lord, when we face Mordred's horde," Gaheris said, his square jaw set firm, his eyes burning with passion.

"This is a sad report, dear uncle," Cado replied. "But take heart; for I have brought my guard of one hundred and fifty to swell your ranks. When do you expect to catch up with Mordred?"

"Tomorrow. He is camped some ten miles from here, his back to a river. I believe he means to make his stand there. With your men, it brings our numbers to above eight hundred – enough for the task. We shall camp here tonight and rise early."

A LOW MIST hung over them as they broke camp, dew dripping from the horses' harnesses onto a silver carpet that shimmered with an eerie glow, lighting their way. Arthur had dreamt of Guinevere, her radiant face smiling at him as they walked amongst flowers in a sunlit meadow. But soon the sky had darkened and Herrig's scarred and weathered face filled his vision, his brooding silence eliciting a sense of foreboding that caused Arthur to wake with sweat on his brow. Now the morning was filled with preparations, and he sheathed Excalibur, ruffling the hair of his squire who had sharpened and polished the blade. "Stay to the rear, boy, in the cook's wagon."

Their path followed the course of a winding river, where willow trees bowed to the water goddess as the ripples of feeding fish spread across the green water in still ponds between stretches of white foam racing over stones. Dragonflies flitted and herons stalked as the lines of silent riders passed, soon followed by marching men, their shields on their backs and spears over their shoulders.

After an hour Arthur started in alarm at the sight of a woodcutter's hut standing before a solitary birch tree that had been spared the axe, its white bark peeling in readiness for the new season. Smoke trails from a vent merged with the fog, indicating it was occupied. It was a scene from his vision when he had stood before the head of Brân in the White Castle. Arthur called a halt and dismounted.

An old man appeared in the doorway, his gnarled knuckles gripping a staff.

"Hail fellow, what is this place?" Arthur asked, approaching him.

"This meadow beside the River Cam is Camlann, lord," the old man replied through shrunken gums that had long been bereft of teeth.

"Camlann," Arthur repeated, rubbing his hand on the trunk and dislodging flakes of bark. "Why does this tree remain standing, alone?"

"An old druid comes here to harvest the bark, lord. He told me to leave it, calling it a sacred tree."

"The bark is used by healers to reduce swelling on wounds," Bedwyr said, leading his horse to the reflective king.

"I saw this hut, and this white tree beside it, in my vision before the head of Brân," Arthur said, slowly turning to look at his friend.

"I was there and saw you swoon under the evil influence of Merlyn's powder. Your mind was playing tricks on you, my lord. I doubt it has meaning."

"But it must have been of a vision of my future, Bedwyr, for here I am, at the very spot I envisaged."

"Then it must be a portent of your impending victory, my lord. This is your day, when you finally remove the pestilence of Mordred and unite all Britons under your banner of the bear and dragon. It is the day of your destiny, King Arthur."

The old man gasped at his royal company, and bowed awkwardly.

At that moment a pair of solemn and curious eyes peering through dark curls appeared under the woodcutter's arm, when a little barefoot figure in a colourless tunic sidled out from the gloom behind him. Arthur's heart knotted in unexpected angst at the child's likeness to his daughter Gwen.

"Oh Bedwyr," he said, shaking his head as the two of them walked over to the old man's well to fill their flasks. "A knee-high poppet shielded by her grandfather. But what have I done to my children?"

"They are safe, my lord," Bedwyr answered.

"I was lost to them from the instant I looked into my lady's gaze. And they were lost to me. Guinevere was all from that time, and I set my family at naught. The shame I brought to St Alban's sacred memory, feigning illness in his abbey. Hiding so that I would not see the slender shoulders of my forlorn children as they walked to their wagon, hustled from the protection of their father."

"They are well protected, my lord, and this wallowing is no way to ready us for battle." Bedwyr wet his hand and massaged the back of his neck to soothe it, twisting the sinews from side to side.

"I have been a palsied wreck these last weeks, and I thought it was Herrig's loss that weakened me. But now I see that Jesus Christ has forsaken me, as I forsook my family. He has sent a wraith to torment me." He cast a surreptitious look back at the hut.

"Your chaplain will shrive us, my lord. And then relics from the abbey can be sent, with an abundance of your blessings, to shore up your children, who are visiting their aunt with their mother."

Arthur nodded, grateful for Bedwyr's practicality, but when a young woman stepped out to draw the child inside, he saw Gunamara's loving nature in her face and winced. It was for the best that events had kept him from Guinevere. His abstinence might help him back into the Lord's good graces.

"And that little maid is no wraith, unless they eat bread and dripping," Bedwyr added for good measure, pointing to the greasy crust in the child's hand. "We shall forget these qualms and ride to wave the dragon and bear in Mordred's face."

Arthur smiled and patted his most loyal knight on his shoulder. "And you will be there at the end, dear Bedwyr, whatever this day at Camlann holds. I feel a strange sense of unease, nonetheless, but perhaps it is at the prospect of slaying my own kin – my nephew."

"Aye, lord. That would be a natural feeling. But he has a black heart and you must strike him down, otherwise his long shadow will fall across our land."

They nodded to the old fellow, and Bedwyr gave Arthur a leg up into his saddle then mounted his own horse. They continued in slow procession along the river path, passing lines of morbid crows perched on branches, listening and waiting for scouts to return and tell them how close they were to the enemy.

THEY DID NOT wait long. Arthur's scouts reported a large army, at least their match, waiting for them around the next river bend. Arthur instructed his commanders to tell their men to be ready. "Bedwyr, take Lucan and ride forward to request that I talk with Mordred."

The knights rode on, soon enveloped in the veil of fog that hung stubbornly over Camlann. The men were silent, their mood pensive. Horses snorted and pawed the soft earth with their hooves, their breath rising to merge with the mist.

Arthur stared at the rolling clouds before him, recalling more of his vision.

I saw a meadow in the hook of a river, shrouded in mist. The mist lifted slowly to reveal an army of knights on horseback, their faces black holes in helmets, crows sitting on their shoulders, black banners hanging limp, silently waiting...

Bedwyr and Lucan returned and reported that Mordred would meet them halfway, unarmed and with six attendants. Arthur handed his lance and Excalibur to his squire and called on Cado, Bedwyr, Lucan, Caratacus, Gaheris and Adminius to disarm and accompany him. They rode forwards into the mist until they were confronted by a line of seven horsemen.

Arthur narrowed his eyes and clenched his teeth at the sight of his knights, Agravane and Mador, on either side of Mordred.

Mordred laughed at Arthur's look of rage. "Well met, uncle. I see you are angry with these two for riding to my banner. Do not be – I have promised them the lands and silver that you denied them, and extend the same promise to your commanders if they join with me."

Arthur snorted, then responded. "Their reward will be their naked bodies thrown into a burial pit beside you, vile nephew. Your mother is gone to the shadowy netherworld and you will soon follow, bringing to an end Uther's first and most poisonous family."

Mordred's smirk disappeared and he leaned forward in his saddle. "Then there is little more to say, old man. I will look for you on the field." He pulled on his horse's reins and wheeled about, leading his commanders at a trot back to their lines.

It was only then that Arthur noticed they had swords hanging from their saddles. The mist lifted enough for him to see that the enemy front line was not of shield men but of cavalry, ready to charge.

As if on cue, Mordred yelled, "Charge!" and wheeled about, drawing his sword, to face Arthur and his group.

"We have been tricked - fall back!" Arthur shouted and turned Son of Mars to gallop to his lines, yelling as loudly as he could, "Make ready!" A cry echoed by his commanders who scattered to find their men.

The ground trembled and the drum beat of hooves behind them filled their ears as Mordred's cavalry bore down on Arthur's line of shield men. Arthur guided his horse around the side of the shield wall and rode to the supply wagon where his squire awaited with his weapons.

War cries soon gave way to screams as Mordred's cavalry crashed into Arthur's shield wall, knocking men aside or under hoof. Arthur, his tactics in tatters, led his riders around the side of the milling foot soldiers and attacked the enemy cavalry, first impaling a rider with his lance, then drawing Excalibur and laying about him.

Visibility remained poor as the mist continued to swirl, but Arthur was aware of the sound of Mordred's foot soldiers charging into the melee, and his other commanders attacking them from all sides with the cries of their tribal names ringing out, identifying their patch of the battlefield. Crossbow bolts flew through the mist, drawing screams and adding to the terror. Arthur's mounted archers retaliated with volleys of arrows aimed at the body of Mordred's men, scoring few hits due to the poor visibility.

The soft ground soon churned into mud, as men stabbed and slashed at each other, trying to keep sight of a friendly comrade by their side for fear of attacking their own or being encircled by the enemy mercenaries who were hunting in packs. Son of Mars whinnied in pain as a spear was thrust into his chest, collapsing to his side and throwing Arthur clear. Arthur was helped to his feet by two of his men, Excalibur still in hand. He parried the blow of an onrushing warrior, eyes wide and screaming in the hope of a kill that would make his reputation. The perfect balance of Excalibur in his hand, and practised body moves, enabled Arthur to dodge away from counter thrusts and set himself for a downward swing that cut into his opponent's neck, above the shoulder guard and below the helmet. With a scream, the man sank to his knees, dropping his sword. Arthur drew his arm back and rammed the tip of Excalibur into his throat, killing him.

"On me! On me!" Arthur cried, wary of becoming separated from his best warriors in the floating mist.

Before long, all riders had been unseated and the fight continued on foot, as groaning wounded men dragged themselves away and the dead and dying piled up underfoot; many of the wounded drowned in mud. It was impossible not to stand on fallen soldiers or broken shields to gain leverage in striking out at the next foe to emerge from the white clouds. Mistakes were made and some hit out wildly, perhaps partially blinded by blood or sweat, striking down their comrades.

The battle raged through the morning until midday, when a pale sun burned through the dissolving mist, revealing the full horror of a field littered with dead and dying men and horses, blood and gore mixed with mud making for treacherous movement. The intensity of combat gradually lessened with tired limbs - those few remaining sought out their comrades and grouped together, gasping for breath and resting their aching arms.

Arthur rallied his men and groaned at the sight of Caratacus's black bear skin floating above the mud close by, his dead friend's face submerged, a gaping wound at the back of his head. "Who else is lost?" he cried, relieved to see Bedwyr, Lucan and Gaheris make their way through boot-sucking mud to his side.

"I saw your nephew King Cado go down, lord, dragged from his horse and butchered," Lucan said, his troubled face smeared with blood.

"Adminius and the Catuvellauni have all perished, my lord," Bedwyr added, leaning on his sword handle and bending forward to breathe deeply.

"The noble Caratacus, Brian and Viroco have all fallen within my sight," Arthur moaned, lamenting the fate of his brave followers. He looked up at the barely dozen men remaining and added, "I must find Mordred, whether alive or dead, and bring this madness to an end."

He looked across the field of desolation at a small group of Mordred's men at fifty paces distance, and started to slog through the mud towards them, carefully placing his boots in gaps between bodies. His remaining men followed, making

Arthur *Rex Brittonum*

slow progress. After some minutes, Arthur could see that Mordred was there, with a similar number of remaining men. There was no sign of Agravane, but Mador stood by him.

"Mordred! Let us finish this!" Arthur yelled when close enough, his mind a whirl of despair and remorse at the extent of the devastation. The cream of Britannia's men lay slaughtered because of his feud with his nephew, the rest of his family now dispersed. He had one more task to accomplish, focussing his mind and remaining strength on that.

"Willingly, old man," Mordred replied in a casual manner, raising his sword and walking towards him. Their swords clashed in front of their faces, and they circled each other, lunging and swiping.

Lucan made his way to Mador, his age mate and one-time friend, and their swords clashed. Soon, all of the survivors were engaged in combat, as the final scene of Camlann played out like a carnival of madness for the pleasure of demons in the depths of Hell.

Arthur's army fell, killed as they lay in the mud, save for Bedwyr, Lucan and Arthur, who continued to duel despite sustaining wounds. Mordred, impatient to finish Arthur, pulled a broken lance from the ground and rushed at him, screaming. Arthur took a step back and tripped on a dead man, falling on his back. As Mordred's lance pierced Arthur's chest plate, Excalibur, in his outstretched arm, pierced Mordred's gut. Mordred's eyes bulged and he fell, groaning. Arthur gasped for air and pulled the lance tip from his chest. Seeing Mordred fatally wounded, he crawled to him and drove the tip of his sword into his stricken nephew's throat, whispering, "Now it ends."

Arthur pushed himself to his knees and slowly stood, wondering if any of Mordred's men remained to finish him. Swaying unsteadily, and through dimming eyes, he saw two men approach. His hand gripped Excalibur more firmly, but as they drew near, he saw that they were his most loyal knights, Lucan and Bedwyr. Arthur clumsily sheathed Excalibur and signalled them to come and help him from the field. No one

Arthur *Rex Brittonum*

else stood. There were no words, just circling crows cawing their greedy pleasure and a lame horse limping in the distance.

Some wounded men had dragged themselves from the meadow to the trees, and now sat waiting for help as their life blood seeped out. But those in the wagons had been slaughtered, and no one came to them. The knights carried Arthur to a wagon and found a horse standing in the trees to hitch to the coupling poles. Arthur groaned at the sight of his dead squire, long-serving cook, Derward, and the young priest who had accompanied them lying close by. Once in the back, on a bed of cloaks, Arthur beckoned Bedwyr and Lucan to him.

"Take me to the lake at Avalon where Morgaise has her healers…" His voice drifted away and he lay back. Lucan tore some shirts and made a bandage to stop the bleeding from Arthur's chest wound, whilst Bedwyr urged the horse into a walk.

They were not far from that place and reached there before the sun set. The knights ignored their own cuts and bruises to carry Arthur on a shield to the pebble beach by the lake. They called to the island for assistance, shouting Arthur's name, and before long a boat set out towards them.

Arthur motioned Bedwyr to come close. "Take Excalibur, and return her to the lake goddess, Coventina," he croaked through dry lips, the scar standing white on his cheek against his greying skin.

"But my lord!" Bedwyr exclaimed. "Such a fine sword should be passed to your son. I cannot."

"You must. The sword was thrown to the water goddess on Ambrosius's passing, only for Merlyn to reclaim it, and now it must be returned. Do as I command, Bedwyr." Arthur coughed up blood and slumped back, closing his eyes, his face growing paler. Bedwyr took Excalibur and looked at Lucan. The younger knight nodded. Bedwyr swung the sword and sent it spinning over the green waters. The water shimmered in the orange glow of sunset just as the sword hit a floating log, or was it an arm? Ripples spread outwards, their symmetry disturbed by the approaching flat-bottomed boat rowed by two maidens in pale blue gowns.

Bedwyr recognised Morgaise, who sat at the back of the boat. It beached on the shingle and Bedwyr bowed to her. "My lady, it is your brother Arthur, grievously wounded in battle with Mordred."

"And was Mordred vanquished?" she lightly asked, dipping her feet in the shallow waters and wading ashore.

"Yes, my lady. Arthur slew him, and both armies were destroyed to the last man in a madness of slaughter the like of which this land has never seen."

"Then you noble knights must spread the word that Arthur fought to the end to free our land from tyranny. I will take him and nurse his wounds. Now lay him in the boat."

With that, Arthur was laid in the boat, wrapped in a muddy red cloak, and the maidens rowed him to their island, escorted by skeins of geese whose shadows reflected off the still waters. The two knights watched until the sun dipped behind distant trees, pointing shafts of orange and yellow over the lake. They took to the wagon and began their journey back to Camlann, intent on looking for survivors. From there, they knew not where they would go.

Arthur *Rex Brittonum*

Epilogue

BEDWYR AND LUCAN found no survivors at Camlann, only crows and ravens fighting over entrails and eyeballs, and sly thieves who had no doubt cut the throats of the lingering wounded and were busy robbing corpses. They spent a restless night in the woodcutter's hut, waking at the moaning wind, fearful of seeing ghosts of the slain. The next morning, they found another horse in the woods and rode north, encountering King Peredur of the Rheged leading a troop of a hundred riders.

He had come to the battle too late, and cursed himself, saying that Arthur might be alive and his army victorious if he had come in time. The knights told how they had placed Arthur into the care of his sister, Morgaise, and her healers, at Avalon, but they held little hope of his recovery from his grievous wounds. If Arthur by some miracle lived, they would surely find out in due course.

Peredur led them to Caer Gloui, where news of the death of their captain, Gaheris, and his men was a cause of much sorrow. They then crossed the bridge to Gwent and visited Caer Legion where they saw the people busy with rebuilding their dwellings beside the abbey. Abbot Asaph hosted them for a night, and they found some mirth in the story of his escape with Merlyn.

Gildas served them at table, but won few friends with his miserable lament on two tyrannical kings whose pride and lust for power had resulted in an unholy slaughter of the best of their men, clearing the way for pagans to spread across the land and trample underfoot humble Christians like himself.

Asaph apologised for his opinionated novice, who was not even on nodding terms with humility. He reported that Merlyn had gone with his followers into the wild interior of the land. Moreover, Queen Guinevere was rumoured to have been reunited with her people, and received at the fortress of the King of Demetia on the coast of the Hibernian Sea.

Lucan announced he would stay and offer his leadership to the community in their rebuilding. Asaph smiled, knowing Lucan had a family he had kept secret from Arthur, owing to his vow to remain free from ties to travel the land in his king's service. They were all in agreement that the age of high kings was over, that each tribe must make alliances where they could and look to their own defence.

Peredur rode north, accompanied by Bedwyr, giving the news to his sister, Gunamara, and Arthur's sister, Anne, at Caer Cornovia. There was great sadness, and the elderly King Owain fretted over the security of the land. He had sent his captain, Viroco, and two hundred men, none of whom had returned.

Gunamara agreed to return with her brother and children to the northern capital of the Rheged people, on the western edge of the Great Roman Wall. The kingdom of the Rheged remained strong, and their future was more assured away from the troubled south. The children of Arthur would have a secure upbringing there.

No news came of Arthur, leading some to say that he still lived, and his name was sung by bards in halls across the land – a lodestar in a lowering sky, the victor in a dozen battles against his enemies, a fearless warrior who was never bettered.

THE END

Arthur *Rex Brittonum*

Author's Note

Many readers will be familiar with the legend of King Arthur and the knights of the round table, his court at Camelot, the ill-fated love affair between his queen, Guinevere, and Sir Lancelot, and the search for the Holy Grail. These romantic and chivalric embellishments were added by various writers in the Middle Ages to a less glamorous King Arthur in a story first told by Geoffrey of Monmouth in his *History of the Kings of Britain* in 1136 AD. The effect of these additions to an already fantastical tale is to leave the impression that King Arthur is a made-up character, invented to fill the black hole in British history known as the Dark Ages (specifically, the late fifth and sixth centuries).

In the 1970s, two notable academics published books in which they both categorically stated that they believed Arthur to be a real historical figure. The historian John Morris, in his comprehensive work, *The Age of Arthur*, states: "The personality of Arthur is unknown… But he was as real as Alfred the Great or William the Conqueror; and his impact upon future ages mattered as much, or more so. Enough evidence survives from the hundred years after his death to show that reality was remembered for three generations, before legend engulfed his memory."

The eminent archaeologist Leslie Alcock, in *Arthur's Britain* (revised,1989) states in the preface: "This book is about the Arthur of history, and about the Britain in which he lived. It will demonstrate that there is acceptable historical evidence that Arthur was a genuine historical figure, not a mere figment of myth or romance." These two works have given credibility to the search for historical evidence of Arthur, and it can only be hoped that more evidence is forthcoming over time.

Arthur *Rex Brittonum*

Geoffrey of Monmouth did not invent Arthur, as has been suggested. There are earlier sources, mainly from Welsh literature, who mention a valiant military leader named Artur, Arthur (or Artorius in Latin) who may or may not have been a king, possibly based at Caerleon in Gwent. Undoubtedly, one of Geoffrey's main sources would have been Nennius, the first compiler of early British history, in his work, *Historia Brittonum (The History of the Britons* c. 820 AD).

Historian Miles Russell in *Arthur and the Kings of Britain* (2018), describes this work as, "a structurally irregular mix of chronicle, genealogical table, legend, biography, bardic praise poems, itinerary and folklore." It is Nennius who gives us our first tantalising glimpse of a 'real' Arthur in the listing of his twelve battles. Nennius tells us, "Arthur fought... together with the kings of the Britons and he was *Dux Bellorum*." He describes Arthur as a *Dux Bellorum* (a leader of battles), who leads the combined armies of the kings of Britain against their enemies, primarily the Angles and Saxons, naming Octha, son of Hengist, as King of Kent. Some interpret this to mean that Arthur was not a king, just a hired military commander. Others argue that Nennius assumes the reader knows that Arthur is one of the kings of Britain and that as *Dux Bellorum*, he was first amongst equals.

Miles Russell is of the opinion that Geoffrey conflated the legend of King Arthur by taking the name of a real character in Welsh folklore and then deliberately constructing a Dark Ages superhero by piling on his shoulders the deeds of earlier heroic Briton leaders. This was perhaps done to satisfy his sponsors. It was a record of history they would welcome, the story of a Briton hero who fought against the unpopular Saxons whom the Normans had recently defeated and were engaged in dispossessing. His story of a busy and destructive Arthur fuelled the imaginations of later writers, who further

Arthur *Rex Brittonum*

embellished the legend and imbued him with the more romantic, Christian and chivalrous qualities of the day.

In my search for a 'real' Arthur I came across an article by historian David Nash Ford (www.britannia.com/history/arthur) who speculates on the locations of the twelve battles of Arthur as outlined by Nennius. Ford suggests that Arthur's first five battles could have taken place in the modern English county of Lincolnshire. He then places other battles further north in Yorkshire/Northumberland and has a further two, possibly three, battles in Scotland. These locations may or may not be correct, but they suited my storytelling, as I send a youthful Arthur and his comrades on a journey north (in *Arthur Dux Bellorum*) finally arriving at one of the many Roman forts on Hadrian's Wall. From his base on the Great Roman Wall, Arthur fights northern tribes at three locations in Southern Scotland.

In *Arthur Rex Brittonum*, a middle-aged Arthur travels south through the Rheged's northwest lands, arriving at the River Dee estuary close to Chester (Deva) at the start of this book. From there he moves south to Viriconium (Caer Cornovia) where he is based until the build up to the Battle of Mount Badon. Thereafter, Arthur bases himself at Caerleon (Caer Legion) in Gwent for his remaining years as king. Then, I have opted for Somerset and the River Cam as the location of his final battle, Camlann.

I think it perfectly achievable that he could cover such distance travelling by horseback on Roman roads, although some historians find the spread of battles is unfeasibly wide. It is a mere three hundred miles from Winchester in the south to Hadrian's Wall. He had plenty of time, as the two books cover roughly thirty years of Arthur's adult life.

There are other problems with Nennius's list. For one, he mentions Badon Hill, most likely a battle associated with an earlier king such as Aurelius Ambrosius (or, as in my previous book, Uther Pendragon). Also, he doesn't mention Arthur's final battle, Camlann, mentioned by earlier Welsh sources and included in Geoffrey of Monmouth's story. I have accommodated those historians who believe there may have been two battles at Mount Badon – one around 493 (Ambrosius or Uther?) and another around 519 – Arthur. A date is given in the Welsh Annales for Camlann of 539. Could this be the true date of Arthur's death?

My description of Arthur is partly based on the picture I chose for the book cover of *Arthur Dux Bellorum* ('Arthur Dux Bellorum' by Gordon Napier). I was instantly drawn to his superb artwork when I recognised one element of Nennius's scant description of Arthur: "The eighth battle was in Guinnion fort, and in it Arthur carried the image of the holy Mary, the everlasting Virgin, on his shield and the heathen were put to flight on that day, and there was a great slaughter upon them, through the power of Our Lord Jesus Christ and the power of the holy Virgin Mary, his mother." Yes, Nennius was a monk, who was clearly keen to portray Arthur as a Christian leader fighting the pagan Saxons and Picts.

What really happened in the late fifth and early sixth centuries? Perhaps one day a lost manuscript will be found, or archaeologists will uncover a definitive battle site, or evidence of Arthur's fortress (almost certainly not called Camelot), or his burial site (almost certainly not Glastonbury Abbey). A recent theory by historian Graham Phillips in his book, *The Lost Tomb of King Arthur*, makes the intriguing case for the location of Arthur's kingdom, his final battle and burial place, to be in Powys, central Wales. His entertaining, if tenuous, case hangs on the possibility that 'The Bear' or 'ur Arth' was a title given to the kings of Powys, and one particular king was the Arthur of legend. There are still plenty of 'ifs', 'buts' and 'maybes' in his extensively researched and passionately argued case, but perhaps the most lasting impression is his enthusiasm for the search for the holy grail – conclusive evidence for the existence of a real historical Arthur.

'What is Beowulf doing in this story?' you may ask. I decided to knit together the legends of Beowulf and Arthur after I read in the introduction to the old English poem, *Beowulf* (the *Delphi Classics* series, 2015), that "The events described in the poem take place between the late fifth century, after the Angles and Saxons had begun their migration to England, and before the beginning of the seventh century." I was delighted at the suggestion that a possible historical Beowulf was behind the epic poem, and that his timeframe roughly coincides with that of Arthur.

I also learned that some popular folk tales have their origin in early Welsh folk tales that include the stories of Arthur that fed into the *Mabinogion*, including the 'old witch and the poisoned apple' that is familiar from *Snow White*. I could not resist portraying Morgana in this role, nor having Arthur slay a giant – also found in those early tales.

Arthur *Rex Brittonum*

A Light in the Dark Ages

The aim of this book series is to connect the end of Roman Britannia (410 AD is taken as the year of final separation) to elements of the Arthurian legend. The timeline of high kings of Britain in the post-Roman years is taken from Geoffrey of Monmouth's work, *The History of the Kings of Britain* (c. 1136 AD). Further historical research has been undertaken in an attempt to build as realistic and believable narrative as is permissible, given the paucity of hard historical and archaeological evidence for what happened where, when and to whom in the fifth and sixth centuries. Quasi-historical and legendary figures have been fed into what builds to King Arthur's story. The author's wish is to present a believable and 'realistic' Arthur to readers, fleshing out the shadowy outline of a man upon whose shoulders the legend has been built.

Book one – Abandoned
Book two – Ambrosius: Last of the Romans
Book three – Uther's Destiny
Book four – Arthur *Dux Bellorum*
Book five – Arthur *Rex Brittonum*

Printed in Great Britain
by Amazon